LEGACY RESTORED

NUTFIELD SAGA
BOOK 7

ROBIN PATCHEN

JDO PUBLISHING

Print ISBN: 978-1694351388

Large Print ISBN: 979-8842597925

Cover by Lynnette Bonner.

For Dad.
Your faith in Christ was the beginning.
It influenced your children's faith.
Your grandchildren's faith.
The faith of strangers you'll never know.
Your legacy will last to a thousand generations.
Thank you for being a faithful follower of Christ.

ACKNOWLEDGMENTS

As always, I am thankful to my critique partners, Normandie Fischer, Kara Hunt, Jericha Kingston, Candice Sue Patterson, Sharon Srock, Pegg Thomas, and Terri Weldon—you make me look good. I couldn't do this without you.

Thank you, Misty Beller, for your marketing advice.

Thank you, Ray Rhamey, for your editing skills.

Thank you, Eddie, Nick, Lexi, and Jacob, for continuing to support this crazy life.

Most importantly, thank You, Father, for giving me the stories, the ability to write them, the community to help me improve them, and the means to get them into the hands of readers. Everything I am, and everything I do, I dedicate to You.

CHAPTER ONE

Angelica Rossi waited until her customers slipped out of the restaurant before she snatched their receipt from the tabletop and glanced at it. A ten-percent tip on a thirty-dollar ticket. They'd occupied one of her six tables for an hour and a half and left her three dollars.

Fine, then. She wasn't going to complain. This was gainful employment. Well, employment, anyway.

She closed her eyes, prayed for patience, for peace, for faith. Maybe this job wasn't that gainful, but it was legitimate. It was a step in the right direction.

She carried the dirty glasses to the kitchen and set them into the sink to be washed.

This wasn't such a bad gig, and she needed to hang onto it. The job was necessary until she completed her six months at the sober living house. Then, her probation would be completed, and she'd be free to live life on her terms again. She'd be free to go home to her parents and rebuild her relationship with them. Her mother had promised years before that she'd always save Angel a seat at church, but Angel hadn't attended since high school. Someday, when all this was over, she'd gather the courage to slide into the pew beside Mom and Dad. Someday, she'd convince them she was worthy of the family name.

The sober living house was much nicer than she'd expected. Her roommate, Brittney, was fun to hang out with, and the other women were nice enough. Heck, it had to beat prison.

Angel returned to the table, propped the menus back in the rack, slid the salt and pepper shakers to their proper places, and sprayed cleaner on the top. After she wiped it off, she cleaned the first bench seat and moved to the second.

Something black stuck out between the far end of the bench and the wall. She reached for it.

A wallet. A thick wallet probably filled with credit cards and IDs and cash.

Temptation, familiar and powerful, tingled in her fingertips. She could slide it into her pocket, go through it later...

No.

She wasn't that person anymore. She closed her eyes and thanked God for her freedom. Not from prison or rehab or sober living, but from the sin that had led her to this place. She didn't want this wallet. Never again would she steal. Never.

Angel slipped the wallet into the pocket of her apron and finished cleaning the booth. Then, she beelined through the restaurant toward the front to turn in the wallet.

She found the manager behind the hostess station. Angel was still ten feet away when the woman turned to her. She was fifty-something, heavyset, and wore a look on her face that held such hatred, Angel slowed her steps. Contempt she was accustomed to, but this was worse. This manager hadn't hired her and didn't like her. She didn't like any of the people the owner had hired from the sober living house. She didn't trust Angel, and Angel couldn't blame her.

She'd never been trustworthy. That she was now seemed irrelevant to everyone, herself included.

Angel plastered on her best smile. "Hey, when I was cleaning a booth—"

"Empty your pockets," Barb said.

The man who'd left the three-dollar tip stood on the far side of the hostess stand. "If you'll let me go look—"

"I'll handle this, sir." Barb focused on Angel again. "Now."

Angel forced her gaze away from Barb and smiled at the customer. "I found a wallet in your booth. I assume that's what you're looking for." She pulled it out and handed it over.

He blew out a breath. "Thank you. It must have fallen out of my pocket."

"My pleasure."

"You'd better check it." Barb's voice was sharp, loud. "Make sure nothing's missing."

A customer at a nearby table turned to stare.

Angel's cheeks warmed, but she kept her smile in place. She hadn't done anything wrong. This time, she hadn't done anything wrong.

The man looked from Barb to Angel. "Uh, okay." He opened it, picked at the many credit cards, flipped through the cash. "Everything's here." He focused on Angel. "Thanks again."

All that cash, and he'd left her three dollars. On the other hand, he'd given her an opportunity to test her ability to withstand temptation. For that, she owed him. "Have a great day."

The man nodded to Barb and pushed out the door of the restaurant.

Barb rounded on her. "You're fired."

"What?" Angel stepped back. "Why?"

"You're a crook."

"I didn't steal—"

"Only because you got caught before you could go through with it."

"I came straight to you. I was going to turn it in."

Barb's face twisted into an evil smirk. "Right. That's why it was in your pocket."

Angel said, "I stuck it there while I cleaned the booth."

"I heard all about you." Her voice carried, and more customers turned to look. "You're not only an addict. You're a thief and a con-woman."

Who'd told her that? The sober living house wouldn't have disclosed that information.

"Why you're not in prison," Barb continued, "I have no idea, but you're not going to steal from our customers."

Words Angel didn't use anymore rose to her lips as heat flooded her skin. She wanted to defend herself, to fight for her job, to argue. But Barb was right. Angel had been a thief all her life. She didn't deserve this woman's trust.

And she sure as heck wasn't going to beg to keep this crappy job.

She slipped the apron over her head, shoved it into Barb's hands, and marched out the door. The air was hot, too hot for mid-September in Manchester. Angel wasn't dressed for Indian summer in her blue jeans, her sensible black tennis shoes, and the long-sleeved black T-shirt with the stupid restaurant's stupid logo emblazoned on the back. But the heat suffocating her wasn't a result of the temperature.

Shame burned hotter than any New Hampshire day.

She'd been fired. Fired for stealing. That she hadn't actually stolen anything was irrelevant.

Normal people—not addicts, not felons, not crooks—drove along Elm Street and walked past her on the sidewalk. Doctors, lawyers, business people. Store clerks, secretaries, salesmen.

These were the kinds of people she'd never wanted to be like when she was a kid. She'd craved adventure. She'd craved risk.

Now, she'd give anything, anything to be one of them.

"Angel!"

She turned to see the other waitress, Karen, hurrying down the sidewalk toward her.

The last thing Angel wanted was to talk. With a sigh, she stopped and waited.

"What happened?"

"She fired me."

"She said you stole a wallet." Karen tilted her head. "Did you?"

"No, but..." Angel shrugged. "I found it, shoved it in my apron pocket."

"You need to talk to the owner. He'll take you back."

Angel looked toward the restaurant, then touched Karen's arm. "Thank you for checking on me. You've been a good friend."

Karen stepped back, regarded her through narrowed eyes. "You're not going to, are you?"

"Her word against mine, and my word isn't worth anything." Angel plastered on a smile. "It's fine."

It would be, eventually. Angel would get over this. "I'll find something else." She said the words with more confidence than she felt. She had to work if she wanted to stay in the sober living house. She had to stay in the sober living house if she wanted to stay out of prison.

Karen pursed her lips and shook her head. "Last week you went to bat for one of the cooks when he showed up late. You argued with Barb until she let him off the hook."

"His daughter was sick. You don't fire people—"

"Her reason for firing you is even flimsier."

Except Karen didn't know her past. She didn't know the truth about who Angel really was.

"You know what your problem is?" Karen asked. "You think everyone's worth fighting for except yourself."

Angel's bark of a laugh held no humor. "I guess I know me too well."

The restaurant door opened. Barb stepped out, looked around. When she spotted them, she glared.

Karen focused on Angel. "You're wrong." Karen pulled her into a quick hug, whispered in her ear, "It doesn't matter what you've done. You are worth fighting for." She let Angel go, squeezed her hand, and hurried back to her job.

Angel watched her friend walk away. Karen was a nice lady, but about Angel being worth fighting for, she was very wrong.

ANGEL WANDERED up and down Elm Street seeking help-wanted signs. She needed a job, and she needed one fast. She applied at a couple of restaurants, but as the hour grew later and the dinner crowds grew thicker, the managers had less time to deal with wannabe employees.

It was after six, and with the sun on its descent, the air had grown chilly. She shivered and decided she'd resume the job search in the morning. Which meant she had no place to go but back to the house, where the house manager would surely ask her why she was home from work early.

She could lie, of course. Tell the woman they'd let her go early because it was slow or that she'd felt sick. It would be easy to come up with a viable story. Except Angel didn't lie, not since she'd become a Christian. Because the Bible said Satan was the father of lies, and she wasn't willing to be his minion anymore.

She'd be honest and face the music.

She pulled her keys from one front pocket, patted the other, which held her cell, and turned down the dark street beside the restaurant toward the parking lot. She could smell the burgers grilling in the kitchen, a scent she wouldn't be sorry not to carry home with her every day. There was the silver lining.

Fewer cars lined the sidewalk now, though there were a couple between Elm Street and the parking lot. She scanned them, looking for anything out of place. Wednesday night, and this wasn't a dangerous area of town, but anything could happen. She was nearing her car when a man stepped out of a dark sedan.

She froze and stared through the deepening twilight. As the other door opened, she realized who the first man was. Not a killer or mugger or rapist. Her stomach plummeted just the same.

Detective Routhier took a few steps toward her. "How's it going?"

Another man stood near the passenger side but said nothing.

She continued toward her car, and Routhier fell in step beside her.

"Just get off work?" he asked.

"Something like that." Another twenty feet and she could crawl into her beat-up gold Impala and leave him and this whole day behind. She concentrated on the soft thud of their footsteps, on the street noises coming from a block south.

"Problem is," Routhier said, "I called the house where you're living, and they said you worked until eleven."

She glanced at him. "What do you want?"

"Just to talk."

She reached her car and tried to insert her key into the lock. The light was dim, and her hands were shaking. She hadn't done anything wrong, but guilt plagued her anyway. And being stalked by the cop who'd arrested her and thrown her in jail wasn't exactly a soothing experience.

He leaned against her car door, and she backed away and crossed her arms.

His partner watched from beside the unmarked car on the street.

Angel sighed. She had no reason for fear. The guilty feelings were remnants of her old self, not reflections of who she was today. "You need me for something?"

"As a matter of fact, I do." Routhier's dark eyes took her in from head to toe and back. "Sobriety looks good on you."

He knew she wasn't an addict. He'd argued fiercely that she deserved prison. Because drugs—belonging to a friend of her former boyfriend—had been found in the car she was driving when she was arrested, her lawyer had pushed for rehab. The state had agreed, assuming she'd stolen to feed an addiction, and the judge had listened.

Routhier knew all of that. There was no good response to his sarcasm.

He glanced at the back door of the restaurant. "You quit your job—?"

"What do you want?"

"Or get fired?" He must've seen something in her eyes, because his wide face split into a cruel grin. "What'd you do?"

"Unless you're here to arrest me, I'm free to go. And since I haven't done anything wrong—"

"Did you steal something? When I suggested to your manager that she keep an eye on you, I never thought she'd catch you that fast."

"You!" She stepped away. "You told her about my past? Can you really hate me that much?"

"All I did was tell her you were a thief, Angel. You're the one who proved me right."

"I didn't..." Rage rolled over her in hot waves. "Are you here to arrest me?"

"You lost your job, which means I can send you to prison right now if I want to. You know that, right? If you're unemployed, you've violated the terms of your probation. And if I have a little chat with your manager, we can add stealing to your violations." He grinned. "Good bye, freedom, hello, prison."

He was right. Maybe Angel's lawyer could buy her a little time. Maybe, if she hurried and got another job, if she could show she was doing her best.

"But that's not why I'm here," Detective Routhier said. "I have another matter I'd like to discuss with you."

Another matter, as if they were business associates instead of enemies. Her gaze flicked to the other detective, who'd walked closer and now stood beside his partner. "What?"

"We want to talk about Anton Turner."

The name was so unexpected, she thought at first she'd heard wrong. Anton Turner was the founder and leader—president, grand poo-bah, whatever—of Cambridge Homes, the organization that ran the sober living house. She'd only met the man a handful of times in the three months since she'd moved in. She'd seen him at the house a few times and at a fundraiser for all his sober living houses across the state.

"What do you know about him?" Routhier asked.

Not much. Anton came across as a nice enough guy, but the whispers told a different story. She'd heard all sorts of weird accusations about him—that he'd supplied drugs to some of the occupants, that he'd made inappropriate advances to some of the women.

They were only rumors. And besides, Angel had no desire

to help the cop who'd arrested her. Yes, she'd deserved it. Been guilty of the theft that got her arrested and plenty more. That didn't change the resentment that dogged her now. "I know nothing about him."

"He knows about you, though," Detective Routhier said. "Do you know why you were able to get into his house?"

She'd known little about addiction recovery before her sentence. From addicts in rehab, she heard the Cambridge houses were cleaner, nicer than a lot of others, and also harder to get into. She'd counted it a blessing when she'd applied and been approved and hadn't given it another thought. "I figured I got lucky," she said.

Routhier said, "We heard he planted drugs on another resident to make room for you."

The other cop nodded. Apparently, the man didn't talk.

"Why would he do that?" Angel asked. "I'd never met the guy."

"You've never had a conversation with him?" Routhier asked. "He hasn't tried to befriend you?"

Anton had sat beside her at the fundraiser and made conversation. He'd been friendly, but not overly so.

He'd been to the house a few times, too, and chatted with her, but he did that with everybody.

Except... Come to think of it, she couldn't remember him talking to any of the other residents. Just the house manager and her.

Routhier was watching her, nodding slowly. "Thought so."

"It was nothing." Her gaze flicked to the other cop. "Seriously."

Routhier nodded as if he were considering her words. That would be a first. "Eventually, he's going to seek you out. We think he's planning a heist, and he's going to ask you to be a part of it."

A heist? Who used that word? And anyway... "He hasn't said anything to me. And even if he did, I wouldn't do it. I'm done with all that."

"Sure you are." Routhier's glance flicked to the restaurant she'd just been fired from. "I'm trying to help you out here. I'm trying to keep you out of trouble."

"You don't give a flying... fig about me."

He laughed and looked at his partner. "She's cleaned up her mouth, anyway." He focused on her again. "Fig?"

"I don't use bad language anymore. And I don't steal. So you don't have to worry about me getting involved with Anton and his *heist.*"

"But if you did get involved"—Routhier lifted his comically wide shoulders, then dropped them dramatically—"you could really help us out. And then we could help you out."

Ah. Now it made sense. They wanted information. They wanted her to... what? Be a confidential informant? No way. She'd probably end up getting arrested again. Even if she didn't, Anton held her future in his hands. If he told the state she wasn't following the house rules, he could get her sent to prison. "Forget it."

"We could talk to the judge, maybe get you out—"

"Not interested. I'm going to earn my freedom the right way."

"Too late for that, seeing as how you avoided prison."

Another wave of guilt. She braced herself, let it roll over her. "The judge gave me probation with rehab and sober living. I'm doing what the state told me to do. There's no shame in that." She nodded to her car. "If you'll get out of my way."

Routhier pulled a business card from his shirt pocket and held it out.

She shoved it in her back pocket.

Finally, he stepped back.

She stuck her key into the lock, opened the door, and slid behind the wheel. She backed out of the parking space and turned toward the street.

A glance in the rearview mirror told her the cops were watching her drive away.

CHAPTER TWO

The distant ring of Donovan Gilcreast's phone barely stole through his concentration. He brushed it off like a fly and focused on scraping off the old wallpaper in the house's half bath.

An hour passed, maybe two, before he finished. As he tossed the scraper on the drop cloth, his phone rang again.

He stretched the kink in his lower back and headed down the hallway. He'd left his cell somewhere...

The living area of the old Victorian was dark and dingy—dark floors, dark walls, dark woodwork. It would all be bright and cheerful by the time Donovan was done with it, thanks to Jack Rossi's plans. It would be beautiful. Perfect for vacationers. Not as much for hermits hiding from the world.

The phone was on the coffee table where Donovan had left it the night before. It stopped vibrating before he reached it. He checked the call log.

Yup. Ian had called... he scrolled down... ten times. Ten times in three hours. Donovan couldn't be irritated, not when he'd avoided as many calls the day before, maybe more.

The phone vibrated in his hand. Donovan wanted nothing

more than to toss it aside, but it had been a productive day. His mood wasn't going to get any better.

He connected the call. Tried to speak, but his voice came out more like a croak. When was the last time he'd used it? He'd gone to the store a few days before, but he'd chosen the self-checkout line. Hadn't spoken to a soul.

"You there?" Ian's voice was strong. Of course, he never stopped talking. The guy even talked in his sleep, something Donovan had learned when they'd roomed together after college. "Donovan?"

He cleared his throat. "Yeah."

"I've been trying to reach you." His Australian accent came through now, along with a hefty dose of irritation.

"Uh-huh."

"Are you lying dead in a pool of blood?"

"Yes."

He expected his friend to chuckle, but no such luck. "Why are you avoiding my calls?"

Donovan wandered out to the sunroom, his favorite spot in this old house and the only reason he'd taken on this job. He gazed out the window. The lake shimmered in the moonlight. "Nothing to say."

"I have a lot to say. I put my career on the line to get you on the gallery schedule for December. If you don't come through—"

"I'm working on it."

"How many paintings have you completed?"

Donovan swiveled, took in the stacks of canvases leaning against the wall. Completed, though? "None."

"None!" Ian's raised voice almost elicited a reaction. Almost. "Tell me you're joking, mate."

"They're almost finished."

"How many?"

"Twenty, twenty-five."

"Which is it, twenty or twenty-five?"

Donovan took his time counting, pulling each canvas forward, glancing at the work. Landscapes, all of them. Pastels of early morning, bright colors of midday, dark colors of evening. Mediocre work at best. "Twenty-two."

"Twenty-two." Ian's voice was back to his typical business tone. "All right then. We need at least thirty, but I'd be happier with thirty-five. How long do you think before they'll be ready?"

Donovan shrugged. They all needed... something. The something they needed, though, he didn't have. He turned to face the canvas on his easel. That was the painting that would unlock it. If he could finish it, then... then it would all come back.

Katie's painting.

"I'm coming for a visit," Ian said.

"No."

"I need to see what you've done, plan the display."

A flimsy excuse. Ian wouldn't start planning the display until a couple of weeks before the gallery showing. He wouldn't even consider how to show the paintings until they were ready. "No."

"I need to see what you've got."

Ian had stuck his neck out to get Donovan a showing the first weekend of the Christmas season. It was a great time of year and a great location that catered to exactly the kinds of people who liked Donovan's work. If Donovan had known what would happen to Katie, he would have told his friend not to bother. But Ian had bothered.

Each morning found Donovan in the sunroom, squeezing dabs of paint on his palette, picking up his brush, touching the canvas, losing himself in the process. Losing himself in ways house restoration would never achieve. The painting kept him alive. The results, though... Maybe he'd never get it back. Maybe these mediocre paintings were the best he could do now. He didn't know. He only knew he owed it to Ian to try. He couldn't care less right now about his own fledgling career, but Ian was his friend.

When Donovan said nothing, Ian blew out a long-suffering breath. "I want to check on you."

"I'm fine."

"When was the last time you left the house?"

There'd been the grocery store. Two days before? Three? He'd skipped church the previous Sunday. And all the Sundays since he'd returned to New Hampshire. He walked down to the lake sometimes. He jogged a couple times a week. "I leave."

"When was the last time you spoke to another human being?"

"Talking to you now."

"In person."

In person? He had no idea. "I need to get back to work."

"That's what I thought."

"You're not my father."

"He's why I'm coming."

Donovan dropped his gaze from the lake to the crappy peel-and-stick tile beneath his feet and rubbed the back of his neck. What did Dad have to do with this? Donovan was mustering the energy to ask when Ian said, "He called me. He says you hardly answer your phone and refuse to let them come see you."

Donovan fell back on the sofa, a dingy plaid piece of crap that belonged in a dumpster. Springs threatened to poke through the rotting foam, but he ignored them and rested his head in his free hand. "I can't see them."

"I know." Ian's voice shifted to the compassionate tone he used with crying children and angry girlfriends. "That's why I'm coming. You need a friend."

"I need to be left alone."

"I don't think so. I think leaving you alone has only made it worse. I can't come this weekend. We have a big showing, but by the middle of next week I should be able to make the trip. Have at least a couple of paintings finished."

Donovan could try to talk Ian out of coming, but he didn't have it in him to argue anymore. And once Ian set his mind to something, there was no point in trying to change it.

"Gotta run, mate," Ian said, "I'll call you early next week. In the meantime, keep at it. We need those paintings, or both of our careers will be in the toilet."

CHAPTER THREE

The two-story five-bedroom house looked like all the other houses in the quiet North End neighborhood. From the outside, nobody would guess a gaggle of recovering addicts lived there.

Angel climbed the steps to the wide front porch. This outdoor space was her favorite feature. All summer, the girls had gathered on the rocking chairs and in the wicker swing to chat and smoke cigarettes. Thank heaven Angel had avoided that bad habit.

The windows were open to let in the cool evening air, and when she stepped inside, the sounds of the outdoor followed her—the hum of cars on nearby River Road, other normal sounds of evening in the city. Inside, the house was blissfully, unexpectedly quiet. No blaring TV, no women talking on the phone or sniping at each other.

No women at all.

Right. It was Wednesday. Residents who didn't work Wednesday nights were required to attend the weekly meeting, which took place at another one of the houses. Angel had been to a few. The house managers spoke or brought in someone from outside the community to speak on various subjects—job hunting, career development, staying sober after release. They weren't a complete waste of time. She should go. She glanced at her cell phone and realized that by the time she crossed town the meeting would be almost over.

And the quiet... She didn't hate living here, but the constant chatter of the women sometimes drove her batty. She wandered through the house, turning on lights as she went and peeking in the common rooms. Even the office where the house manager worked was empty.

In the kitchen, Angel grabbed a can of soup from the pantry and searched for a pan to warm it. She was setting it on the stove when she heard a thump.

Seemed she wasn't the only one skipping the meeting. Maybe one of the residents was sick.

Then, another thump, this one louder.

And a crash.

What in the world?

Angel hurried to the staircase and ran up the stairs as quietly as possible. Most likely, it was one of the women who lived there. But what if it was a burglar?

The upstairs hallway light was off. She reached for it, then changed her mind. No reason to alert anyone to her presence. Probably, she was about to scare the pants off some unsuspecting resident. Most of the bedroom doors were open. Only the door to the room she shared with Brittney was closed. No light came from beneath it.

Brittney hadn't been sick earlier in the day. And she'd never missed a Wednesday meeting. She'd worked hard on her recovery and was close to going home. She'd do nothing to risk that now.

Angel's heart pounded. Something was wrong. She crept

toward the door, instinct telling her to run away. She couldn't do that. This was stupid. Brittney had probably fallen and—

A man's voice. Angel couldn't make out the words, only the deep tone.

Men weren't allowed on the second floor. Maybe Brittney had thought she'd be alone and had invited a friend over. Angel lifted her hand to knock.

A quiet gasp, a scream, quickly muffled.

Angel turned the knob and pushed into the room.

In the glow of the streetlight streaming through the windows, she saw Brittney on the bed, a man on top of her. His hand was pressed over her mouth.

Angel bolted forward and shoved the man off her friend.

He toppled off the far side of the twin mattress.

Angel grabbed Brittney, barely registering the torn clothes, the look of sheer panic on her face. "Run!"

Brittney staggered, nearly pulling them both down.

Angel pushed her friend out the door. They had to get—

The man caught Angel from behind. Brittney disappeared into the dark hallway.

Angel yelled, "Call the—!"

The man yanked her back from the door and flung her into the room.

She clutched a fistful of his shirt to keep him from chasing Brittney.

He shoved her away, and she crashed into the bureau, sending makeup and jewelry flying.

Downstairs, a door slammed.

Brittney had gotten away.

But Angel was trapped.

The man backhanded her, and she stumbled, almost fell. He gripped her arm and kept her on her feet, then pressed her against the wall.

That's when she saw his face. Short hair, gray at the temples. Blue eyes. Rimless glasses. He looked like he could be a Baptist preacher.

It was Anton Turner. The owner of the house, the man who held Angel's freedom in his hands. "That was a very foolish thing to do."

"I-I didn't know it was you. I would never have..." What? Stopped him from attacking her friend? She scrambled to come up with a story, something that would get her out of here. There was no story that would explain away what Anton had been doing. "I don't want any trouble. I won't say a word."

He leaned down until his face was inches from hers. "You won't. Not if you want to stay out of prison." His breath was hot against her face, the scent of liquor unmistakable as he inched closer. "Maybe I'll get what I want from you."

Think. She had to...

"Brittney must have called the cops," she blurted. "You should go before they get here. I'll tell them I didn't see your face."

His eyes blazed with evil. He mashed his mouth against hers. Took her lip in his teeth and bit until she tasted blood.

She turned her face to escape him, but he pushed his hand against the back of her neck, stilling her. The hand slid to the front, pressed against her windpipe. She gasped for air.

"If you tell anybody anything, I will take you out." He shoved his lips against hers again.

Far away, a siren whined.

Anton backed up, looked toward the window.

She tried to yank away, but he held her body against his, tightened his grip. He squeezed his thumb against a vein in her neck.

She saw stars, struggled to stay conscious. The room darkened.

He stepped back, and she fell, disoriented.

Anton stood over her. "Keep your mouth shut and stay put. You and I aren't done."

He kicked her in the side, and pain exploded.

He stomped out.

She lay there in the dark room, listening. Downstairs, a door slammed.

The sound of the siren faded. It hadn't been coming here. Angel wasn't surprised that Brittney hadn't called the police. Her sobriety depended on Anton, too. If Angel had to guess, Brittney wouldn't tell a soul he'd attacked her. She was too desperate to be free. She'd put up with anything.

Angel would never be that desperate.

She sat up, inventoried her injuries. Her arm ached where he'd grabbed her. Her side throbbed.

She stood, hunched over, and held onto the bureau through a wave of dizziness. Everything hurt. She forced herself to stand up straight.

"Ow..." She pushed her palm against her side. That kick had done damage. She forced a deep breath.

She had to leave before the women returned. She had no idea how she could explain this, but if she weren't here, nobody would question her. They'd assume she'd been at work. Which would give her time to...

What?

Right now, she had to get out. Without turning on the lights, she found her duffel bag and shoved as many of her things into it as she could gather. The pain increased as the adrenaline wore off. She didn't even have half her clothes, but she was running out of steam.

She hefted the bag with her good arm and hobbled down the stairs and outside. In her car, she locked the doors, then double-checked them. She scanned the area. Was he here? Was he watching to see what she'd do?

She'd do nothing, not yet. Not until she figured out the right move.

She took back roads out of the neighborhood. Only when she was safely hidden in the crowd of cars on Elm Street did she risk stopping. She pulled in front of a drugstore, away from the door and the lights, and parked.

She checked again... Her doors were locked.

She was safe here.

And then, it all came back. She sucked in a breath, another. She'd never been so afraid. Never been so vulnerable. He could have beaten her, raped her, killed her. And... she hated to think it, but Brittney probably wouldn't have told a soul. Because Anton held Brittney's freedom—all the women's freedom—in his grimy hands.

He held Angel's, too.

Keep your mouth shut and stay put. You and I aren't done.

She couldn't think about that. Couldn't think about facing him. And she wasn't about to go back to the house. She couldn't. He had access, too much access to her and to all the women.

The memory of his lips against hers... She touched the cut with her tongue. One more pain to add to all the rest. No. No way was she going back there. Ever.

She had to call the cops. Except they wouldn't believe her. The word of a thief and, as far as the authorities were concerned, an addict, against the word of an upstanding member of society? She had no chance of convincing them. If she called them, and if they confronted Anton, she'd get kicked out of the house for sure. If she had a job and could show she was doing her part...

But she'd been fired.

She'd go to prison after all. Which was what she'd deserved all along.

Her eyes were squeezed shut, but tears escaped anyway. *Oh, Lord, what should I do?*

Routhier. She should call him. The thought felt like an answer from above. *Thank you.* Gingerly, she shifted in order to pull the detective's card from her back pocket. Her side protested, but she pushed through the pain.

She called the detective, who answered on the second ring.

"It's Angel Rossi. I need to see you."

THIRTY MINUTES LATER, Angel waited in the far corner of the mall parking lot. She'd wanted to go somewhere nobody would look for her. She'd backed into a spot that enabled her to see most of the lot, and she'd chosen an empty area below the lights, irrationally afraid of the dark. As if Anton could find her.

Trying to convince herself she was safe, she scanned the area. No people, no cars moving about.

A few minutes after she parked, Routhier's unmarked sedan pulled in beside her.

She stepped from her car, wincing at the pain in her side, as Routhier and his partner climbed out of theirs. She faced them under the flickering light.

Routhier's face held only suspicion, but the other man must have seen something in the overhead light. He rushed forward and took her arm to steady her. "Whoa, what happened?"

But he'd gripped her left arm, and she winced and pulled it to her side. The detective's eyes widened slightly. She said, "I'm—"

"She's fine," Routhier said.

His partner ignored him and waited until she was leaning

on her car before letting her go. "I'm Detective O'Donnell. We didn't meet properly." He was shorter and slimmer than Routhier and had Opie-Taylor looks.

"Angel Rossi."

"What happened?" The look of concern on Opie O'Donnell's face surprised her. Didn't he know she was the enemy?

She looked past him to Routhier, who was leaning against his sedan, arms crossed. "You wanted something on Anton Turner?" she asked.

He pushed off the car. "Not exactly. We want—"

"When I got home tonight, he was in the process of..." She swallowed, tried to come up with a better way to say this. The right word was ugly and scary. "He was sexually assaulting my roommate. I pushed him off her. He attacked me."

Opie's jaw opened, then closed. He swallowed and looked her up and down. "Did he rape you?"

Blunt much? At least he seemed to care. Angel shook her head, her cheeks burning as if she had something to be ashamed of. "He kissed me." Though *kiss* was the wrong word. Her lip stung with the memory. "And then he got spooked and took off."

The younger detective lifted her chin and studied her face. "He hit you. Tell me what else hurts." The kind words raised tears to her eyes and only added to her headache. She needed to think, think. She wasn't here for a medical exam. But she was shaking, trembling with cold.

She tried to answer his question. What hurt?

Her head. Her arm. Her face. And... she pushed her palm against her ribs. That pain rose to the surface, and she inhaled sharply.

Opie turned to Routhier. "We need to get her to a hospital."

Both Routhier and Angel said, "No."

Opie said, "She's injured."

"Pretty convenient, if you ask me." Routhier's lip curled as if he'd gotten a whiff of rotten food.

Convenient. He didn't believe her. And here she'd had this bizarre idea that he might. She breathed slowly, in and out, and tried to focus. "How do you think I got hurt? And what could I possibly have to gain by making up this story?"

He shrugged. "Haven't figured that out yet."

She tried to hold his gaze as tears stung her eyes. What was happening? How could she have lost so much in the space of a couple of hours? Her job, her home, now her freedom. She'd done nothing wrong. Nothing to deserve it.

But oh, she'd done plenty to deserve it. Maybe not today. Maybe this was punishment for all the things she'd done before she'd met her Savior. Maybe grace only kicked in after karma.

If that even made sense.

She didn't have the energy to think, to fight, to deal with any of this.

She slid down and sat on the asphalt, pulled her knees in and rested her head on them. "I can't go back there. Ever. That man is... He needs to be stopped." She looked at Routhier. "I came to you because I thought you wanted to bring him down." She faced Detective Opie. "Will you take my statement?"

"Yes," Opie said.

"No," Routhier said. "You have to go back. It's a condition of your probation."

She tried to stand up and failed. "You're going to have to take me to jail, then. I'm not going back to that place."

Opie's quiet "She's injured" barely registered as Angel tipped her head back against her car and closed her eyes. The cool metal felt good.

Routhier crouched in front of her. "You can help us."

"I'm not going back."

"If what you say is true, then you have something on him. You can use that."

She opened her eyes. "You're not listening. I'm not going back." The thought of entering that room again, where he'd touched her, kissed her... "Never."

"Okay. So you call him. Meet him somewhere. Make a deal."

The tears she'd been fighting spilled over, trailed down her cheeks. She didn't have the energy to fight them or wipe them away. "I just want..." But they didn't care what she wanted. She was a criminal. She'd made a deal to stay in rehab and sober living or go to prison. She was trapped. And now, thanks to Routhier, she'd be a pawn.

Routhier said, "I'll talk to a judge, make a deal for you. You don't have to go back. All you have to do is help us bring him down."

"I don't even know what he's doing."

"I told you. He's planning something. And he wants you to help him."

"You're crazy."

But Anton's words came back again. *You and I aren't done.*

"Let's say you're right," Angel said. "What do you want me to do?"

"Work with him. He'll have you and at least one other partner involved. We need him to get away with the goods and take them back to where he keeps them."

"Why?"

Routhier sighed. "Boston PD thinks he pulled a job last year in the city. They don't have enough evidence to bring charges, but they're sure it was him."

"So you want him to get away with another theft? That doesn't make sense. Just catch him in the act."

"We need to prove he did the last one, which means we need to find the stolen goods."

"Why?"

Routhier stood, looked at his partner. "We just do."

"You're not going to tell me why?"

"He's not a good guy," Routhier said. "He's not worth protecting."

The pain throbbing in her side was evidence of that.

When Routhier said nothing else, she reached for the door handle to pull herself up, wishing she'd not given in to the temptation to sit. The pain wasn't worth it.

Opie gripped her right arm and lifted her.

She brushed off her backside as well as she could with her uninjured arm. "Thank you." She stepped toward Routhier.

The detective was a huge man, probably a foot taller than her five-two frame with shoulders as wide as a compact car. She looked up into his face, refusing to back down from his size or that intimidating stare. "I'm not doing this unless I know why."

He glanced at O'Donnell, who said, "She deserves to know the truth."

Routhier smirked. After a moment, he said, "Fine." And then he was silent for a beat, two beats. "He killed an off-duty cop."

Whoa. *Killed?* She stepped back. This was way above her pay grade. She'd been a thief. She'd never associated with people like that.

Anton, a murderer?

She closed her eyes, could feel him against her. She rubbed her neck, thought of his hand jammed against her windpipe. He could easily have squeezed, left her for dead.

But he didn't. Why? Because... because his fingerprints would have been all over the room. Because he'd never have gotten away with it.

But he could now, if he wanted to. If he got his hands on her, he could kill her. What could Angel do to stop him?

Maybe prison was a better idea. She'd be safer there.

She started to say just that, then kept quiet. *Prison.* Instead of being free in six months, she'd spend two and a half years behind bars. Thirty months before she could get her life back.

Worse than that, though... How could she face her parents? She'd promised them, promised them she would clean up her act. She'd sworn she was done with her foolishness. She didn't blame them for not believing her. How many times before had she made the same promises? And now, if she got sent to prison, they'd think she'd broken the law again. After all they'd done for her—paying for a rehab she didn't need, supporting her despite her poor choices—now she'd have to tell them she was in prison?

She didn't know what to do. She was faced with two bad choices. "I need to think."

"Your time is short," Routhier said. "Once your house manager reports you missing, I'll have a hard time helping you."

"Can you just give me until tomorrow? If it gets called in, can you... do whatever you people do to not arrest me?"

Routhier glanced at his watch. "It's nine-thirty. You have twelve hours. If I don't hear from you in the morning, I'll issue the arrest warrant myself."

Angel glanced at O'Donnell hoping he'd suggest more time, suggest some alternative to this. He narrowed his eyes but said nothing.

Fine then. Neither good cop nor bad cop cared about her. At least she knew where she stood.

CHAPTER FOUR

Angel should have phoned her brother. She had his address, thanks to their mother, who'd texted it to her when Jack had moved, along with the suggestion that she *drop him a note*.

Because Angel hadn't spoken to her brother in years. Or, perhaps it would be more appropriate to say he hadn't spoken to her. The further she'd drifted into her previous life, the more distant Jack had become. Which was why his house was the perfect place to go tonight. She didn't have enough money for a hotel, and she wanted out of Manchester.

Thirty minutes later, Angel turned onto a quiet street in the tiny town of Nutfield. The house was a charming two-story Cape Cod. The porch light was on, but otherwise, the house was dark. In the driveway were a pickup truck—Jack's, no doubt —and a sedan.

Probably Jack's wife's car. Angel had never met her, hadn't been invited to the wedding. But Mom had kept Angel apprised of her brother's life. Maybe this was a terrible idea. The last thing newlyweds needed was a felon knocking on their door in the middle of the night.

If she'd had anywhere else to go, she'd have chosen it. But if Anton was looking for her, he'd start at her parents' house in Nashua. Her sister lived close enough that he'd check her house next.

Eventually, if Anton wanted to find Angel badly enough, he would locate Jack. Which meant she couldn't stay here. But right now, she needed a blanket and a place to rest until she figured out what she was doing.

She shuffled up the walk. The pain in her side overshadowed all the other minor aches. She could hardly straighten. Gripping the railing, she climbed the steps to the door, then rang the bell.

A lamp turned on in an upstairs window, spilling a tilted rectangle of light on the tree-filled yard. A moment later, the door opened.

Her brother stood there in pajama pants and a gray T-shirt. He was handsome, even with the sleep-tousled hair. "Angel? What are you—?"

"I'm sorry," she said. "I have nowhere else to go."

A woman called from behind him. "Who is it? Is everything OK?" She inched beside him and looked out. Her hair was messy, and she wore yellow pajamas and fuzzy slippers. Even so, she was blond-haired, blue-eyed, and drop-dead gorgeous. "Hi," she said. "I'm Harper."

Angel glanced at Jack, who turned to his wife and said, "My sister, Angel."

"Oh!" Harper smiled as if delighted. She bounced her hip off Jack's. "Get out of the way and let her in."

He did, although the frown on his face was far from delighted.

Angel stepped inside as Jack flipped on the overhead light. She squinted in the sudden brightness.

Harper's smile faded. "What happened? Oh, honey. Come

in. Sit down." With a hand on Angel's back, she guided her into the living room—a pretty space with hardwood floors and over-stuffed furniture—and settled her onto the sofa

Jack followed. "What's wrong?"

"Get the lamp," Harper said. "She's hurt."

"I'm fine." But she wasn't. She could hardly keep her eyes open. Her ribs throbbed. Her arm ached. Her head pounded.

A second light came on, and her brother moved to stand beside his wife. As soon as he got a good look at her, he crouched down, reached toward her.

She flinched.

Jack very gently brushed her hair back and peered at her face. "Who did this to you?"

"It's a very long story," Angel said.

"I'm calling the police."

Angel grabbed his wrist. "No, don't."

Jack yanked his wrist away and stood, but Harper hooked her arm around his. "Let's give her a minute to get settled."

He rounded on his wife. "Someone beat the crap out of my sister. And I'm going to find out who."

Oh. That protectiveness... She remembered that from when they were kids. The kindness brought tears. It was both sweet and undeserved. "I already talked to the police."

Both Jack and Harper looked her way.

"They know. They don't care, but they know."

Harper crouched down beside her. "What hurts?"

She pulled back the T-shirt sleeve on her left arm. This was her first opportunity to get a look at it in the light. A bruise was forming around her wrist.

Jack muttered something under his breath.

"What else?" Harper said.

Angel shifted, lifted her shirt to see her ribs. A faint dark spot marked the place where Anton had kicked her. A pathetic bruise considering how badly they hurt.

Harper sucked in a breath. "Do you think they're broken?"

"No idea," Angel said. "Never had broken ribs."

"Me, either," Harper said. They both looked at Jack, whose face had turned an angry red.

"Who did this to you?"

Angel pulled in a breath. It was starting to hurt even to do that. She focused on Harper. "That's it, really."

Harper brushed Angel's hair back. "And this. He hit you?"

She nodded as she met her sister-in-law's eyes. Sister-in-law. She'd known Jack was getting married, but she hadn't actually processed the sister thing.

"Jack, get the ice pack and Tylenol, please."

He stomped off. When he'd disappeared into another room, Angel said, "I shouldn't have come."

Harper squeezed her hand. "I'm glad you did. The problem is, we don't have a place for you except this couch. There are three bedrooms upstairs, but one is being used as an office, and the other is... We're redecorating it."

"The couch is perfect. I don't think I could climb those stairs right now anyway."

Jack returned, and Harper stepped out of the way. He set a glass of water on the coffee table and handed Angel an ice pack.

She pressed it against her side. The cold stung, but maybe it would numb it. Numb would be a huge improvement.

Jack sat beside her and opened his fist to reveal two pills. "This guy. What can you—?"

"The cops know who he is. It's not your problem."

"I want to help."

She took the pills from his palm, tossed them back, and then sipped the water he'd brought.

Harper said, "I'll get some blankets and a pillow."

Jack said, "Thanks, babe."

Harper stood. "You need pajamas or a T-shirt to sleep in?"

"My bag is in the car."

"I'll get it in a minute," Jack said.

Harper turned toward the staircase.

It was the angle that made Angel realize...

When Harper had gone upstairs, she said, "She's pregnant?"

"Five months."

"Congratulations."

He didn't smile. He looked furious.

"I'm sorry I barged in like this. I didn't think you'd be asleep so early."

"She's tired all the time. I go to bed when she does."

"I bet you're a good husband."

He shrugged and looked away. When he looked back, his eyes were narrowed in suspicion. That didn't take very long. "Aren't you supposed to be in jail?"

"Mom doesn't tell you much, does she?"

He shrugged. "I guess you got out."

"I was in a..." She didn't want to tell him she'd gone to rehab. He already thought very little of her. The last thing she needed was for him to think she was an addict. "It was like a halfway house."

"You were released?"

She looked past him. Stories that would explain her presence at his house filled her head. Lies. Telling the truth would do her no good. He wouldn't believe her anyway. But the truth was all she had. "I was attacked. The guy was in the house."

Jack blinked, swallowed. He touched her cheek. "What was he trying...?" Jack seemed to struggle to find a gentle way to ask the question Opie had blurted out.

"It wasn't like that." Jack already looked murderous. Telling him what Anton had been attempting wouldn't help anything. Except she'd not been honest. Was that okay? A half-truth to give her brother some peace?

She closed her eyes, tried to think. Finally, she tossed up a quick *Forgive me* and continued her explanation. "I called the police, but I didn't go to the hospital. I just want to sleep. I'm going to talk to the detective tomorrow."

She watched Jack's face, waited for him to accuse her of lying. He had every right to. Until she'd invited Jesus into her life a few months before, nearly every word out of her mouth had been a lie. But Jack only regarded her. "It sounds like you've got it under control."

Not even close.

"Why did you come here?" he asked.

"I'm sorry. If I'd known Harper was—"

"I'm glad you came." He brushed her hair back from her face and met her eyes. "I'm not saying you shouldn't have come. I'm just wondering why here. Why not go home?"

Again that battle—should she tell the truth or lie? The truth would be harder to say, harder for him to accept. But a lie... was a lie.

"I'm afraid the guy who attacked me will look for me at Mom and Dad's. And... I know it's a lot to ask, but can you not tell them I'm here. It's hard to explain, and I promise I'll tell you everything eventually."

Jack's eyes narrowed.

"They'll only worry about me. They think I'm safe. There's no reason to let them know differently." Jack started to speak, but she pressed on. "I can't stay here, either, but it'll take him time to track me down here. And by then, I can find someplace to go."

"The police should help you."

The short laugh was both humorless and painful. "They won't."

"Here we go." Harper carried a blanket and pillow down the stairs.

"Thank you," Angel said.

Jack stood. "Is your car locked?"

She patted her pockets. "I hope not. I think I left the keys in the ignition."

He chuckled. A real, honest-to-goodness chuckle. From her brother. Who hated her. Except maybe he didn't.

"Be right back."

Ten minutes later, Angel was tucked onto the couch, a glass of water and two Advil on the table should she need them. Jack and Harper had bid her good-night and gone upstairs.

Now, it was just Angel and her thoughts and memories. And that big looming decision. Work with the cops—and thus with Anton—or go to prison.

Which wasn't exactly lullaby material.

THE SCENT of bacon and coffee wooed Angel to consciousness along with the scrape of a chair, the setting-down of a cup.

The sun shone through the bay window. How had she slept all night?

She shifted to a sitting position on the sofa. Yup, ribs hurt, but that pain was tolerable. She bent her left arm, then turned the wrist in a circle. Again, tolerable. Carefully, she pushed to her feet and pulled in a breath. She was okay. She'd survived. And somehow, she'd slept.

In the little half-bath where she'd cleaned up the night before, Angel got a look at her reflection. Her lip was swollen and cut. A smudge of purple on her cheekbone indicated where

Anton had backhanded her. She studied the marks on her neck. Fingerprints, a thumbprint.

Acid filled her stomach, and she closed her eyes. He could have killed her.

She could be dead right now.

Her parents at the morgue, identifying her body.

Thank You. Thank You, God, for sparing my family that grief. For sparing me. I know I don't deserve it.

As cleaned up as she could get without a shower, Angel padded to the breakfast table, where she found Jack.

He looked up, and a dark expression crossed his features. He masked it quickly with a smile. "Morning."

"Do I smell coffee?"

"Sit." He stood and nodded to a chair. "I'll get it. How'd you sleep?"

"Like a rock." With the words, a thought occurred to her. "What did you give me last night?"

"Tylenol PMs. Figured you could use the rest. I meant to tell you before you took them, but, with everything... I hope that was okay."

That explained the sleep. "Definitely. Thank you."

He poured her a cup of coffee. "Cream and sugar?"

"Sugar."

He set the cup and a sugar dish in front of her, and she dropped a spoonful of sugar in and stirred.

"You still like pancakes?"

"You don't have to feed me."

He leaned against the peninsula countertop that separated the breakfast area from the kitchen. "I'd like to, though, if you're hungry."

She was hungry. In all the craziness of the night before, she'd skipped dinner. "Pancakes were always my favorite."

He winked. "I remember."

While he worked, she took in the space. The house was small but lovely. This room had gray tile floors, what looked like brand new white cabinets, and a light gray patterned backsplash. The granite countertops were dark and marbled. "Did you do all of this?"

He focused on whisking ingredients in the bowl. "Redid almost everything in the house."

"It's beautiful."

His smile looked genuine. It'd been a long time since she and her brother had had a conversation, even longer since they'd had an amicable one. "Thank you," he said. "I'm pleased with how it came out."

"Did you pick out all the"—she spun her finger—"decor?"

His eyebrows lifted. "Surprised?"

She shrugged. "I knew you were handy, but I had no idea you were artistic."

"I copied pictures I saw on Pinterest."

"Did Harper help?"

"I did most of it before we got engaged, but I asked for her input. We have similar taste." He grabbed a pan and set it on the stovetop.

"Harper's really sweet," Angel said. "I like her."

He glanced over his shoulder. "Me, too." That was clear in the way his eyes crinkled at the corners when he talked about her. Seemed Angel's brother had found true love. She was glad for him. Someday, if she ever got her life together, maybe she would, too.

"She was sorry to miss you," he said.

"Oh. I assumed she was sleeping." The clock on the stove told her it was a little after seven. "Where does she work?"

"She cares for her grandfather. Well, he's not actually her grandfather, but... That's a long story. She likes to be there when he wakes up. He's got someone who spends the night with him, but she spends her days over there."

"Huh. I figured she was a model or something. Some job where her looks..." Angel chuckled. "She is ridiculously pretty. I'm trying to figure out how she ended up with you."

Jack lifted the whisk out of the pancake batter and made like he was going to flip it at her.

She held her hands up and laughed. "I'm kidding."

He chuckled. "I caught her in a moment of weakness."

"Nah," Angel said. "You're a catch. How many guys can fix up the kitchen and then prepare a gourmet meal in it?"

"She married me for my cooking skills. She's the only person I know who can ruin canned soup."

Jack cooked a couple of pieces of bacon in the microwave, then set the bacon and pancakes on the table, along with butter and real New Hampshire maple syrup. He added two plates and silverware. "You need anything else? Juice, water?"

"Nope. This is perfect."

She forked a couple of pancakes onto her plate, spread the butter, and added a ribbon of syrup. The first bite was like heaven on her tongue. "Mmm..." She closed her eyes, savored, swallowed. "How in the world do you get them that fluffy?"

He sat across from her with his own plate. "Secret family recipe."

"I'm in your family. Mom never made them like that."

He winked. Apparently, the recipe was going to stay secret.

They ate breakfast, her asking him about his life, about how he and Harper had met. "Long story. We'll tell you about it sometime."

Vague much? But then, she hadn't told him her story, either.

Their new addition was a girl, apparently. Jack's smile lit up when he talked about her.

Her brother wasn't just happy. He was euphoric.

When they finished their meals, she stood to clear the table, but he nudged her back down with a hand to her shoulder. "I got it. You need to rest."

"I could get used to this."

He threw a look over her shoulder—this one less amused and more worried.

"I'm kidding," Angel said. "I'm not planning to stay."

He set the dirty dishes on the counter and faced her. "Where will you go?"

She lifted her right shoulder, careful about the left. That whole side of her body ached. "I don't know yet. I have no idea about this guy... Anton. Maybe he won't come after me. I don't know why he would, except he sort of told me..." What exactly? That he wasn't finished with her. What did that mean? "But maybe he will. And... I mean, this time yesterday, I'd have told you he was this sweet, gentle guy. Today..."

"A boyfriend, or—?"

"No, no. Nothing like that. He..." She started a deep breath, stopped when her ribs ached.

"You need to breathe deeply." Jack walked into the living room and returned with the ice pack and the pillow she'd slept on the night before. He handed her the pillow. "Hold that to your chest. It's supposed to help with the pain. I looked it up."

She did, tried another deep breath. It did help.

"No need to go to the ER for the ribs," he said. "Seems there's not much they can do, and whether they're bruised or cracked, the treatment is the same." He opened the freezer door, tossed the ice pack in, and pulled something out. "You can ice them the first couple of days. Take over-the-counter medications —Tylenol, Advil. Rest often." He handed her the something he'd grabbed, a bag of frozen corn. "Move around when you're not resting. And breathe deeply to keep your lungs clear. Otherwise, you're at risk for pneumonia. If you think breathing hurts..."

She held the frozen corn against her side. "Coughing will be torture."

"Exactly."

She imagined her big brother searching the internet to learn about her injuries, thinking about her, worried about her. The thought made her eyes sting. She held out her hand to him, and he took it. "Thank you. It means a lot."

"Of course. You're my baby sister."

"I thought maybe you'd disowned me by now."

His smile was slight this time. "Never. Been pretty fed up with you at times, but I never stopped loving you. And I never stopped praying for you."

She squeezed his hand. "Thank you. You should know, your prayers worked."

His eyebrows lifted.

"I..." She wasn't sure the right way to say it without sounding all churchy. Finally, she settled on, "I gave my life to Christ a few months ago."

"Oh!" He crouched beside her, rested his hands on her shoulders, and squeezed gently. "I'm happy to hear that. I can't even tell you..."

She leaned into her brother's chest. "Me, too. I have a lot to learn, but I'm trying. I read my Bible every day and pray and go to church."

He settled in the chair beside her, keeping her hand in his. "This is the best news I've had since..."

He seemed to falter.

"Since the baby?" she suggested.

"Better." He touched her chin to raise it. Studied the bruises on her neck. Swallowed. "Was he trying to kill you?"

"I don't think so."

"What can I do?"

She sat back.

"Why would this guy look for you?" Jack swallowed. "Is it like a stalker thing? We have a little experience in that area."

She raised her eyebrows.

"Part of that story we'll tell you someday. I'm just saying, we might be able to offer advice."

"Not a stalker. He was hurting my roommate, and I got in the middle."

"But you told the police. They should arrest him."

She looked away. This was too complicated to explain, and if she did, Jack would only get angrier. That the police would use her like this? It made her angry, too. She glanced at the clock. She had less than two hours to make her decision.

But the decision was made. She wasn't going to prison, not if she could help it.

She turned back to her brother. "It's a long story."

"I have no place to be," he said.

She pushed back in her chair. "Well, I need to get out of your hair. If, on the off chance this guy does look for me, I don't want to be anywhere near you or your wife."

Jack stood. "Where will you go?"

An idea occurred to her. "I could go to a woman's shelter. They'd take one look at me and offer me a room. That's why those places exist, right?"

He was shaking his head before she'd finished. "You're not doing that."

"It's not like I have a lot of choices."

"I want you close by. Far as I know, there are none near here. And anyway, I have options."

"I can't stay here. I can't risk..." And then she remembered that Dad said Jack owned apartment buildings. "If you have a place... I mean, I can't pay you yet, but I'll get a job, and—"

"You're not paying me. You're in trouble." He looked past her, seemed to be thinking. Muttered, "But she'd need a bed..." He wasn't talking to her. Then he snapped his fingers. "I can do better than an apartment. I own a furnished house. I got a guy living there right now, fixing it up, but there's plenty of room for you. Let me make a call."

CHAPTER FIVE

Donovan had known he might have to see her. When he'd heard Jack Rossi had bought this old place on the lake where Donovan and his family used to vacation, when he'd reached out and offered to fix it up in exchange for being able to stay there, he'd known there'd be a slight, practically nonexistent, chance he'd run into Jack's little sister, Angelica.

As he tossed the phone back onto the coffee table, he scoffed at his stupidity. Run into her? That he could have managed. Maybe. This... this was too much. Way too much.

He wandered to the sunroom and looked out the wall of windows to the blue sky above.

No, Lord. You can't be asking me to do this.

As usual, God seemed silent.

Donovan's dad had told him that Angel had "gone away for a while." As if she'd taken an extended cruise to the Mediterranean. That was Dad's way, though. Like when he'd gotten fired because he'd missed work too many times to take care of Mom, he'd said he'd decided to "move on to new opportunities." And when, after Katie's death, Mom slipped into depression and refused to leave her bedroom for months, Dad had said she was "taking a much-needed break." He'd explained selling their home to pay for Katie's last—failed—stint in rehab by calling it "downsizing to something cozier."

How would Dad spin Donovan's life? Donovan could hear the man's voice now, that deep timber, always gentle, always generous, like the man. "Donovan's living on a gorgeous lakeside property, feeding his muse and painting the views."

True. Also not true. It wasn't as if Dad would come out and tell their friends that Donovan couldn't get over his sister's death. That he was hiding in a big rambling house to avoid contact with all human life.

When Dad said Angel had *gone away for a while*, Donovan had assumed she'd finally been arrested. A quick Google search had confirmed that.

She was supposed to be in prison.

So why was she on her way to his house?

Not *his* house, though. That was the problem.

He had no right to deny Angel entrance.

He'd been avoiding people for months, and now he had to face the one person he'd hoped to never see again. The only person in the world he hated more than he hated himself.

He'd just have to ignore her. Pretend she wasn't there. He could do that.

He picked up his paintbrush. He'd finally gotten the green exactly right for those dark pines. He had to hurry. Soon, the leaves would start changing colors, and he'd have a short window of opportunity to capture the beauty. He focused on the evergreens, dabbing at the canvas. Except... That didn't look right. Gazing at the tree-covered hill across the lake, he took the scene in, then returned his attention to the canvas.

Angelica Rossi.

The vision of the trees was pushed out by the face of the girl he'd once known. He couldn't do this now. Couldn't focus on Katie's painting when Angel was on her way here.

How was he ever going to do this with her hanging around?

He dropped the paintbrush, cleaned his supplies. He'd try again tomorrow. Tomorrow, he'd be able to focus.

Today, he had to steel himself to face her.

CHAPTER SIX

Glad Jack had insisted on driving Angel to the house—seemed her constant wincing in pain had convinced him she needed help—Angel peered at the lake between the cabins and tall trees. The sunshine glinted off the water. The forecast had promised more warm temperatures, but by the weekend, autumn would return.

They passed the marina and a couple of lakeside restaurants. Based on the lobster painted red on one sign, it looked like a seafood place. The other—Kathy's Kountry Kitchen—seemed casual. Both had outdoor seating that took full advantage of the beautiful view.

"The restaurants are new," Jack said. "Since they broke ground on the country club and golf course on the far side of Clearwater Lake, new businesses have been springing up."

"It's charming."

He glanced at her. "I love it here. A lot different from Nashua, though. I know how much you always liked city life."

She had, before. Right now, this place felt idyllic. "Tell me about this house where I'll be staying."

"I bought it a couple of months ago. It's an old Victorian in need of repair, but it's got good bones."

"Are you and Harper going to move into it when it's finished?"

He chuckled. "Not a chance. It's way too big for a single-family home."

"How big is it?"

"Hold on and you'll see." He turned away from the lake and snaked along a narrow drive that barely interrupted the forest on both sides. A moment later, they entered a clearing.

Angel gaped at the house in front of her. It was enormous, the kind of place that would be converted into an apartment building in the city. A wide front porch wrapped around the whole downstairs. The second floor was as large as the first. The third story was smaller, standing above it all like a sentry. She counted three chimneys. "You *own* that?"

She glanced at him to see him gazing at the building as well. "Eight bedrooms. And there's a full basement that I'm planning to finish. It opens on the side to the backyard."

It was amazing in spite of the signs of neglect, the fading green paint and peeling white trim. Someone needed to take pruning shears to the bushes and a hammer and nails to the sagging porch.

"What in the world are you going to do with such a big house?"

"Repair it, then flip it. I think it'll make a great B&B."

"Why sell it, then?" She turned to her brother. "Why not run it yourself?"

"Harper has no desire to own a B&B, and my passion is real estate. I'd get bored running a place like this."

Bored? She looked at the building again. As a kid, she'd longed for city life, for adventure. Now, what she really wanted was security and peace. Freedom. Everything a place like this offered.

He opened his door. "Stay put. Let me come around and help you out."

She pushed her door open, thinking she could manage by herself, but by the time she got one foot out of the car, Jack was there. Pain made her groan, and she took his hand before shifting on her seat to get her other foot onto the ground.

"Take it easy," he said.

After a deep, painful breath, she pushed to standing. Her ribs protested, but she made it.

Jack held her until she was steady. "You okay?"

"Piece of cake."

He snatched her duffel from the backseat, tossed it over his shoulder, and wrapped his hand around her upper arm. "I wish you'd stay with us for a couple of days. We could take care of you."

"I'll be fine here."

Together, they started up the walk—flagstone pavers that were nearly covered by the encroaching grass. Now that she was on her feet, the pain wasn't so bad. And she was enjoying her brother's comforting presence, especially as she felt a little apprehensive about this situation. Jack hadn't told her much about the guy who lived here, except that he was someone Jack had known in high school who was staying in the house while he fixed it up.

"You're sure he won't mind me moving in?"

"I'm doing him a favor." They were almost to the steps when Jack stopped and faced her. "If he gives you any trouble at all or makes you feel uncomfortable, you let me know, and I'll toss him out."

"Oh, I don't want—"

"This is my house"—Jack leveled a serious gaze in her direction—"and you're my sister. Donovan's a good guy. Everything I know about him tells me I can trust him, but he's not exactly personable. If he's a jerk to you, he can go."

"Don't you need him?"

"I can do the work myself. He needed a place, and I had one. And honestly, he's a strong guy, and from what I know of him, he's pretty protective. If you won't stay with me"—he shrugged, gazed at the house—"I don't mind the idea of leaving you with him." Then he regarded her again. "Just remember, my loyalty is to you."

She didn't deserve Jack's loyalty. *Lord, help me to not ruin this.*

"You hurting? I can carry you—"

"No, no." She looked at Jack, at his kind eyes. "I'm just... Thank you for all you're doing."

He smiled, but it didn't stick as he glanced at the house. "I'd really rather you stay with me."

She patted the hand he'd wrapped around her arm. "I can take care of myself, Jack. Believe me."

With raised eyebrows, he gave her ribs a look, a good point he was kind enough not to press. "Promise me you'll let me know if Donovan doesn't stay on his best behavior."

"I promise."

Slowly, they climbed the steps while she considered the name. She'd known a Donovan once, a long time ago. She couldn't place his face, and she couldn't remember how she knew him.

It probably wasn't the same guy, anyway.

They had just reached the porch when the oversize door flung open. A man filled the space. She first noticed his high cheekbones and strong chin, though much of his face was covered with days of whiskers not quite thick enough to be a beard. Straggly dark brown hair brushed his shoulders. He was tall, though not as tall as her brother. He wore jeans and a white T-shirt, both of which were covered in paint splatters. His slim T-shirt failed to hide muscles that, if she used her imagination, she could picture on the cover of a romance novel. His stance was wide, his arms were crossed.

His eyes blazed with pure hatred. The look passed quickly, covered by a closed-mouth smile that didn't reach his eyes.

He didn't seem familiar, except there was something in the set of his chin... Was this the Donovan she'd met before? She doubted it. Surely she'd remember this handsome, scruffy, brooding man.

He focused on her brother and held out his hand.

Jack shook it. "Donovan Gilcreast, this is my sister, Angel."

Angel held out her hand, and Donovan barely touched it before backing up to allow them to step in.

Gilcreast. Donovan Gilcreast. Of course. This was Katie's older brother. She and Katie had been friends in middle school and freshman year. They'd gone their separate ways at that point, but Angel had met Katie's geeky older brother many times. He'd been skinny and worn glasses, and he'd always been sketching something. Even back then, he rarely talked.

Now, he swiveled and walked away, his footsteps fading as he disappeared in the dark space.

She whispered, "Friendly fellow."

"He's not much of a talker. He was always shy, but..." Jack shrugged. "Come on."

She stepped into a hallway wider than her childhood bedroom. The walls were lined in dingy yellow floral wallpaper, the woodwork dark and chipped. But the space... It was lovely. Hardwood floors led into rooms off both sides. In front of her, a darkly stained staircase curved to the second floor. She peered up and saw that the staircase rose another level.

Silently, she moved to the room on her right, a parlor, she

assumed. More dingy wallpaper and old drapes darkened the space, but the bones... Tall baseboards. Intricate crown molding. A stone fireplace. And a bay window with a built-in seat. Someone had shoved all the furniture into the middle of the room and covered it with a cloth. She lifted one corner, saw the beautifully carved legs of a Victorian-style sofa. The fabric was worn, but the piece itself was impressive.

"It came furnished." Jack's voice startled her. She'd forgotten he was there.

"Have you had the furniture appraised?"

He shook his head. "Been focused on the house. Do you think it's worth anything?"

She lifted more of the sheet. "If it's authentic." She didn't know much about antique furniture, but she had developed an eye for quality. That skill had been integral to her livelihood, such as it was. No sense risking her freedom stealing a fake.

"I'll do that," Jack said. "Thanks for the tip."

She twisted to face her brother, and pain shot through her side.

He hooked his hand around her right arm. "We'll save the tour for when you're feeling better. Let's find Donovan."

Where had the man run off to?

She walked beside Jack down the hall and into a room at the back of the house. Dark paneling lined the walls. A sofa and two chairs faced a black TV screen, which was perched on an old table beside another fireplace. Beyond the room, a wall of windows opened on a sunroom, where she spied an unfinished painting resting on an easel.

Jack led her to the couch. "Here, sit. I'll go find him."

Her phone trilled a reminder. When she was settled and Jack gone, she glanced at the time.

She had five minutes to contact Routhier. She couldn't talk

to him right now, but a text should hold him off for a few minutes.

I'm in. Can't talk right now. I'll call soon.

She saw those dancing dots that told her the detective was already responding. Had he been waiting, phone-in-hand, to call for an arrest warrant the moment her twelve hours were up?

More likely, Routhier had been waiting for her to agree to his crazy scheme. A moment later, his text came through.

When can we meet?

She sighed. She'd prefer she never saw Routhier—or Anton Turner—again. She responded with *Tomorrow. I'll text you a location.*

She'd better enjoy her one day of freedom. Tomorrow could very well be the beginning of the end of it.

CHAPTER SEVEN

In the downstairs half bath, Donovan focused on a particularly stubborn section of paper between the toilet and the pedestal sink, using his putty knife to gently scrape it off. Last thing he needed was to ruin the plaster.

Back here, he could barely hear the voices.

He'd always liked Jack Rossi. Unlike a lot of kids in high school, kids who either ignored or picked on a skinny, geeky kid, Jack had been kind to Donovan. They hadn't been friends—Donovan hadn't had many of those until college—but they'd been in some of the same classes. They'd gotten along.

Angel was another story. She was four years younger than Donovan, and he only knew her through his sister. He knew enough about Angel to know she'd drawn his sister into trouble. Only Katie was gone now.

And, in a twist of irony, Angel was here, alive and well.

Although *well* was an overstatement. Donovan might have missed the bruise on her cheek if his gaze hadn't snagged on the cut on her lip. She was injured and in trouble. Jack had said she needed a place to stay. Maybe she needed a place to hide.

Someone like her probably had all sorts of people to hide from. Thieves, liars.

Cops.

Who knew what she was into?

Why Jack would want her in his house, Donovan couldn't fathom. Maybe if Donovan had been as good to his own sister...

He pushed too hard on the putty knife and gouged the wall. *Great job, Gilcreast. Make more work for yourself, why don't you?*

He set the tool down and sprayed more wallpaper stripper, then turned to a section he'd prepared earlier and started to peel. This wallpaper had to have been on the walls for decades. He'd tried to steam it off, but the old-fashioned spray-and-peel method was working faster. Even still, it was coming off inches at a time.

A knock came on the open bathroom door. "You want to tell me what that was about?" Jack's voice was low, nearly a growl.

Donovan kept stripping. "You need something?"

"Is this going to be a problem?"

Donovan still didn't turn. No need to let Jack see the hatred he was trying to hide. Though Angel had seen it when he'd first laid eyes on her. He knew by the surprised reaction in her eyes. Served her right. He continued with the wallpaper, managed to get a good strip peeling off. "Your house. Your sister. I'll stay out of her way as long as she stays out of mine."

"You have something against my sister?"

The strip tore. He balled it up and tossed it into the bag he'd propped in the corner. "Barely know her."

"Have you two had a run-in in the past?"

"Nope."

"Stop what you're doing for a second."

With a huff, Donovan stood and faced him.

Jack stepped forward. This bathroom was barely large enough for one man, way too small for two.

Donovan crossed his arms. "What?"

"I like our arrangement, but if my sister's presence is a problem, you can find somewhere else to stay. I won't stop you."

Donovan wanted to shove Jack's *arrangement* down his throat, but the painting... He had to finish Katie's painting, and he couldn't do that from anywhere else in the world. He needed at least three more weeks in this house. He'd take longer if Jack would give it to him, long enough to get all the paintings done for the show in December. If he didn't finish Katie's painting, though, none of the rest would be completed.

"Well?" Jack said.

He swallowed his retort. "It's not a problem."

Jack dipped his head once. "Where do you want her? She's injured. I was thinking the room down here, if it's not in disarray."

Down here. Donovan was hoping to keep her as far away from himself as possible. "I'll clean it out."

"I can help. Have you been working in there?"

He shook his head. "Sleeping."

"I don't want to displace you, but—"

"She's hurt. It's fine. If you'll..." He nodded, and Jack stepped back.

Donovan passed him and headed down the hall to his bedroom. He didn't know what this room had been used for originally. Not a bedroom, that was for sure, but the previous owners had converted it to a master suite complete with a full bath. It was only fair that Angel sleep here. Donovan could lie awake and stare at the ceiling in any room in the house.

He gathered his things, which he'd unpacked into the bureau that had been left from the previous owners, and shoved them into his suitcase. Five minutes later, he hefted it upstairs to the first bedroom he came to. Dust everywhere. He'd covered all the furniture with drop cloths when he'd first started working on the place, so at least the bed wouldn't be too dirty to sleep in. There was a bureau. A working bathroom down the hall. This would be fine.

He was tempted to go straight back to the wallpaper, but Jack hadn't left. Donovan should play nice.

He found Angel in the living room with a pillow hugged to her chest. She looked up when he walked in. Her eyes were narrowed, her mouth pinched.

"You okay?"

"Bruised ribs. Jack tells me I have to breathe deeply or I'll get pneumonia."

"Car accident?"

She shook her head. "Not exactly."

What did that mean? Had she fallen? Or... He thought of that bruise on her cheek. Had someone hit her?

It was instinct, that rise of protectiveness. Who would hit a tiny little thing like her? Yeah, maybe she was a thief and worse, but she couldn't weigh more than a hundred pounds. He could bench press her and barely break a sweat.

Since when did Donovan care about what happened to Angelica Rossi? He shoved those stupid feelings aside. From what he knew about Angel, she could take care of herself.

She peered past him. "Where's Jack?"

Footsteps in the hallway answered the question. A moment later, Jack stepped into the living room. "I put your bag in your bedroom. Come on and I'll help you down there."

She started to stand. Her wince had Donovan crossing the room to offer a hand. He reached for her left arm, but she yanked it away, and, in the process, fell back onto the sofa. So the arm was injured too.

Jack regarded her. "Maybe you should rest awhile."

She closed her eyes, nodded. "I feel like I've used all the day's energy, and it's only ten o'clock."

Donovan returned to his place by the doorway.

"You need to take it easy," Jack said. "Your room is down the back hallway and on the right. Only bedroom downstairs."

Her eyes rounded, and she looked past Donovan to the entry. "There's another hall?"

"Behind the staircase," Jack said.

"I can show you."

They both turned to Donovan.

"Later. When you feel like getting up again."

Her smile was beautiful. She was beautiful. Always had been. She'd always been a nightmare, too.

"Thank you." She focused on Jack. "I'm sure you have other things to do today. Don't hang around on my account. I'll call an Uber to take me to my car."

Jack leaned down and kissed her cheek. Her smile widened as if she were surprised by the gesture. "Harper and I will run it by tonight. You don't need to go anywhere today, do you?"

She shook her head. "But I hate for you to—"

"It's no trouble, sis." He squeezed her shoulder. "See you tonight."

Jack turned, caught Donovan's eye. Though he didn't speak, the message was clear. *Be nice, or you're out of here.*

Donovan nodded, and Jack continued on his way. A moment later, the front door closed with a dull thud.

And he and Angel were alone.

CHAPTER EIGHT

Angel awakened on the too-soft mattress and rubbed her ribs. The old house was unnaturally quiet. Or maybe the quiet was natural. After rehab and the sober living house, quiet felt foreign. She hadn't had her own room for months.

The thought of roommates brought Brittney to mind. After her shower the night before, Angel had tried a few times to call her, but the woman never answered.

Was she okay? Had she told the police about Anton? Angel seriously doubted it.

She'd given up reaching Brittney and gone to bed. And stared at the ceiling for hours, listening to the creaking of the old house. She'd slept some, thank heavens.

As soon as the black sky started to brighten beyond her windows, Angel padded across the bedroom's cold hardwood floor into the bathroom. This room had been almost completely redone. A claw-footed tub sat atop light-colored tiles, which also lined the new shower. Rimless glass shower doors showed off the workmanship within. The only glaring issue was the vanity.

Donovan had explained that the new vanity had come damaged, and he'd had to order another one.

She brushed her teeth and her hair. The bruise that had been slight the day before was more pronounced today, but the cut on her lip was healing, and the swelling had gone down.

Her ribs were painful but bearable. Her left arm was better, too. She'd iced them both the day before, off and on, while watching TV and dozing in and out.

Jack and Harper had brought Angel's car late in the afternoon, along with bags of groceries and a couple of casseroles Jack had pulled from his freezer. She'd been ravenous, had nearly cried at their kindness.

Donovan had wandered through a few times but had barely spoken to her. He didn't like her. Maybe he knew she'd been arrested. Maybe he didn't like criminals in general—she could understand that—but this felt personal. It was a conundrum she hoped to get to the bottom of today. She didn't want to live in a house with a man who loathed her. And she wasn't about to complain to Jack. Jack would send him away, and she wouldn't do that to either of them. She wouldn't be here long enough to ruin the deal they had going.

Finished in the bathroom, she flipped on the bedroom's overhead light—the only one in the sparsely furnished space—and then opened the curtains. There were four oversize windows, two on each exterior wall. The side windows looked across a weedy lawn toward a forest beyond. The back windows gave her an amazing view of the lake. The sun hadn't crested the horizon yet, and the world was bathed in varying shades of gray. With the fog lifting from the lake, the scene was eerie and ethereal, yet somehow peaceful.

She dressed and headed toward the kitchen but was sidetracked when she reached the living area where she'd spent the previous afternoon. Beyond the windows, Donovan stood in the sunroom in front of his easel, gaze transfixed on the vista in front of him. He wore his brown hair in a ponytail over a white T-shirt and blue jeans.

She stepped into the room behind him, the pungent scent of oil paint and turpentine filling her nostrils. She thought she'd say good-morning. He didn't seem to hear her walk in.

This was the first time she'd been in the sunroom, and she peeked beyond Donovan's shoulder to the canvas. He'd sketched the lake, the trees on the hill on the far side, even the cabins near the water. Now, he was dabbing at the trees with dark green paint.

She turned, saw more canvases stacked against the walls all around her. Beautiful landscapes—a lake, a cabin in the woods, a lighthouse. Even in the dim light, she could see the paintings were exquisite.

Donovan Gilcreast was a true talent.

He hadn't heard her behind him. Not that she was being sneaky, but with the hum of the heater, her slight sounds were muffled. Plus, he seemed engrossed in his work. She sat on the plaid sofa, trying not to disturb him.

And, if she were honest, to observe. As soon as he noticed her, he'd no doubt banish her from the sunroom altogether.

She watched him work, eventually slipping down to a reclining position. The couch was old and worn out, but if she shifted away from that one aggressive spring, it was comfortable. The air in the sunroom was chillier than in the rest of the house, but a crocheted afghan had been draped over the arm of the couch. She pulled it over herself and watched him paint. And then, her eyes drifted closed.

"What the...!"

She sat up. Her ribs exploded in pain, and she doubled over, crossed her arms, breathed through it.

"What are you doing here?"

She glanced up to see Donovan glowering down at her and wielding a paintbrush like a dagger.

What *was* she doing there? She must have fallen asleep. And by the looks of the room, quite some time ago. The sun was up beyond the windows. The painting he'd been working on had dark pines where only pencil marks had been before.

He saw what she was looking at and shifted to block it. "Why are you here?"

"I didn't want to disturb you." She hated the crack in her voice and cleared her throat.

"You could have *not* disturbed me from any other room in the house."

"I thought you might want coffee."

He sniffed the air. "You didn't make coffee."

"I-I was going to, but then I was fascinated watching you."

"So fascinated you fell asleep?"

Okay, that was a bit odd. She'd lain awake half the night and then fallen asleep in the presence of a total stranger, a stranger who hated her. What was wrong with her?

Except, she remembered those moments just before she'd drifted off. She'd felt at peace, certainly more peaceful than she'd felt sleeping on Jack's couch and a whole lot more than she'd felt in the locked bedroom the night before. What was it? The sunroom? The paintings? The windows?

That feeling of peace couldn't have anything to do with the man who was practically snarling at her.

She swung her legs to the floor—ugly vinyl tiles—and pushed to her feet. "I'm going to make coffee. Would you like some?"

He glared, turned back to his easel, and ignored her.

Fine, then. He could make his own.

She stepped into the living area and through the door that led to the kitchen, where she flipped on the overhead lights. The room was bathed in a soft white glow, thanks to the bulbs recessed in the ceiling and the sun shining through windows that faced the lake. This was the only room in the house completely finished, and Donovan had done an artful job. It was an industrial space, not meant for eating in but large enough to prepare food for a crowd. He'd installed new cabinets, which ringed three walls, and an island with two stools pushed beneath the overhang. The cabinetry was a soft gray and contrasted beautifully with the white subway tiles that made up the backsplash. The hardwood floors continued into this room, giving the sleek space a homey feel.

Angel found the coffeemaker and prepared enough for four cups. Donovan was grumpy and inhospitable, but that didn't mean she needed to be. While the coffee brewed, she opened the refrigerator—an oversize stainless steel side-by-side—and found the ingredients she wanted.

While bacon fried on the stove, Angel chopped a bell pepper and an onion and grated the cheddar cheese. Like Jack, she'd always loved cooking. When they were kids, they used to fight over who would get to help Mom in the kitchen. Their older sister, Gloria, always offered to do the dishes, uninterested in learning to cook.

Fifteen minutes later, with crispy bacon cooling on a plate beside the stovetop, she poured herself a cup of coffee and cracked eggs into a bowl.

She turned in search of a whisk and caught sight of Donovan in the doorway. She gasped and covered her chest with her hand.

"Don't like people lurking about?" His gaze cut toward the sunroom. "Find it annoying?"

She dropped her hand. "I was trying not to disturb you."

He shrugged, leaned against the door jamb, and crossed his arms.

"This kitchen is beautiful."

One of his shoulders almost lifted in a half shrug.

"Coffee?"

He crossed the space, poured himself a cup.

"I thought maybe you didn't drink it, since you've been up for hours and hadn't had any."

He stepped to the far side of the island and looked out the window at the same view he'd been studying when she'd *lurked* in the sunroom earlier.

"You're pretty focused when you paint," she said.

He sipped the brew, said nothing.

"You want something to eat?"

He glanced back, first at her, then at the food on the counter. That shoulder lifted again.

"I'm making scrambled eggs. Do you like that?"

A nod.

"Don't talk so much," she said. "Let a girl get a word in edgewise."

He turned back to the windows.

Fine, then. She cracked a few more eggs, whisked them, and poured them into the pan. She added the veggies and, when the eggs were nearly done, the cheese.

Maybe he didn't dislike her. Maybe he disliked people in general. Except... She couldn't stop seeing the look he'd given her the day before when they'd first arrived. That had felt personal.

She thought back to their childhood. She couldn't remember having been anything but cordial to him the many times she'd gone to Katie's house. He was her friend's geeky older brother. Not cute, not cool, but not mean, either. Certainly nothing like the guy brooding at the windows.

Maybe this wasn't Katie's brother. Maybe she'd never met

this guy before. Except... Donovan Gilcreast? It wasn't exactly a *John Smith* sort of name, was it?

When the food was ready, she put a couple of plates on the bar, scooped the eggs onto them—a spoonful for herself, the rest for him—and set the plate with the bacon in front of them. "Soup's on." She skirted the island and sat on one of the two bar stools there.

He walked around the island, pulled the plate across to himself, and ate standing up.

Wow. He wouldn't even sit with her.

Their forks clinked against the heavy plates in the otherwise silent room. She focused on her food until she'd scraped the last bite. Only then did she steal a glance at him. He was staring at her with naked hatred.

She almost confronted him. At the fury in his eyes, she lost her nerve, swallowed, and asked, "Aren't you Katie's older brother?"

His eyes narrowed an instant before he averted his gaze. How could her question have made him angrier?

For a moment, she thought he wasn't going to answer. Then he nodded.

"I thought so," Angel said. "You used to paint back then, too."

Another nod before he shoveled food into his mouth as if he were in a race.

"Your paintings are amazing."

No response.

"How is Katie?"

His fork stilled, hovered over the plate. He stood, dumped the rest of his breakfast into the trash, and headed for the door.

What in the world? Angel should let it go, let him leave and quit trying to befriend him. But behind the anger, she'd seen a glimpse of something that twisted her heart. Raw pain. "Is she okay?"

Donovan froze at the threshold. He turned and glared at her. "Katie died of an overdose three months ago."

∼

DEAD? Katie was dead?

Angel could only watch helplessly as he stormed from the kitchen. She was stunned by Donovan's words.

Her friend was dead.

Okay, maybe they hadn't been friends in a long time, not since ninth grade. They'd both dreamed of adventure back then, but Angel's idea of adventure had been very different from Katie's. Neither of their ideas had been good, safe, or wise. Angel had started shoplifting, perfecting her skills of deceit and manipulation. Katie, on the other hand, had started using drugs. She'd tried to pressure Angel into trying them when they were about fifteen. Angel hadn't refused out of some sense of morality. She'd avoided drugs because she needed to be sharp, not dull-witted, to get away with her increasingly clever and high-value schemes.

It was when Angel had not only refused to try drugs but had encouraged Katie to give them up that their friendship fell apart. They started hanging with different crowds and lost touch. After graduation, Angel had hardly thought of Katie again.

And now, she was dead.

A seed of guilt tried to take root in her heart, but she yanked it out. Angel was no more responsible for Katie's choices than Katie was for Angel's. Rather than let guilt pull her down, she closed her eyes and prayed for Donovan and his parents. She couldn't imagine the pain they must be going through.

And maybe that explained Donovan's bizarre behavior. He'd always been socially awkward, and now he was socially awkward and grieving. Her presence, an old friend of his sister's from before the drugs, likely made the process more difficult.

She had problems of her own, but as long as she was sharing a house with Donovan, she would do everything in her power to be kind to him, to forgive him his angry looks and refusal to talk to her. She'd never lacked for friends and had always been able to charm even the most cynical of people when she wanted to. She used to use those skills to lull people into believing she was trustworthy, but not anymore. Now, she would try to use her God-given pleasant personality to bless Donovan Gilcreast.

Whether he liked it or not.

Decision made, Angel cleaned the kitchen until it gleamed and returned to the bedroom. Thanks to her aching ribs, it took longer to shower and prepare for the day than usual, but she was ready in plenty of time to leave to meet Routhier. She grabbed her cell phone and keys and followed sounds of scraping to the room next to the parlor. She hadn't done more than glance in here the day before. Now, she studied the space. It was small and cramped with the cloth-draped furniture in the center. That strangely shaped item could only be a grand piano.

So this was the music room. She itched to pull back the covering to get a look at it. If it was anything like what she'd seen the day before, it would be gorgeous.

Donovan stood on a ladder near the back of the room running some sort of tool over the faded wallpaper. He'd added a baseball cap to the outfit he'd worn earlier. His T-shirt rose and fell with his motions. His broad shoulders V'd down to a slim waist. He certainly was attractive when he wasn't glowering at her.

She knocked on the entryway—no need to be accused of lurking again.

He turned, but not quite enough to see her, nodded, and continued the work.

"What are you working on?" Not that it wasn't obvious, but maybe if she could get him to answer…

"Stripping wallpaper."

"What's that thing in your hand?"

He blew out a tortured breath. "It scores the paper, helps the liquid get in."

"Water, or…?" She let the question hang in the air while he ran the tool over the wallpaper. A couple of minutes passed while she watched him work. She was sure he wasn't going to answer as he climbed down from the ladder, tossed the round tool on the floor, and sipped from a bottle of water.

Then he picked up a spray bottle. "Wallpaper stripper. Dissolves the glue." He climbed back up the ladder and sprayed.

"I've got to go out for a little while."

He turned, eyes narrowed beneath the brim of his ball cap. "Where?"

"Meeting someone. I shouldn't be gone long. You need anything while I'm out?"

"Don't you need to recuperate after your…" He turned back to the paper and shook his head slightly.

"My arm is already feeling better. That was a sprain, I think. The ribs hurt, but if I keep moving, it's not that bad after a while."

He sprayed, sprayed, sprayed.

After another minute, she said, "Do you need anything as long as I'm out?"

"Don't know where you're headed."

"Manchester."

He climbed down from the ladder and set the spray bottle on the floor, then lifted his cap and wiped sweat from his brow with the hem of his T-shirt, revealing those abs she'd imagined the day before. The reality far surpassed the picture she'd conjured.

Every gesture was like poetry. Donovan moved with grace and fluidity, not at all like the awkward teen she remembered.

He snatched a rectangular can off the floor and turned to face her. "Could use more of this, if you pass a hardware store."

She hadn't thought he'd take her up on the offer. When he did, her heart did a little flip. Maybe they could be friends after all.

She snapped a photo of the can with her phone. "Anything else?"

He shook his head, sipped his water again.

"Okay, then. I'll pick it up. I should be back in a few hours."

He grabbed a tool that looked like a putty knife and started working on a different section of wallpaper.

Dismissing her. They hadn't exactly conversed, but he'd only glared at her once. She'd call it a win.

In the car, Angel called Jack, who'd texted asking how she was feeling. They chatted while she drove to a hardware store, him questioning how she felt, her assuring him she was recovering and that Donovan was being nice. Not entirely true, but she could handle him. After purchasing the wallpaper stripper, Angel snaked her sedan up to the third floor of a parking garage off Elm and found a spot on the outside half-wall between two oversize SUVs. She'd hoped to beat Routhier and Opie O'Donnell, but the detectives approached as soon as she opened her car door.

By the time she'd climbed from the car, the pain in her ribs sharp, the men were standing behind her car, blocking escape. Her heartbeat thumped. A flash of memory from the other night, trapped in the bedroom with Anton, had her backing up.

The redheaded detective must've seen something in her expression, because he said, "It's okay. You're safe."

Routhier shot his partner a smirk before focusing on her. "This spot was your idea."

"I know." She took a deep breath. This was a good meeting place. Public, but they wouldn't be seen talking. She swallowed the irrational fear. Or maybe it was rational fear, considering these guys held her future in their hands.

Routhier looked around at the parked cars before turning toward her. "You decided to work with us?"

Her heart was racing. What she wanted was to run away, pretend none of this was happening. Pretend the events of the other night had been nothing more than a bad dream. Unfortunately, the pain she experienced with every breath reminded her that the attack had been very real. The attack by a man these guys wanted her to... what? "I think so," she said.

"You *think* so?" Routhier's eyebrows lifted. "You'd better know so, or you're going straight to prison."

As if she didn't understand the power he held over her. Her probation would be yanked and her suspended sentence unsuspended if Routhier told the judge she'd both lost her job and left the sober living house. "Where is this theft supposed to happen?"

Routhier said, "No idea."

At the same time, Opie said, "Somewhere nearby." He glanced at his partner. "We think."

"And how do you know this?" she asked.

The men glanced at each other. "We have a guy," Routhier said, "a confidential informant like you."

"I'm not a CI."

Routhier ignored her. "Anton told the guy he's planning something big."

"They're old friends," Opie said. "They worked together a few years back."

"And why do you trust this CI?" Angel asked.

"Trust? Hardly." Routhier shrugged. "So far, his information's been good."

A car drove by. Angel looked down and away. The chances that it was someone she knew were slim, but she wasn't risking it. Though probably nobody would see her past these two men. When the car was gone, she said, "What information?"

"Different cases. Not important." Routhier said.

This wasn't helpful. "Look, if you're not going to tell me everything—"

"You're going to have to trust us," Opie said.

Her burst of laughter was anything but amused and had her holding her hand against the pain in her ribs. "Why would I be dumb enough to do that?"

Routhier pulled a set of handcuffs from his pocket. "Turn around. We'll take you in."

She didn't move.

The detectives didn't, either. They needed her, but she needed them too.

"Fine." She really didn't want to go to prison. "You said something about talking to a judge?"

"I can get you a deal," Routhier said.

A deal. A deal that would set her free? Really and truly? "What do I have to do?"

Routhier held out his arms in a no-big-deal gesture. "Contact Anton and work with him."

"Why would I do that? The guy tried to... The guy attacked me."

"He thinks he holds your freedom in his hands," Routhier said. "You'll call him, ask him if he turned you in for not coming home the other night. Tell him that if he does, you'll report him for attacking you."

"Did he? Turn me in?"

"Not yet," Routhier said. "Not as far as we've heard."

"So you want me to threaten him? Nobody would believe me. He knows that."

Opie's voice was low, gentle. "It's the only leverage you have, Angel. You have to try to use it, or he's going to be suspicious."

That made sense.

Routhier said, "You'll have to threaten to go to the cops. He won't be scared. He's going to make a counteroffer, try to get you to help him with something. You agree to it, and you're in."

In, when all she'd wanted, all she'd prayed for months, was to get out of the old life she was trying to leave behind. She backed up a step, crossed her arms. "What if you're wrong?"

Routhier smiled at his partner. "We're not."

They looked a lot more confident than she felt. "What aren't you telling me?"

Routhier said nothing.

She focused on Opie, who shrugged. "That CI we told you about? Anton asked him if he knew anybody who could help him with a heist. He said he'd look into it and get back to him. Then he told us."

"We gave your name to the CI, who passed it on to Anton," Routhier said. "A week later, a spot magically"—he air-quoted the word—"opened up in his sober living house, and you were accepted."

Wow.

So they'd set this whole thing in motion.

Routhier had gotten her fired.

Which had resulted in her going back to the house early, which had resulted in her getting attacked. Not that Routhier could have known that would happen. At least she'd rescued Brittney. That was something, but...

"You've been setting me up from the start," she said.

"This is going to be good for you." Routhier smiled, showing his teeth like a predator watching his prey.

Prison, or go along with this crazy scheme? Work with a man who'd attacked her. Work with a man who'd tried to rape her friend. And if what Opie had told her two days before was true, she'd work with a man who'd murdered a cop.

But on the other hand... prison.

She didn't want to go to prison.

She really didn't want her parents to visit her in prison.

The detectives watched her, Routhier with that predatory smile, Opie with squinty concerned eyes. As if he cared. She wasn't dumb enough to fall for their good cop/bad cop routine. They were both using her. They were both sending her into danger.

As if he could read her mind, Opie said, "I promise we'll do everything in our power to keep you safe."

In their power. As long as it didn't get in the way of their operation. Because, as a CI, she'd only be valuable as long as she was feeding them information. If Anton found her out, she'd be useless. They'd write her off and find someone else to use.

But... prison.

And she was good at what she did. She could convince Anton to trust her. She could do this.

"I want a clean record, no matter how it ends up. No felony conviction. Nothing hanging over my head. Free."

Routhier was shaking his head before she finished her statement. "If we get a conviction—"

"Forget it." No way was she risking all of this under those circumstances. Too much could go wrong. "It's not worth the risk."

The men looked at each other. Routhier sighed. "You'll call Anton today?"

"I don't have a number for him."

"Look up Cambridge House on your phone, call the main number, and leave a message. He'll get back to you."

"I'm not meeting with him until I see the deal."

Routhier nodded. "Fair enough. We'll be in touch."

SHE HATED TO ADMIT IT, but Routhier was three steps ahead. After he and Opie—she figured the younger cop would hate the moniker, but it was stuck in her head now—left, she climbed into her car and found a number for Cambridge House. A woman answered the phone, and Angel asked for Anton. He wasn't in, but the woman took her number and promised to pass it along.

Maybe he wouldn't call back. Maybe... maybe the cops were wrong about all of this.

Angel turned her car toward Nutfield. She was exhausted, her ribs aching with every breath. She needed ibuprofen and a nap.

She'd not even reached the highway when her phone rang. She snatched it from the console and looked at the screen. A local number, no name.

She pulled over and answered. "Angel Rossi."

"I knew you'd come crawling back." Anton's low voice tinged her nerves.

"I'm not crawling anywhere," she said.

"You will be. And I can't wait." He exhibited none of the Baptist-preacher persona he'd put on the first few times she'd met him. This was the real Anton.

"I went to the hospital," she said. "All I have to do is file a police report—"

"You won't, though. Because it'll be your word against mine. The word of an addict, a thief, who'll say and do anything to keep from going to prison, versus the word of an upstanding citizen."

"A rapist."

He tsked. "Now, now, let's not throw accusations you can't prove. Accusations nobody will back you up on."

"Brittney will."

He chuckled. "Brittney came back before curfew Wednesday, Angel. She had a very interesting story about how a total stranger had mugged her. Poor thing's been hurting, but I've been giving her something. She's feeling no pain now."

Angel closed her eyes. *Oh, Brittney.* The woman had worked tirelessly to get free of her addiction, and this man had stolen that freedom from her. Attacked her, used her, and then offered her drugs to soothe the ache. Tears dripped from Angel's eyes as she prayed for her friend. Prayed Brittney would get free of Anton and free of the drugs.

She opened her eyes. "You're a monster." She had to keep her cool and do what she'd promised to do. Suddenly, she wasn't only in this for her freedom. Anton needed to be caught. He needed to pay for what he'd done to Brittney. How many other women had he purported to *help*, only to use their need to his advantage?

Anton was dangerous. If Angel could help take him down, she'd do it.

A surge of confidence had her mind racing. How should she play this?

Scared, needy. That's what he'd respond to, but she couldn't be too obvious. She had to pretend...

"Is there a warrant out for my arrest?" she asked.

"Not yet. I told your house manager that I'd given you a pass to visit your family, that there'd been an emergency at home. If you're not back tonight, there will be."

Tonight. No chance that was going to happen. "I'm not coming back."

"I think you are."

No. She wouldn't sleep in a house where Anton had the key. With the injuries he'd already caused, she wouldn't be able to fight him off again. "I can't," she said. "I..." The tremor in her voice was a nice touch. If only it weren't authentic. "I'll turn you in, take my chances with the judge."

His laugh held genuine amusement. "You wouldn't dare."

"Maybe they won't believe me, but if I turn you in, then the next time somebody does, there'll be a trail. Maybe I can't take you down alone, but eventually you'll show your true colors." She stopped talking, took a breath.

It was time to let him talk.

He was quiet, though. Only his heavy breathing on the other end of the phone indicated he was there. Finally, he broke the silence. "I may have another idea."

Routhier had been right. Of course he had.

Anton continued. "I'm looking for someone to help me on a special project, someone with your particular skills."

"What skills?"

"We both know you're no addict, Angel. We both know you convinced the judge you were stealing for drugs to get sent to rehab instead of prison. That's one of those skills—the ability to lie convincingly. To ingratiate yourself with strangers. To blend into a crowd and look innocent, when we both know you're far from it."

"What kind of project are we talking about?"

"No details on the phone. We need to meet."

"I'm not coming back—"

"I'll tell the house manager you transferred to a different sober living community, one closer to home because of your family emergency. I don't need you here, but you and I are going to be spending a lot of time together."

The fear that rose in her heart made perfect sense, and she didn't try to hide it when she spoke. "Alone?"

"Are you afraid of me?"

Terrified. "I can take care of myself."

He chuckled. "There'll be another guy on the team. He'll act as our chaperone."

A good guy, or another guy like Anton? The last thing she needed was to be in the arena with two lions.

But in this case, the head lion had all the power, and he knew it. "I need a couple of days to recover."

"I'll call you in two days."

Two days. Routhier should have the paperwork completed by then. Which would mean she'd have no excuse not to meet with Anton. She touched the cut on her lip and shuddered. What was she doing?

CHAPTER NINE

Donovan had finished stripping the wallpaper in the parlor and then started on the library's ugly floral print. Whoever invented wallpaper should be drawn and quartered. And he wasn't going to think about how he'd chosen to tackle this room next because it gave him a view of the driveway. He wasn't going to think about how he'd probably have finished earlier if he hadn't had one eye out for Angel all afternoon.

Why did he even care where she was or when she'd get back? She wasn't his problem.

Except, she was injured. The bruise on her cheek this morning, though slight, had been darker than the day before. The cut on her lip was healing. And the way she moved... Who'd done that to her? A boyfriend? A rival of some kind? Wondering about it was making him a little crazy. Donovan didn't like her, but she was a tiny thing. She wasn't capable of defending herself against any man—or most women.

Where was she?

And for the thousandth time that day, he wondered why he cared. She was trouble. Her injuries... She'd probably been up to no good and paid the price. He should be happy about that, considering what she'd done to his sister. On the other hand, what kind of man could ever glory in a woman's being assaulted? Donovan wasn't a monster.

He attacked the wall, tried to focus on the stubborn paper, tried not to think about the woman he shared this house with.

Tires crunching on gravel had him glancing outside to where Angel parked her ugly gold Chevy.

Before he could stop himself, he was on the porch and headed her way. And, though he'd like to scold himself for it, when he saw her trying to get out of the car, he jogged forward. "Let me help."

She smiled at him, that sweet, guileless smile he couldn't let himself believe, and took the arm he offered. Her expression turned pained as she stood and held her free hand against her ribs.

"You okay?"

"Too long in the car," she said. "I need to walk it out."

When she was steady on her feet, he stepped out of her way.

"I got the wallpaper stripper." She motioned toward the backseat.

He opened the rear door, pulled the cans out, and set them on the driveway next to her car. She'd bought three, though he'd only asked for one, enough to tide him over until he could work up the energy to make a run to the store himself.

"I figured with all that ugly wallpaper, you'd use that much and more."

"Probably." He took her good arm and walked with her to the house.

"I can get there myself." But she held on to him anyway.

He helped her up the front porch steps, then opened the door and walked her inside. "Where to?"

She glanced up at him, her brown eyes sleepy and vulnerable. "The living room?"

"Shouldn't you lie down?"

"Yeah, but..." She looked away, shrugged. "I think I'll rest more in the living room."

He stayed with her until he had her settled on the sofa, then snatched the afghan from the sunroom, the one she'd used that morning, and draped it over her. "You need anything else?"

She cuddled under the blanket, wincing as she got settled.

"Painkiller?" he suggested.

"I left the ibuprofen in the kitchen."

He retrieved it and a glass of water, then stood there while she downed a couple of the pills. When she was finished, he took the glass and set it on the beat-up coffee table. He wanted to ask where she'd been, but it was none of his business. He handed her the remote to the TV. "Anything else?"

"No, thank you. I really appreciate your help. I was wrung out."

After retrieving the wallpaper stripper from outside, he returned to his work. Only now, instead of watching for her car to return, he kept looking at the door to see if she was standing there. It was ridiculous how distracting one tiny woman could be. After working a little while, he wandered through the living room toward the kitchen to get a glass of water, and, if he were honest, to check on her. Her eyes were open, glazed, as she stared at the game show playing quietly. He sat on the La-Z-Boy. "Thought you'd be asleep."

"Me, too."

He sat there a minute, staring at the TV and wondering what thoughts kept Angel from drifting off. He knew why he couldn't sleep. As soon as he closed his eyes every night, memories of his sister bombarded him. Katie at six, messing with his paints, begging him to let her use his brushes. His sharp, "Go away" resounded in his consciousness.

Katie at nine tagging him at a neighborhood barbecue with a shout of, "You're it!" His thirteen-year-old self shrugging her off. "I'm not playing."

Katie at sixteen calling him at college, asking if she could visit him for the weekend. His impatient, "Too busy. Maybe next month."

He'd never had time for her. He'd never made time for her.

What he wouldn't give to have every one of those moments back.

No matter how many times he confessed and repented of his selfishness, he'd never be free. Because he could never fix it. Katie was gone, and there was nothing he could do to bring her back.

But it wasn't only his fault. Angel'd done her part. Donovan glanced at her now and saw that her eyes had closed. Her breathing had evened out. While he'd been thinking of Katie, Angel had drifted into sleep. Her face held no hint of the guilt she should feel.

Anger propelled him to his feet. He stared down at the sleeping woman. She was beautiful, no doubt. On the outside, but he didn't like her and didn't trust her and would never forgive her.

He stalked out of the room and attacked the wallpaper as if it, too, had played a role in Katie's addiction and death. He turned music on to play softly, new songs he didn't particularly care for, but at least they didn't remind him of Katie. Anything to keep him from the memories.

He finished with the library quickly, since most of the walls were lined with bookshelves, and tackled the front hall. He worked hard, never stopping to eat or drink or think. By the time he got the last of the paper off, the sun was dimming beyond the front windows, and his stomach was growling.

He passed through the living room without peeking at Angel—no easy feat, that—and opened the refrigerator. There were three casseroles. One looked like chicken cacciatore. Not his favorite. Another... some kind of beef and onion something. The third looked like an Alfredo lasagna. Score.

Jack had written the instructions on the foil that covered the pan. Donovan started the oven and popped in the lasagna. Angel would share, and Jack had told Donovan to help himself when he'd dropped off the casseroles.

While the meal cooked, Donovan showered and made a plan of attack for the following day. When an hour had passed, he returned to the kitchen and checked on dinner. The white sauce bubbled around the noodles. It smelled delicious as Donovan pulled the pan from the oven and set it on the bar. He turned at movement in the doorway and saw Angel standing there in mid-yawn.

When the yawn passed, she said, "I was going to announce myself."

He nodded. "Hope you don't mind. I figured you'd be hungry."

She padded across the tile floor in her socked feet and peered at the food. "My brother's a great cook."

Sure smelled like it. Donovan pulled a plastic container of salad from the fridge. Jack must have brought that too. Donovan faced her with the salad in hand and raised his eyebrows.

"Sure. Let me help."

"Sit."

"I can set the table, or—"

"I got it."

He prepared the salad and an Italian loaf—also from Jack— and set the places on the island while Angel chatted. She talked about the house and how beautiful it was going to be. He had to agree with her about that. It would be exactly the kind of place he'd like to live someday. The kind of place where he could be free to paint and create in peace.

He served the meal, choosing to sit beside her instead of stand at the island as he had that morning. His feet appreciated the rest. While he ate, she chattered about the game show she'd been watching earlier and some of the questions that had come up.

The lasagna was delicious, salty and creamy. Bits of chicken gave it heft, and the layer of spinach added color and flavor. The Italian dressing was tangy, the salad crisp and cold. All in all, it was the best dinner he'd eaten in weeks. Months.

After the best breakfast he'd eaten in about as long.

Having Angel here was a nightmare, but at least he was eating better.

She continued to talk, now about some book she was reading. Honestly, he had no idea even the genre of the book, much less what it was about. As much as he'd avoided people since Katie's death, Angel's constant chatter was... calming, somehow. Like background noise.

And the good food didn't hurt his mood.

"How about you?" she asked.

"Uh..."

She took a bite of her meal—she'd hardly eaten anything. Hard to eat with a constant stream of words coming out of your mouth. She was watching him now. After she swallowed her tiny bite, she asked, "You have no idea what I said, do you?"

"Sorry."

She faced forward again, took another bite.

Apparently, she wasn't going to explain. Fine, then. He speared another bite. He would need a second helping soon enough.

The silence in the room grated on his nerves. The question she'd asked hung in the air, along with his rudeness in not answering. He should ask her to repeat herself. How hard could it be to talk? He could talk. He used to be able to, anyway.

This was ridiculous.

"I'm sorry." There, that wasn't that hard. "Could you repeat your question?"

She glanced at him. "I talk too much. Not usually, but with you... Maybe because you're quiet. You make me feel..." She shook her head, focused on the meal again.

What? Wasn't she going to finish her sentences? The woman never shut up, and then when he wanted her to talk... "Feel what?"

She shrugged, kept her focus on her food. "Comfortable. I don't have to keep my guard up with you. Even though you hate me."

He wanted to tell her that wasn't true, but it was. Only... He didn't know what to say. Didn't want to lie. Didn't want to tell the truth and open the conversation. He took another bite of his meal.

She sighed. Sipped her water. Buttered a tiny piece of bread and ate it.

He focused on his dinner. Wished he hadn't spoken. Things were better when he kept quiet.

"I was talking about finding a church," she said. "Jack and Harper go to that little one downtown. He likes it but said it's pretty old-fashioned. He said there's a non-denominational church I might like, but he's never been there. I was asking if you had. Really, I was digging to figure out if you were a Christian. I know your family went to church, and I just thought... It's none of my business. Forget it."

Oh. Now he really felt like a bonehead. But... was she a

Christian? How could that be, considering all he knew about her? She was a thief, a liar, a druggie.

Right?

But maybe she'd changed. He had. If God could change him, He could change Angel.

Donovan swallowed his latest bite, took a breath. "I haven't found a church since I've been in Nutfield."

"Have you looked?" she asked.

He shook his head. He knew he needed to get back into the family of God. Knew isolating himself was only making his grief worse. But he hadn't had the courage to face people, to stand in a worship service and try to praise God while he was so... angry. Defeated. Guilty.

"Do you want to? I mean, is that something you'd be interested in? Because I thought I'd try that one Jack was telling me about on Sunday, and I wouldn't mind not going alone. Unless... I mean, there's no pressure. If you're not a Christian—"

"I am." Not a very good one, but God wouldn't reject him for his grief, right? Even Jesus wept when Lazarus died, and He was about to raise him from the dead. Donovan's grief was okay, but maybe the way he was handling it wasn't.

"Okay, then," Angel said. "Let me know. I don't know about you, but ever since I became a Christian, I feel like I need church, you know?" She stared at her glass. "When I miss church, even one week, I feel like the past is right there, nipping at me, trying to grab hold. Not to pull me back into... well, into all the stuff I used to do, but to pull me into the mire of guilt. When I go to church..."

She turned toward Donovan, who hadn't taken his eyes off her through her monologue. He couldn't get over how sincere she sounded. Maybe it was true. Maybe her faith was genuine.

Why did the idea of it irritate him?

"Church is vital, for me, anyway." Angel held his gaze, unashamed. "It helps me remember who I am."

She'd only been a girl when she'd introduced Katie to drugs. He had no right to hate the woman she was today, the Christian she was today, because of a stupid choice she'd made when she was, what, fourteen? Fifteen?

He swallowed the anger that was trying to rise, thought of something he'd heard in Bible study back in college. *It's God's job to judge. It's the Holy Spirit's job to convict. It's Jesus's job to save. It's our job to love.*

He'd been judging and convicting Angel since she'd arrived. If he were honest, he'd admit he'd been judging her and finding her wanting ever since Mom had told him about his sister's drug addiction and Angel's part in it years before. It wasn't his job to judge her, though. That was God's job. And based on Angel's words, God had forgiven her.

Did Donovan have any right to withhold his own forgiveness, in light of God's?

"I don't hate you."

His words had her freezing with her fork halfway to her face. Slowly, she turned to him. Eyebrows lifted, waiting.

He wanted the words to be true. They weren't yet, but they would be. He'd work on it. He'd try. *Lord, help me with this. Because I do hate her. I shouldn't, but I do.*

Finally, she said, "Okay," and slid the bite into her mouth.

Did he owe her an explanation for his feelings? Maybe. Probably. If she wasn't smart enough to understand why he struggled with her being there, he could explain. Not tonight, though. He'd used a weeks' worth of words tonight. He was spent.

CHAPTER TEN

Sunday morning, about an hour after Angel heard water running through the pipes—her clue that Donovan was awake—she sneaked out to the sunroom. She couldn't see much of what he was doing from her spot on the sofa, a good fifteen feet away from where he'd set up his easel. The heater humming above masked her sounds like it had the two days prior. And like the two days prior, Donovan was engrossed in his project and didn't hear her.

She fell right to sleep after tossing and turning all night long.

Only this day, she'd set her alarm on her phone. When it went off, she awoke to find Donovan glowering at her.

"Sorry." She silenced the alarm.

"Why are you here?" He didn't add *again* to his statement, but she heard it nonetheless.

She sat up on the lumpy couch and stretched as well as she could without paining her ribs. "I couldn't sleep."

"Looked like you were sleeping fine."

"I mean, in my room, but here..."

"I can clean out another room for you, or switch out your bed."

She didn't blame him for wanting her out. Painting was something he did in private. It wasn't as if she'd bothered him or even watched him, though. And she needed the sleep. "It's not that. It's that... I don't know why, but you make me feel safe."

"You don't even know me."

"True."

"I could be a serial killer."

He wasn't, though. He was gentle. Everything in her spirit told her she could trust him, despite his obvious dislike of her. "I've never seen you kill any cereal, but the way you attack your eggs is pretty scary." She'd cooked breakfast for him two days in a row and planned to do so again today. She hoped the words would bring a smile.

He turned his back, stared at the vista he was recreating on the canvas. She peeked at his painting, amazed at how it had transformed in the days since she'd arrived. There was a lot to do before it would be completed, but what he'd done already was beautiful. She couldn't wait to see the finished piece.

When he said nothing else, she stood, pressed her hand to her ribs, and breathed through the pain. Maybe it was slightly better today. Duller. She headed for the kitchen to start breakfast.

She'd gone to the grocery store the day before to supplement what her brother had brought. Though she wasn't a fan of big breakfasts, Donovan seemed to be, and mealtime was the only time he opened up to her. She liked it when he talked, little though he did.

She started the coffee, then set the sausage links she'd fried the day before into the microwave. She cracked eggs and searched the refrigerator for vegetables. When she turned, she found him standing in the doorway.

"Hope you're hungry."

"You don't have to cook for me."

"Seems the least I can do, considering how generous you are about letting me share your sunroom."

His eyes narrowed, and one corner of his mouth twitched as if he might smile.

It wasn't nothing, that near-smile. She'd take it.

"I'm excited about church today," she said.

He grunted and poured himself coffee.

"Pour me a cup, would you?"

A few moments later, he set the mug she'd been using—a delicate blue-and-white one—on the counter near where she was working.

She turned toward the sugar dish, but he said, "I added it."

She sipped the coffee. How kind, not only that he'd taken that extra step, but that he'd noticed how she liked it. "Thank you. I really appreciate that."

He shrugged. "It's only sugar."

Embarrassed about being nice. What a funny man.

"So I'd been going to this church in Manchester, and I liked it okay," she said. "A couple of other people in the house went there, and it was nice to go with friends. That church never felt like home, though. I hope this one does. I haven't had the opportunity to find a real church home since I got saved."

He sipped his coffee.

She put the pan on the stove and sprayed it with cooking spray. "I'm not really sure what to look for in a church. When I was a kid, we attended a Methodist church. That really old one —you know the one I mean?"

No answer.

"I didn't like it, but then, I wasn't a believer." She poured the eggs into the pan. "Maybe I'd like it now. The one in

Manchester was a little more lively and less steeped in tradition. Not that there's anything wrong with tradition."

Again, no response. She didn't look, but she knew he was there.

She pulled a couple of plates from the cabinet and set them out. Then, she started the microwave to warm the sausage "How about you? Do you prefer a traditional church or a more modern one?"

She glanced his way. He was studying her, eyes narrowed. A moment passed before he shrugged. "My last church was... lively, I guess."

He'd used her word. She turned away before he could see her smile. It was ridiculous how happy that made her.

She continued babbling as she finished the omelet and served it. The day before, she'd made one huge one and cut off a small portion for herself, leaving the rest for him. The system seemed to work well, so she did the same today and set the plates on the island, along with the dish of sausages.

She sat beside him and reached for her fork, but he touched the top of her hand—so gently she almost missed it. "Maybe we should"—he cleared his throat—"pray."

Oh. What a good idea. She hadn't gotten into the habit of saying grace, but she wanted to. She wondered if he expected her to do the praying, considering she did all the talking, but before she could...

"Thank you for this food." His voice was deep, rumbly, as he added, "And the hands that fixed it. In Jesus's name, amen."

"Amen." She faced him, added, "Thank you."

He shrugged and started eating.

Okay, then. She dug into her meal and resisted the urge to fill the silence. She wasn't usually such a talker, but something about Donovan made her want to share—about herself, about her life, about her past.

After a few minutes, he spoke. "How did you become a Christian?"

Now, there was a loaded question. She could lie. She could adjust the story. Or she could tell the truth. She hated that she always considered lying first.

"I got arrested about a year ago." She cut her sausage link into tiny bites while she talked, mostly to keep from looking at Donovan. "I managed to avoid prison by agreeing to go to rehab. Honestly, I shouldn't have done that. I don't use drugs, and I deserved prison, but at the time, I didn't care that I wasn't being honest. Whatever I had to do to stay out of jail." She glanced his way to find him watching her, eyes narrowed.

She focused forward again, sipped her coffee. "It turns out, rehab was the best thing for me. Because even though I'm not addicted to drugs, I was totally addicted to the rush of stealing. It was a Christian center. My parents had chosen it and paid for it, and I wasn't exactly in a position to argue about where I should go. One of the counselors was always talking about God and faith. At first, I thought it was ridiculous, but the longer I was there, the more I saw how people who embraced God got better while people like me—people who were convinced they were in control and needed to stay in control—fell back into their old ways. You know, addicts are taught to trust in a higher power. I always thought it was stupid to believe in some nebulous higher being, but then I learned about God. You know, the real God, the God of the..." She glanced his way. His expression held a look of pure fury, and her words faltered. "What? What's wrong?"

He stood, dumped the rest of his eggs in the trash, and started toward the door.

She stood. "What happened? What's—?"

"I'm done."

"But... Wait. Are you going with me to—?"

"No." He walked toward the door, then turned to add, "sorry."

What in the world?

Maybe he was disgusted to learn she was a thief. Fair enough, but now she was saved. And he was, too. He had to understand that she wasn't that person anymore.

Or maybe he understood more than she did. Maybe he understood how the urge to lie, to steal, to cheat was never far from her mind. Maybe he guessed that she didn't deserve to live in this house or have her freedom. Maybe he saw the truth about Angel that she didn't even want to face. That, despite her nickname, she was no angel, no saint, and she never would be.

ANGEL FORCED herself to dress and go to church, even though the remnants of her conversation with Donovan—if one could even call it a conversation—hung on like the scent of turpentine in the sunroom.

During the first worship song, Angel forced herself to focus and be present. By the end of the second song, she remembered that, despite Donovan's unkindness that morning, she was saved and redeemed and purchased by God's love. By the third song, her arms were lifted in praise, and tears streamed down her face. Because she'd been lost, and now she was rescued, and nothing Donovan or anybody else said to her, no thought they had against her, could separate her from the love of Christ her Savior.

Maybe the service would have been better if she'd had a friend with her, but she'd felt welcome and included as much as any newcomer probably could. In fact, by the time she was walking toward her car, she felt downright buoyant.

She deflated when her phone rang. Anton.

She'd hoped he'd leave her alone on the Lord's Day, but no such luck. She answered the call.

"There's an abandoned factory on the West Side. I'll text you the address. Be there in an hour."

"I can't be there in an hour." It wasn't true, but the lie emerged before she could stop it. She checked her spirit. Did she need to repent and tell the truth? No. The entire operation was going to be a lie, yet she was convinced she was supposed to go forward with it. She sent up a quick prayer for wisdom and felt—and maybe it was wishful thinking, but it was the only feeling she got—that it would be all right to be dishonest in order to put Anton away. Anyway, she sure hoped so, because she was in it now. And she had to assert her independence and get this relationship onto level ground.

After a moment of silence, he asked, "How soon can you get there?"

Score. "I'll need an hour and a half, at least. We won't be alone, right?"

"You don't have to worry," he said. "As long as you cooperate with me and do your part in this operation, I'll behave."

The unspoken words might as well have been broadcast on a loudspeaker—*if you don't do what I say, all bets are off.*

"Why should I trust you?"

"Because we're going to be partners, and partners have to trust each other."

Right. Partners. As if. "You told me there'd be someone else working with us. I'll be happy to join you when he's available."

Anton blew out a long breath. "He'll be there. I'll text the address."

On the way home, Angel called Routhier. He answered on the second ring. "What's up?"

"Anton wants to meet today."

He swore under his breath.

Not a good sign. "Did you get that deal for me?"

"I'll have it tomorrow."

"I need it now."

"It's the weekend," Routhier said. "We're doing the best we can. Meet him today. Tomorrow, you and I will—"

"Forget it. You said—"

"The judge agreed to the deal. It takes time to write these things up. And your lawyer will need a copy, too. We don't want to rush it. We want to do it right."

That was true.

"It should be ready first thing in the morning," he said.

"Fine. I'll put him off."

"Don't do that." Routhier's voice, usually demanding, turned placating. "Find out what he's planning. You and I can meet first thing tomorrow to sign the deal."

She didn't want to meet Anton at all, certainly not without some assurances that it would be worthwhile. If she put him off, would he suspect her? She'd agreed to work with him, and the man did have a job he had to show up for Monday through Friday. Maybe the partner did, too. Maybe Sunday was the only day they could do this.

Was she willing to risk this deal? Willing to go to prison over it?

"What's in the deal?" she asked.

"If you work with us in good faith, your record will be clean. No felonies. As long as you stay out of trouble, there won't even be a lingering traffic ticket."

Not that she'd ever had one of those. Traffic laws were about the only ones she'd ever obeyed.

"I'm offering you your freedom," Routhier said.

"In return for working with a monster."

"For putting away a monster for good."

There was that. She turned onto the narrow tree-lined drive that led to the house.

It wasn't as if she had a choice here. "Fine. What time tomorrow?"

"Same place as before, ten o'clock."

"I'll be there, but if the deal's not what you promised, I'm done. No information for you."

"No freedom for you. Don't forget why you're doing this."

As if freedom were ever far from her mind.

Angel changed her clothes, ate a sandwich, and left again without ever seeing Donovan. He was there, and it looked as if he'd been working in the hallway. He must have seen her pull up and run upstairs to avoid her.

Coward.

The more she thought about their morning conversation, the more irritated she became. She'd been a bad person, no doubt, but she'd never done anything to Donovan. There were a lot of people who had every right to hate her, victims of her thievery, her lies, but Donovan Gilcreast wasn't one of them. What was his problem?

She didn't have time to dwell on it as she headed to Manchester, worry twisting her stomach and her meager lunch with every passing mile.

She reached the address Anton had sent and parked beside the open door on the back side. It was an old brick factory, probably once used in the textile industry. Most had been refurbished, but based on the disrepair on the exterior, this one hadn't been. Tall windows lined the four-story building. A black Audi was parked in the rutted lot. She'd seen it before. It had to be Anton's. Which meant the third partner wasn't there yet. She settled in to wait.

Anton had picked a good spot to meet. Even if it weren't Sunday, they'd be well-hidden here. The factory was flanked by similar buildings. Behind them, overgrown brush and trees blocked the buildings on the next street.

If Anton got out of hand, nobody would hear her scream.

Anton emerged from the building carrying a trash bag and headed her way. He wore khaki pants and a long-sleeved golf shirt. With the rimless glasses, the round face, the little paunch in his middle, everything about him screamed *trust me*.

The sight of him had her heart pounding. She breathed through it, but her ribs protested, throbbing to remind her how dangerous he was.

As if the memory of the night the previous week didn't replay every time she closed her eyes.

She locked her doors. When he knocked on the window, she cracked it.

"Come inside," he said.

"Not until your friend gets here."

Anton called toward the factory, "Mason!"

A man stepped into the doorway. "Yeah?"

Anton turned back to her. "He's here." He pulled her door handle and found it locked. "Open up, Angel."

"Back off."

He sighed, stepped back. She waited until he was a good ten feet away, then unlocked her door and climbed out.

"Brittney packed up the rest of your things." Anton held up the trash bag. "She didn't have any spare luggage. I'm going to put it in your backseat, okay?"

She stepped out of the way to give him a wide berth, and he tossed the bag into her car.

She shoved her keys and phone in her pockets, locked the

door, and faced Anton. "As long as you keep space between us, this will work. Get any closer, though, and I'm done."

The man in the doorway cocked his head to the side and called, "Everything okay?"

"It's fine." Anton focused on her and lowered his voice. "We're going to have to find a way to work together. I understand that, if you'd known it was me with Brittney the other day, you wouldn't have attacked me."

Angel'd attacked *him*? The arrogance, the nerve... She swallowed her retort and said, "That's one way to look at it."

"And if I'd realized sooner that it was you who'd rudely interrupted us, I would have been more forgiving."

"Why?"

He shrugged. "I like you, Angel. That night we met at the fundraiser, I found you charming."

"I guess Brittney wasn't charming."

His nostrils flared. "Brittney and I have a deal, which is none of your business. You should have stayed out of it." Then, his lips stretched into what some would call a smile. "I forgive you for attacking me. I want us to be friends."

He must've thought she was an idiot.

"Please?" he asked.

She took one step toward him, wanting to show her courage. Wanting to prove she wasn't intimidated—but she was. She froze. "I will never be your friend. And you'll keep your distance, or I'll tell the cops everything."

His smile only widened. "I don't think so." He swung his arm toward the warehouse door. "Ladies first."

"That's okay. I'll bring up the rear." No way would she turn her back on him.

"Suit yourself." He stalked toward the warehouse.

She breathed a prayer for bravery and stepped into the space, her eyes adjusting to the dimmer light. The windows, though in desperate need of a cleaning, spilled sunshine onto the wooden floors. Brick pillars, a few trash piles, and a card table were the only things that broke up the space. As she'd suspected, the building hadn't been refurbished, but it could be beautiful one day. With elbow grease and TLC, it could be amazing.

"Angel, this is Mason Baldwin."

The guy she'd seen in the doorway approached, his hand held out. He had longish dirty-blond hair and deep dimples. He was maybe five-seven, probably early twenties, and couldn't have weighed more than a hundred and thirty pounds. If she'd hoped for someone who could protect her, her hopes had been dashed.

He shook her hand. "If all the angels are as pretty as you, I'd better clean up my act." The smarmy line was accompanied by a goofy grin.

She couldn't help an answering smile. "Nice to meet you."

He took his hand back, held it to his chest. "The angel speaks with heavenly tones."

Anton cleared his throat. "This isn't a night club, Baldwin. Get your head in the game."

"Not sure I can, not with an angel in our midst."

"Then you can go," Anton said, "and we'll find someone else."

Mason's amusement faded. "Don't get your briefs in a bunch, dude. I'm only joking."

Anton glared until Mason stepped away and lifted his hands in surrender.

"Your party. I'll shut up."

"Good idea." Anton walked to the card table, where a glossy brochure was opened. "This is our target."

She wandered closer, got a glimpse of the name. *Nightingale's Treasures Museum and Gift Shop.*

What could possibly be contained in a seacoast museum that was worth prison?

"Don't be fooled," Anton said. "It's small, but it houses some valuable art." He pushed his glasses back on his nose, his tone slipping into that of a high school history teacher. "The museum was founded in the fifties after the wreckage of a ship—the *Nightingale*—was discovered not far from the Isles of Shoals. The story goes that it was an old slave ship that had left off its cargo and was on its way back to England when it was hit by a violent storm. All the passengers were killed. The gold and treasures were lost with the ship."

Mason didn't even try to hide his bored yawn. "Dude, if I wanted a history lesson, I'd have gone to college."

Angel's interest was piqued, though. "I've heard of it. Divers have been searching the wreckage for years."

"And a lot has been found," Anton said. "In fact, the guy who owns the museum was one of the first. He and some of his family members have been diving every year since, trying to uncover more."

Mason gave Angel a *whatever* glance before he spoke to Anton. "What's the job?"

Anton pointed at a bronze sculpture in the brochure. Angel leaned closer. It depicted a man, standing, extending his hand toward a woman who was bowed at his feet.

"Jesus and the woman caught in adultery," Anton said. "The story goes that the ship's captain bought the sculpture many years before but never understood its meaning. While in Boston, he met a man who'd told him about his religion and explained who the woman was, and the captain supposedly repented of his slave-trading ways. He was on his way back to England to hand over the profits and then, presumably, quit slave trading altogether."

Angel lifted the brochure, studied the sculpture. The detail work was amazing. She traced her finger over the bronze fingers that reached up to Jesus, the face of the Savior beaming down at the woman. "Who's the sculptor?"

"Andrea Pisano."

She sucked in a breath. "Oh, wow." She'd heard of him, but she'd never seen his work.

Mason looked over her shoulder at the photo. "Old guy, I guess."

Angel ducked away from the younger man. He wasn't creepy like Anton, but she was feeling too antsy to be that close to anyone. She stepped into the light streaming in through the window and turned to him with an apologetic smile.

His dimples disappeared. He lifted his hand toward her face, and she leaned back.

"What happened?" Mason asked. "Who did that to you?"

Without thinking, she glanced at Anton, who didn't even flinch. "It was nothing."

Mason looked from Anton to her. All playfulness leached from his expression. "Seriously. What happened?"

"She said it was nothing." Anton's voice was low. "You need to focus on the task at hand."

"I like to know what kind of people I'm working with."

Anton gave Angel a look that clearly said *fix this.*

Because of course it was her job to clean up his mess. "Really, it's nothing." She touched Mason's arm, and he turned back to her. "Let's try to focus."

Mason studied her another minute, then shrugged. "Whatever."

"Anyway," Anton said, "Pisano did most of his work in the fourteenth century. Which would be the thirteen-hundreds."

"Duh," Mason said. "What's it worth?"

Angel had to smile at the kid's single-mindedness.

"I have a buyer lined up. He's willing to pay two hundred grand."

Mason whistled. "That's not nothing."

Anton had probably been promised twice that. She wasn't dumb enough to think Anton was planning to share all his profits.

Mason's eyes were bright. "A third of two hundred grand—"

"You're not getting a third," Anton snapped. "I get half for setting it up and planning it. You each get half of what's left, fifty grand apiece."

Mason's cheeks tightened around his dimples. "Whatever. Fifty grand isn't bad for a couple hours of work."

"What's the play?" Angel asked.

"Simple." Anton pointed to Angel. "You're going to start hanging around the gallery, get to know the staff, study the guards and see what you can find out about their security." He turned to Mason. "You're going to figure out how to disable the alarm."

Seriously? This kid could do that?

Her questions must've shown in her eyes, because he winked at her. "I got skills, baby."

"So do lots of other people," Anton said. "Focus."

"You got it, boss."

"So I'm going to be the face of it," Angel said. "After the robbery, when the cops ask if there's been anybody new hanging around, I'm going to be the person they point to. I'll be the one who gets arrested."

"If you get arrested, you'll give me up in a blink," Anton said.

No doubt. She held his eye contact, said nothing.

Beside her, Mason shifted, but for once held his tongue.

Anton broke the silence. "You'll have to figure a way for them to believe you're on their side, not against them."

"How am I supposed to do that?"

"How should I know?" Anton asked. "You're the con artist."

She hated the moniker, even though it fit.

And in the long run, it wouldn't matter whether she did the job well or not, because she was working with the cops. She was only playing along on this job.

Looking at Anton, at the raw greed and power that showed on his face—things which he'd kept well-hidden during their first few meetings—she wondered if her deal with the cops would be able to save her.

CHAPTER ELEVEN

Donovan had been stripping wallpaper in the back hall when he heard Angel's car in the driveway. He retreated to his bedroom, where he paced and prayed.

She'd left again minutes later. Good thing, because his anger still hadn't subsided.

He returned to his work in the hallway, picked up the scraper, and fumed. By the time he faced one clear section of stripped wall, he had to admit his anger was irrational and unfair to Angel. Yet the feeling remained, harder to scrape off than this stubborn wallpaper.

He'd been attacking the mess for hours, first the back hall, then the entry. When he finished that, the common rooms would be ready for him to start priming and painting. Jack had chosen a soft gray with a hint of beige, which would complement the stained woodwork. Donovan was ready to start the improving aspect of this project. He needed to focus on a beautiful future for this home, not the ugly past.

True in his life, too. His past was ugly enough. Would there be beauty in the future, or was he destined to this dull-toned existence forever? His high school days had been colorless. Being the art-geek hadn't won him any friends, and, with zero social abilities, he'd been unable to break out of the mold the other students had shoved him into. In his mind's eye, he saw those days in tones of gray and white, tasteless, joyless.

But Katie... His sister had been the one exception. They'd always been very different, she with cheerleading and partying and popular friends, he with video games and studying and painting. She'd made efforts to spend time with him, efforts he'd mostly rebuffed. But sometimes, he'd let her play Call of Duty with him. She was terrible, but she'd tried. And she'd tried to understand his art. His memories of his sister, when he wasn't pushing her away or ignoring her, were jewel-toned, deep purples and emerald greens and ruby reds.

College, though... That's where the true color came in. At school, Donovan's talent set him apart. He'd met people like himself, people who understood him and liked him for the person he was.

Leaving the drab gray-and-white world of high school, in Boston he'd found everything swathed in color. The pastels of evenings on the banks of the Charles, the blues of the John Hancock building reflecting a clear sky, the greens of springtime in the Public Gardens. And there were the bright colors of the college students swarming all over the city.

In college, he'd discovered who he was. When he and Ian, his closest friend, had shared a loft, when he'd worked beside those tall windows in his bedroom-slash-studio, he'd truly discovered his talent. Everything about those years had glowed with color.

And then, Katie...

He'd known she was in trouble, but he hadn't cared enough to reach out to her with more than an occasional text. Sure, he'd been there for the intervention that had convinced her to try rehab that first time. Unfortunately, after years of focusing on his own life and ignoring her, he'd had little influence on his sister.

And when she'd left rehab and relapsed that last time, he'd gotten angry, called her selfish and greedy, blowing through Mom and Dad's money faster than the drugs she couldn't give up. Accused her of not caring about anything but herself. He'd shouted those words, eliciting a gasp from his mother, a low *calm down* from Dad. But Donovan hadn't calmed down. Hadn't apologized. He could still see the pain in Katie's face, still picture the way she'd stormed out of the house, peeled out of the driveway too fast, and driven away.

Maybe, if he'd been more understanding... Maybe if, when he'd surrendered to Christ, he'd reached out to Katie, told her about this amazing Savior he'd met...

He'd planned to. Figured he'd apologize for his outburst and tell her about Jesus when he saw her next. The family always got together for birthdays, and Mom's had been coming up in July. He'd figured it could wait until then.

But Katie had died in June.

He'd missed his chance. And lost his sister.

He pulled the last of the wallpaper from the plaster and surveyed his work. It was a mess right now, but it would be beautiful soon enough.

His life wouldn't be refinished that easily.

The front door opened, and Angel stepped inside.

She froze when she saw him, then pasted on a smile that seemed as genuine as the lips on a Mrs. Potato Head. She looked at the stripped walls. "You've been busy."

He nodded, then scooped some bits of paper off the floor and shoved them in the trash bag.

She passed him and rounded the corner toward her bedroom.

He waited for some remark about that hallway, which he'd also stripped, but she said nothing. His anger came back then, dark and heavy.

Because Angel was alive and well. Angel was healthy and beautiful. Angel had found Christ in rehab when she wasn't even an addict.

But Katie... Katie was gone. It was too late for her. Maybe she'd accepted Christ. Someone who'd come to the funeral told him and his parents that Katie had become a believer in rehab, but her conversion hadn't changed her, not that he'd seen, anyway. Was it real? Was Katie in heaven waiting for him now?

Or not?

He couldn't consider the alternative.

He took the tools to the small utility room off the kitchen and the trash bag to the back door.

He stepped outside and stopped. The sun shone, the air was cool, the promise of autumn flitting in the breeze. The world was bright and cheerful.

Overhead, a flock of geese headed south, fleeing the oncoming winter.

Katie was gone, and Angel was here. It wasn't fair. It wasn't right.

But...

But today was fresh and clean. He'd spent time on his painting and been happy with the results. He'd finished stripping wallpaper and could start painting tomorrow. He was filled with sorrow and optimism. How could they exist at the same time?

Somehow, life was both cyclical, like the seasons, and final, like Katie's death.

But also eternal.

Like God.

Did Donovan trust that God knew what He was doing, or didn't he? Was he a believer, or wasn't he?

If God was sovereign, then He'd let Katie die, and He'd brought Angel here. It didn't make sense. And it never would. Maybe it wasn't Donovan's job to understand. Maybe it was Donovan's job to live with it. To learn to have faith despite it. Or through it.

He grumbled as he walked around the house to the trash bin.

Grumbled as he thought about what he had to do next.

After he dumped the trash, he returned to the house and headed down the hallway to Angel's bedroom. The door was closed. He lifted his hand, breathed a quick prayer, and knocked.

She pulled the door open, stepped back, and crossed her arms. "Can I help you?"

"I was a jerk this morning."

"I'm aware," she said.

He'd expected her to be more forgiving. Not that he deserved it.

"The talk about rehab... It's hard to explain. I don't really know why it makes me angry." Not entirely true, but it wasn't his place to lay the blame for Katie's death at her feet. That was between Angel and God. "Katie went to rehab. She really was an addict, though. And they say she got saved there, but I don't know. It's not like I ever saw any change in her, not that I saw her..." He was babbling. Very unlike him. "Anyway, what you said today brought that back. My worry, that is. About where..."

He couldn't finish. Felt like an idiot. His cheeks burned. He turned to go.

"Wait."

He stopped. Didn't turn back.

"That makes sense." Angel's voice was gentle. "You weren't mad at me."

Not true, but no reason to correct her.

"You were upset about Katie, and you took it out on me."

He swiveled to face her. To tell her the truth. That he was angry at her, because it was all her fault, her fault for introducing his sister to drugs in the first place.

Except that wasn't true.

And when he saw Angel's face—guileless, kind, forgiving—the words died in his throat. "Sorry."

She tilted her head to the side. "I can't imagine what you're going through. I think my being here is making it harder for you. Maybe I should find someplace else to stay."

Could she? That would be better. Her presence was agonizing.

But then, he thought about the pain he saw in her face every time she moved too quickly, the bruise on her cheek. He'd caught a few on her neck that morning during breakfast.

At the time, he'd been irate at her words and hadn't let the truth of those bruises penetrate.

But someone had wrapped his hands around her neck, choked her. Maybe that someone had been trying to kill her.

Donovan didn't like Angel, but he'd never wish her harm.

And sometimes, he did like her. Sometimes, he couldn't take his eyes off her. When he lay in bed at night, he didn't only think about Katie anymore. Now, thoughts of Angel distracted him. His anger toward her, yes, but also, the way she smiled, the way she moved.

He'd slept more the previous few nights than he had since Katie's death.

What was wrong with him? His own feelings were a mishmash of clashing colors. He couldn't differentiate between the gunmetal gray of hatred and teals of curiosity and the reds of...

Ugh. Why would desire be in there?

He was confused. He spun away, was halfway down the hall when he remembered her offer.

"You can stay. It's fine."

Donovan studied the lake, the play of light on water. Blues, grays, silvers… He was working with silver right now, catching the reflection of dawn. He focused on the canvas, dabbed his brush into the paint, then onto the work.

The painting was coming together. When the leaves turned, he'd capture their beauty, too. He'd find that elusive thing that was missing from this painting, from all of his recent works. He'd figure it out. He had to, or the gallery showing would be a flop, and his once thriving career as an artist would come to an abrupt halt.

This gig as a fix-it man was supposed to be temporary, but if he didn't figure out how to create beauty in his grief, he'd be painting a lot more walls than canvases in his future.

He studied the water again. Katie would have loved it here.

When he painted, he remembered his sister as a child. They'd vacationed at this lake. He could picture her diving off the floating platform, climbing back up, and doing it again. The two of them used to race from the platform to the beach. She had no chance against him, of course. Sometimes, he let her win, just to see the look of triumph on her face.

Their parents would watch, smiling and shouting encouragement and whispering to each other.

Those were some of the best days of their lives.

Somehow, when he painted, he could stand the memories. When he wasn't painting, they were sharp, swathed in uneven lines and dark shadows. When he had a paintbrush in his hand, though, the memories were softer, the pastels of nostalgia.

He stayed at it until the image he'd kept in his mind blurred. He stood and stretched. His too-long hair fell in his face, and he pushed it behind his ears. He should've stuck it in a ponytail. He needed to do something about that. He'd get a haircut tomorrow.

He'd been telling himself that for months, but barbers liked to talk, and Donovan didn't have it in him to make conversation. Or even listen to it.

A glance at the old lumpy sofa revealed Angel, sound asleep.

Though she'd accepted his apology the afternoon before, she'd made no effort to join him for dinner.

So he'd eaten alone. Told himself he liked it better that way. Even though the silence had closed in, and his mind had raced with thoughts and memories and fears. He'd realized last night that he'd become accustomed to Angel's chatter. It helped him relax.

Why did the woman affect him like she did?

He stared down at her. The bruises on her face and neck were hidden by the way she lay. Was her arm hurting her? He'd watched her enough to know she moved as if she hurt, flinched when she turned too fast. Ribs, even bruised ribs, took weeks to heal.

Messy curls framed her peaceful face. The one eye he could see was puffy and underlined with a dark swath. What kept Angel from sleeping? Did she agonize over poor choices that could never be undone? Or did she lie awake trying to figure out her future? Or maybe it was simpler than that. Maybe fear of whoever had left those bruises kept her from closing her eyes when she was alone.

Maybe that was why she crept out here every morning.

Except... How could she trust Donovan when he'd been unkind to her?

Angel Rossi was a mystery, one he certainly wasn't going to solve by watching her sleep.

Quietly, he cleaned the painting supplies and went to the kitchen, where he started a pot of coffee. She'd fed him breakfast every day since she'd arrived. He dug through the cabinets and found what he was looking for. He was no cook, but he could read a recipe. Or, in this case, the back of a box of Bisquick.

Pancakes sounded good, and she must like them, too. She'd bought the mix and maple syrup, hadn't she?

When the batter was ready, he sat with his phone and read the headlines. The world was a mess... No news, that.

Finally, Angel stepped into the room. Why had he been waiting for her? She froze at the threshold and yawned. "You let me sleep."

He stood and rounded the island to the coffee, where he poured her a cup. He set it and the sugar dish on the island. "Making pancakes."

Her eyebrows lifted as she slid onto a barstool. "You cook?"

"No." He turned on the burner, heated the pan. Prepared to pour some pancake batter in.

"Wait!"

He glanced her way. "What?"

"You might want to add butter or spray it with cooking spray or something."

Good point. He found the cooking spray and used it, then added the batter.

He could feel her watching him, but he didn't turn to see. Instead, he guarded the pancake as if it might run. It didn't, but it didn't cook right, either. When he flipped it, some of the batter splattered out.

"The first one's always a throwaway," Angel said.

Was that true? He had no idea, but he threw the mess in the trash and tried again.

"When the top stops bubbling and looks dry," she said, "that's when you flip it."

Dry? That didn't even... Oh. He saw what she meant. When the whole thing looked dry, he flipped it. "Huh."

She said nothing. He glanced her way and caught her smile.

She was enjoying this.

Weirdly, he was, too.

While he stacked pancakes on a plate, she set plates and silverware on the island and added the butter and syrup. They sat side by side and dug in.

"Delicious," she said.

So maybe he puffed up a little. Beautiful woman compliments your cooking—of course he was proud. He said nothing, but he did nod—that counted as a thank-you, right?

"This was nice of you," she said. "And thank you for not ordering me out of your sunroom this morning."

"Not *my* sunroom."

"You had it first."

True, but it would be petty to agree.

"What are you working on today?" she asked.

"Painting." He ate a bite, swallowed it. Thought of what that meant... a trip to the store for paint. He'd only bought a pint for them to test the color. Maybe there was more wallpaper he could strip instead.

No. He needed to get out of the house. He'd been holed up here for... days. "Thought I'd start in the parlor, work my way toward the back."

"I can't wait to see it."

He nodded, ate more.

"I was wondering..."

He glanced her way, caught her worrying her bottom lip. *Sexy.*

No. He looked back at the pancakes, but the image lingered. "What?"

She sighed. "Never mind."

He faced her again. At least she'd quit that lip thing. Now she looked annoyed. "What?" he asked again.

"I have an appointment this morning, but I was thinking later... There's a museum in Portsmouth I've always wanted to visit. It's from that shipwreck—"

"The Nightingale."

"Yeah." Her eyes lit up, apparently pleased he'd heard of it. He was an artist, after all. He'd been to every museum and gallery in the area.

"I'm planning check it out later. I thought you might like to go with me."

Why would he want to do that? He had work to do. And he hated leaving the house, hating having to talk to strangers. Although, if he was with Angel, she'd do all the talking. And maybe they could stop by the paint store on the way home. She could do the talking then, too. Save him the trouble.

Hadn't he told himself he had to get out of the house? He hadn't left since...

The grocery store a week prior.

Ian had questioned him about it. Ian, who'd threatened to come this week. Maybe that would be good. Ian and Angel could talk, and Donovan could ignore them both. Ian would like Angel. In fact, they'd probably be good together.

No.

The word seemed to growl up from someplace deep inside, someplace he'd locked away years before. A place of pale blues and bright reds—tenderness and desire. He preferred to pretend those things didn't exist. Because his life was his art. Any feelings he had, he needed to pour onto the canvas, not lavish on some woman.

Certainly not a woman like Angel, a woman he didn't even like.

But the image of her red lip caught his gaze. That same lip that had been purple and abused only a week before. A protective rage exploded in his chest.

Ugh. He shook his head. He was losing his mind.

He glanced her way to find her staring at him. She said, "I take it by your silence that you're not interested."

Oh, he was interested, but unless she'd been reading his mind... Oh, right. The museum. She'd invited him. No way. Too much to do. However, he did need to get that paint. And maybe the light blue and bright red were messing with his logic, because he said, "Could we stop by the paint store on the way back?"

"Sure!" She smiled, and all those colorful feelings mixed together again. Lots of red. Way too much red.

CHAPTER TWELVE

Angel parked on the same level of the garage as she had on Friday, and like on Friday, Routhier was at her door by the time she climbed from the car. The only difference was, Opie wasn't with him.

Fear crawled up her spine, but she shook it off. Routhier had never hurt her. Even when he'd arrested her, he hadn't been rough.

Anton's fault, that fear. The memory of that night had her shuddering. "You have it?"

Routhier held out a manila envelope. "Right here."

She slid the papers out. There were eight sheets, all written in legalese. She flipped through them and realized there were two copies. One for herself, she assumed, and one for the court. Both copies were already signed by the judge.

She leaned against the car and started to read.

"It's what we agreed," Routhier said. "It says if you work with us—"

"I'll read it myself." The guy must have thought she was an idiot. "You can go sit in your car if you want."

He leaned beside her and crossed his arms.

She refused to be intimidated. In fact, if anything, she read more slowly to irritate him. It took her ten minutes to digest the words in the contract. Routhier was right—the agreement was exactly what they'd discussed.

A little flame of hope flickered to life in her heart.

"Basically," Routhier said, "you do your best to aid Anton Turner. You'll report back to me twice a week, at least, on that extra phone I gave you."

"I won't keep that phone with me all the time."

"I don't expect you to. I do expect you to tell me everything and do exactly what Anton asks you to do."

"Within reason. I won't hurt anyone, and I won't let him hurt me."

"You don't trust me." Routhier said the words matter-of-factly.

She pushed off from the car and faced him. "You blame me?"

He shrugged. "I'm a cop. It's my job to catch bad guys. You're a bad guy."

"Was." She took a deep breath, ignored the pain in her ribs. "I *was* a bad guy. Now, I'm not."

"You got fired for stealing a week ago."

"I didn't steal anything. I got fired because you told my boss I was a thief. "

He uttered a short chuckle. "If you say so."

She wanted to argue the issue, to convince him she wasn't the person she used to be. What would have been the point? The only way to prove she'd changed was to show she'd changed. And even if she did, he'd never see it. And she didn't blame him. She didn't deserve to be seen as anything but what she'd always been.

"If you hold up your end of the bargain," he said, "your record will be cleared completely."

Cleared. Completely. That's what this contract said. Not only this conviction, but all the previous arrests would be expunged.

They must really want to nail Anton Turner.

There was a niggling issue, though. She considered all she'd read and the conversations she'd had with Routhier in the past. And then, it came to her. "You said your goal is to find the other stolen goods, the one from the Boston robbery."

"Right."

"How do you know they haven't been sold yet?"

He looked past her. "We don't. None of the items has shown up for sale, but it's not like they'd be advertised on eBay. After the guard's death, we hope he decided to hang onto them, wait until the heat dies down."

"What if they're gone?"

"Then they're gone. Won't be your problem."

"But if you fail to catch him this time, then I'll have done all of this, and he'll still be free."

"We'll get him, Angel. If not for the other robbery, at least for this one."

"But why would he trust me with the location of his secret hideout, wherever that is? He won't, you know. He won't take me there at all."

The detective nodded. "He'll go there eventually. We'll be tracking him until he exposes himself."

"It's a risky game."

"Not for you," Routhier said. "You do your part and leave ours to us."

She scoffed. "Except if he gets wind I'm working with you, I'll be his next victim."

"It's not going to come to that."

She wished she shared Routhier's confidence.

"I hope you caught the caveat on the last page," he said.

She flipped to the page, skimmed the words.

Routhier summed it up for her. "Where it says that if you tell anybody about our deal, it's off."

She looked up to meet his eyes. "I saw it."

"Nobody can know about this, Angel. Not your parents, not your friends, not your boyfriend."

Boyfriend. As if. "I get it."

"It's to protect the operation, but more than that, it's for your safety."

"Kind of you to worry about me."

He smirked. "The only people who know are O'Donnell, the judge, you, your lawyer, and me."

Angel's lawyer had called that morning. She'd called it a "sweet deal" and had, like Routhier, stressed the part about Angel keeping quiet.

"I'll keep it to myself."

Routhier smiled. Unlike the triumphant smiles she'd seen often on his face, this one seemed genuine, almost kind. He pulled a pen from his breast pocket. "Ready to make it official?"

She snatched the pen and set the contract on the trunk of her car. After another glance at the words, she sent up a quick prayer. This was right, though. She'd been praying about it for days, and she was confident God wanted her to go forward. What Anton had done to Brittney would be paid for. The police officer's life he'd stolen would be avenged.

It felt good to be a part of something bigger than herself. She wasn't doing this for purely selfless motives. Yes, she would gain her freedom, but she wanted to bring Anton down. With God's help, she'd be part of seeing justice done. Maybe her motives weren't a hundred percent selfless, but God could sort all that out.

She was a work in progress, and He'd promised to continue that work until completion.

She signed the paperwork and handed one copy to Detective Routhier. She slid the other into the manila envelope. She'd mail it to her post office box and leave it there. She couldn't think of a safer place to store it.

"So, what's the target?" he asked.

"The Nightingale Museum in Portsmouth."

He squinted. "Never heard of it."

"It's a good choice," she said. "Most of their displays aren't very valuable. It's not the kind of place that gets a lot of traffic. Just a sleepy little out-of-the-way museum. Their security will be nothing like what you'd find at one of the major art museums." She shared what she knew about the Pisano.

"Dinky little place like that has a sculpture worth that much?"

"According to the website, they have a lot of treasures, most of which didn't actually come off the shipwreck, but the sculpture is the most valuable."

"So what's your job?"

She caught him up on what she knew "I'm going to see it this afternoon."

"And you're seeing Anton again when?"

"Don't know yet, but I'll text you when I do."

Routhier pushed off from the car. "Looking forward to working with you."

She wasn't looking forward to the work, but the work would lead to her freedom. And she couldn't wait for that.

ANGEL CLICKED ON HER SEATBELT. "I didn't figure you for a pickup kind of a guy."

Beside her, Donovan shrugged. He'd pulled the truck

around from the far side of the house. "Bought it used when I took on this project."

"Why don't you park it in front?"

"I prefer to unload to the utility room."

That made sense. "What'd you drive before?"

He started down the narrow driveway. "Didn't need a car. I lived in Boston."

"But what about when you visited family?"

"I took the bus. Dad would get me at the station, or I'd grab an Uber."

"Huh." She couldn't imagine life without a car. "You captured the sunrise beautifully on your canvas."

Donovan glanced at her, nodded.

"You're preparing for the leaves changing color, yes?"

Another nod. She stifled a sigh. This was going to be a long day if he wasn't going to talk to her. "This painting is larger than the others you've done. And broader in scope. Is there a reason?"

For a long moment, he said nothing. She stared at his profile, at the sharp angles of his jaw, his straight nose, his full lips. The only thing off was the long hair—which he'd pulled back in a ponytail—and the scruff of his beard. Not that they didn't look good, but they seemed... out of place on Donovan. He was tidy in every other area of his life. The scruff didn't distract from his beauty. She was accustomed to seeking quality and authenticity, seeking works of art. Donovan was a work of art. He moved no more than was absolutely necessary. Right now, he brought to mind a statue. If Michelangelo had ever sculpted David driving a truck, it might look like Donovan right now.

One might mistake his silence for a flighty mind, but no. She thought he was contemplating. What thoughts went through that brain of his? Was he debating what to tell her, debating whether to answer her? Or was he trying to find words to put to voice what he was trying to create on a canvas?

Or maybe he was wishing he hadn't come along.

That seemed likely as seconds ticked into minutes.

She faced forward again. If he didn't want to talk, fine. She could be quiet, too.

"Katie loved the lake," Donovan finally said.

That he'd spoken made her inordinately happy.

"We came to Nutfield every summer to enjoy the lake," he said. "We didn't come every fall, but a few times to see the leaves change. I remember one day, I woke up early. I was maybe eleven or twelve, which made her about eight. I looked out back and saw her sitting on a picnic bench staring across the water. I didn't join her but stood in the house watching her watch the sunrise. She was always active, chatty."

He glanced her way. She knew what he was thinking. *Like you.*

He didn't say it, though. "To see her that calm, that mesmerized by the view... I'll never forget it."

So he was recreating a scene Katie had loved. He must have adored his sister. How his heart must have broken at her death.

Poor Katie. She'd craved fun and adventure and had ended up with nothing. Maybe, if what that person had told Donovan at her funeral was true, maybe she was having the adventure of her life in heaven.

Lord, is she there with You?

There was no audible answer, but Angel remembered when she and Katie had gone to church together as kids. They'd have sleepovers back then. Whether they were at Angel's or Katie's house, they were expected to attend church in the morning. They'd both complained about it, but the truth was, they'd also both enjoyed it. They talked about God back then, talked about their faith. Katie's had been real, despite all the foolish mistakes she'd made. Angel's had been contrived, but Katie had believed. And maybe she'd walked away from the Lord for years. Maybe drugs had pulled her away. If Katie had rededicated her life to God in rehab, Angel believed it was real.

Right, Lord?

Peace filled her heart, seemed to expand to fill the space.

Should she share her feelings with Donovan? She glanced his way again. His jaw was ticking with tension. Maybe not right now, but sometime, she'd tell him. Maybe she could share some of her peace with him.

That was, if he quit hating her.

She could see he was trying. She wasn't accustomed to people having to work at liking her.

"It's beautiful, your painting," she said. "Katie would have loved it."

His jaw did that ticking thing again. She let the subject drop.

Portsmouth had long been one of Angel's favorite places. The city was quaint and artsy with lots of shops and galleries and restaurants. Prescott Park lined the waterfront, and the Strawberry Banke Museum, with its historical buildings, rested a block behind.

Donovan parked outside a white clapboard Victorian. It had been built as a single-family home in the late eighteenth century, according to the website. The oval sign hanging above the door was the only indication they'd arrived.

"It's little," she said.

"There's more to it in the back." He led the way to the front door and held it open for her.

She stopped in the entry. It truly did feel like a house. A staircase rose in front of her, a red velvet rope blocking it off, along with a sign that read *Closed to the Public*. To the left was a gift shop. Angel stepped into the room on her right, where a desk was set up, brochures all around. Donovan hung back, gaze on the gift shop in the other direction.

A woman on the far side of the desk stood. "Welcome to the Nightingale." She was tall, heavy, and had medium-brown hair. She seemed to be a little older than Angel, maybe mid-thirties. Her smile was bright and kind.

Angel returned the smile as she stepped forward. "Glad to be here. I've heard good things."

"Oh, you'll love it," the woman said. Her name tag identified her as Mary Lynn. "Two tickets?"

Angel reached for her wallet. "Yes, please."

Donovan stepped into the room, his heavy footsteps loud in the quiet space, and handed Mary Lynn cash.

"I can get my own—"

"I got it," Donovan said.

Mary Lynn's smile froze at the sight of Donovan. She seemed almost nervous as she made change and handed him the tickets.

Nervous because he was gorgeous, or nervous because he was intimidating? Likely both.

Mary Lynn pointed toward the room to her right. "Start this direction." She gave Donovan another look. "Be sure to check out the local artists' gallery on your way out. The path'll take you in a circle, and you'll exit through the gift shop."

Donovan nodded.

Angel said, "Thanks," and followed Donovan into the next room. They were the only people there, maybe not surprising on a Monday. They read about the Nightingale's shipwreck, saw drawings of the original ship and underwater photographs of the wreckage. She'd researched the shipwreck, and what she saw now matched what she'd learned. It truly was fascinating, the whole *treasure hunting under the sea* thing. In another life, she could see herself doing that. What an adventure that would be.

There was no guard in sight, but then, there were no treasures in this room, either. And Mary Lynn was just on the other side of the doorway. A camera in the corner presumably was tracking their every movement. Was it recording? Was there someone watching the footage even now?

She highly doubted it.

The house's original back door had been replaced with a wide opening. She and Donovan stepped through it and down two steps into the addition, which looked more like a museum and less like a house. The addition had high ceilings, white walls, and soft overhead lights. It was broken into separate rooms with wide openings between them. Angel caught sight of a guard in the far doorway of the first room. He glanced in, then turned to the next room.

One guard here.

A camera in the corner, as expected.

The first room displayed plates and silverware that had been pulled from the wreckage. A few silver serving dishes, which had likely belonged to the captain, along with pewter plates and other common objects. Again, she read all the placards. The silverware was the most stunning to her—real silver, not the stainless steel she was accustomed to. The detailing was beautiful.

Beside her, Donovan seemed engrossed in a chalice.

"Beautiful," she said.

He nodded.

They moved to the next room, which displayed recovered firearms and swords. The next room displayed tools of various kinds. Though these things were interesting and had value, they weren't works of art, and she had to force herself to seem interested.

The guard moved steadily between the various rooms.

The fourth room was the smallest. Along the edges, glass

cases displayed small items that had been recovered. A comb, a razor, a few little boxes. But in the center of the room, a pedestal displayed the museum's pride and joy.

The Pisano.

It stood about twenty inches tall. Bronze. She'd seen the photograph, but that hadn't done this masterpiece justice.

Jesus stood, hand outstretched, to the woman caught in adultery, who was on her knees, reaching up to him.

Jesus's face held such tenderness, such compassion. Such love.

The woman's, such wonder.

Wonder, that the Son of God would reach out for her, would accept her.

The photograph had been a pale imitation of this sculpture. And this sculpture was a pale imitation of God's love for His children.

That He'd reached out to Angel with that same compassion...

Emotions, too strong, too many to name, filled her. Her bottom lip quivered.

What kind of a God reaches out to the wretched, the lost? What kind of a God sends His Son to redeem the unredeemable?

Joy unspeakable washed over her, through her.

She was saved. Because of the love of God, the sacrifice of His Son, she was a new person. The old sinful, thieving liar was gone.

She'd never been an angel, despite her name. Now, according to Scripture, she was a saint.

She felt the smile on her lips, the tears dripping down her cheeks, and she didn't care. Because this was Truth.

God was good, and He'd chosen her.

CHAPTER THIRTEEN

Donovan couldn't take his eyes off Angel. He'd realized as soon as they walked into this room that the real reason he'd agreed to this little field trip was to see this sculpture again. Last time he'd visited, he'd appreciated the beauty and craftsmanship of it fine all by himself.

This time, though, he'd made the mistake, the colossal mistake, of glancing at Angel to see her reaction.

Her eyes were wide. And then she blinked, closed them. Tears streamed down her cheeks. She made no move to wipe them, didn't seem to realize they were there.

What was she thinking, this enigma? The sculpture had touched him the first time he'd seen it. Touched him today, but not like that.

Here was a woman who felt things, saw things, knew things. For all her chatter, the river of her thoughts ran deep, deeper than he'd imagined. Where were those thoughts now? On the beauty of the sculpture? Or was it more than that? Was it the beauty depicted beyond the bronze, the Savior reaching for the lost?

He'd thought the sculpture beautiful. It was nothing compared to the woman beside him.

Feelings he'd buried for years pushed their way to the surface. Tenderness, protectiveness, desire. The anger he was supposed to feel for her was gone, replaced with this... this affection.

He should look away. He had to look away, now. Before the feelings overwhelmed him and he did something colossally stupid like reach out for her. Touch her.

And with that thought came an image, clear as the trembling of her lower lip. Her, in his arms, head thrown back, hair blowing in a breeze. Her gaze on him. Smile like that one. He could imagine himself bending to touch his lips to hers. Feel their softness. Her arms would slide around his neck, her fingers would dig into the hair at his nape.

Oh Lord, help. He was in trouble.

Look away, he commanded himself. *Look away now.*

But he couldn't. She was a work of art beyond anything in this room, in this gallery. It wasn't her looks that drew him now, though she was beautiful. It was her heart, which shone on her face. It was her depth and complexity. Like all works of art, she needed to be studied, understood.

Treasured.

Her eyes opened.

He snapped his gaze to the sculpture, thankful she hadn't noticed him staring.

For the second time that day.

"It's... it's magnificent." Her voice hitched, filled with emotion.

"Yes."

She gazed at it a few more moments before—reluctantly, it seemed—she moved into the next room, which was twice as wide as the previous and signaled the far end of the addition.

This room was filled with paintings of the New England seacoast and ships at sea. Artwork, some quite valuable, but nothing like the Pisano.

He stayed beside her as she studied each piece, read each placard. He found himself trying to guess which pieces would touch her the most. She kept surprising him. Her gaze didn't linger on the ships in the stormy seas but did when she saw the idyllic landscapes of the shore. She seemed to take in each piece. With each one, he took in a little more of her.

This was a dangerous game, but he couldn't seem to make himself stop.

They moved through the gallery into the next room. Finally, they came to the gallery of local artists, the one he'd been dreading. He hoped she'd give this one no more than a cursory glance, but no such luck.

Again, he studied her face as they went from painting to painting.

Then she saw it.

Boston Light at Dawn.

The sun shone on the lighthouse, the island, and the skyline behind it. An old man and a small boy were fishing off the stone pier.

Angel stopped. He knew right away that she loved it. By the way her eyes widened. The way her mouth opened a touch. The way her gaze never wavered as it took in the piece.

And he saw when she noticed the signature.

D.H. Gilcreast.

Surely she wouldn't put it together.

Except Angel had surprised him at every turn today. She had an eye for art, an eye for beauty and authenticity. She was savvier than he'd given her credit for. If he'd known, he'd never have agreed to accompany her today. Because even if she didn't recognize the name and style, when his gaze flicked to the placard, he knew he was sunk.

His photo was plastered beside the little write-up.

She turned to him, eyes as wide as they'd been when she'd first seen the Pisano. Wonder—that's what he saw there. And admiration.

His heart thundered. He shouldn't love that look. He shouldn't be thrilled she'd figured it out.

But he did. And he was. And, God help him, he was in trouble.

"It's yours."

He forced himself to focus back on the painting.

"I knew you were talented," she said. "The canvases in the sunroom... But this is..."

Better than anything he'd done in months. He knew that. Knew his work was lacking... What? Something. Even Angel could see that.

He'd not given Angel nearly enough credit. She could see much more than he'd imagined.

Her fingers flitted across his arm, the lightest touch. It penetrated his thin shirt and sent sensations through his body.

He jerked, stepped away.

She recoiled. "I'm sorry. I didn't mean—"

"No. My... problem. My... I didn't think you'd realize."

"You didn't want me to?"

"No." *Yes.*

"I don't think that's true." Her head tilted to the side. "I think you like that I know. And you hate that you like it."

How did she read him so easily? Throughout their time at the gallery, he'd followed her, gone where she went, looked where she looked. Now, he stepped away, irrationally annoyed. He marched through the final gallery, barely glancing at the amateur sculptures displayed there, and reentered the house, which led to the gift shop. He found a book—one of those glossy coffee-table books people would buy and never look at again. He opened it, tried to get engrossed in it. Tried not to be aware of Angel as she stepped into the room and perused the selections. The curator must have heard their footfalls on the old hardwood, because she came in and stood behind the counter at the register.

Angel approached her. Within seconds, the women were having a conversation. He tried not to listen but somehow discovered Mary Lynn—Angel had called her by name—was an aspiring artist. She'd sculpted one of the pieces in the room he'd marched through. Angel had noticed it, seen the artist, somehow remembered the curator's name, and now asked if the piece was hers. The woman was delighted. They got into a discussion about sculptures, techniques, and of course, the Pisano.

The women chatted like old friends. Angel laughed, and the sound colored his imagination, a kaleidoscope of emotions.

"He seems engrossed in that book." Angel made no effort to keep her voice low.

He didn't look, but he knew they were watching him.

Mary Lynn lowered her voice, whispered something he couldn't hear.

Angel laughed again.

His ears burned.

"Do you know who he is?" Angel asked.

He slammed the book shut. "Are you ready?"

Angel glanced between him and the curator, whose eyes were bright with curiosity.

He carried the book to the counter. He couldn't very well put it away after acting as if he were engrossed. "How much?"

The woman rattled off a price, and he handed her his credit card.

Angel stood beside him, and though he didn't look, he could tell she was amused.

Which irritated him.

He snatched the plastic bag from the woman's hands and headed toward the door. Then, he remembered his manners and turned to Angel. "Are you ready?"

"Where are we going to eat? I'm starving."

"Uh..."

"Oh," Mary Lynn said. "Have you tried the new place..." And she was off, describing some restaurant that overlooked the marinas on the harbor.

"That sounds perfect," Angel said. "Doesn't it, Donovan?"

He shrugged. He hadn't planned on having a meal with her. Told himself he didn't want to.

She said good-bye to the curator and promised to stop back by another time. Finally, she headed for the door.

He held it open for her. When she stepped into the sunshine, she stopped and smiled. "I really am hungry. I haven't eaten since those pancakes."

He hadn't either. It was midafternoon, and the air had warmed into the low seventies. And now that they were outside and he could breathe again, the idea of lunch didn't seem scary. In fact, the idea of lunch with her sounded almost... pleasant.

He wouldn't allow himself to analyze all the emotions that colored his vision right now. He nodded toward the harbor. "Let's go."

Donovan led the way toward the restaurant, his pace slow. Angel seemed to be moving better today than she had the week before, but every once in a while she winced and tried to hide the pain in her ribs.

If he ever got his hands on the man who'd roughed her up...

Except he wasn't supposed to care about that or about her.

"It's quaint, isn't it?" she asked. "I love Portsmouth."

He did, too. Always had. There was something about the town that drew a person, made him want to stay forever. Of course, a lot of New England towns were like that. Nutfield was, too. Small, friendly. With tall trees all around, it felt protected from the world.

Maybe if Katie had lived in a little town like Nutfield instead of in Nashua... Except, little town or big, trouble was everywhere.

They meandered past houses that had been there for centuries. To the right, the trees of Prescott Park overlooked the water. To the left, Strawberry Banke, with its quaint buildings that made up the living history museum, reminded people of the town's storied past.

Others wandered along the sidewalk, some hurrying, some taking in the scenery.

"You ever been there?" Angel's gaze was on a small building that was part of Strawberry Banke.

"Field trip."

"Oh, yeah. I forget we went to the same school."

He nodded, kept walking.

"Are you always this quiet or only with people you hate?" Her words were spoken matter-of-factly.

"I don't hate you."

"Fine. Dislike. Barely tolerate."

"I don't..." He couldn't exactly blame her for picking up on all the emotions he was trying to hide. Trying to do away with, because they weren't fair.

They walked another block. He should have insisted they eat somewhere closer or take the truck. A ten-minute walk there, ten minutes back, plus the time at lunch... How would they fill it?

"At the Nightingale," she said, "did you recognize the curator's name on that sculpture?"

She had to know he hadn't. He'd barely glanced at the sculptures in that room, but maybe she hadn't been as focused on him as he'd been on her. "Not until you said something."

"Did you notice how she reacted when I asked her about it?" Angel's question seemed innocent, but he'd bet anything she had a point to make.

"I did."

"That's how normal people react when you compliment them on their art." Amusement laced her voice. "They say thank-you. They talk about their work. They're happy to be recognized."

"So I'm not normal."

She giggled. "You're a lot of things, Donovan Gilcreast, but normal isn't one of them."

He had no answer for that. Because she was right, and because he didn't care. He used to. When he was a kid, he'd wanted to fit in, to be liked. And when he went to college and met friends, he loved that he'd found other people like himself. There, he'd felt *normal*, at least for the artsy crowd.

But since Katie's death, none of it mattered.

Soft fingers brushed his arm. "I've offended you," Angel said. "I'm sorry. I didn't mean anything by it. I was teasing, trying to..."

He waited for her to finish, but her hand dropped to her side, and she said nothing else.

They crossed the intersection at Scott Street and continued onto Bow. More buildings, more people to contend with. Little shops lined the narrow road. The restaurant would be up ahead.

He'd like to feel relief at the thought, but that only meant they'd have to face each other and talk rather than walking side by side. What had he been thinking?

She started across the intersection of an alley barely wide enough for two to walk side by side. From the corner of his eye, he spied a bicycle careening toward her from the narrow space. He grabbed her shoulder and yanked her back. The bicycle missed her by inches.

She gasped, and her hands flew to her ribs. She doubled over.

He rested a hand on her upper back. "I'm sorry. I didn't mean—"

"You mind?" A man's voice cut him off as a family of tourists sidestepped them. The man muttered something under his breath that sounded a lot like *idiot*, and Donovan's hands clenched into fists. Instead of punching the jerk, though, he urged Angel toward the brick building beside them. "I should have been more careful. I reacted."

"Not your fault." She paused, blew out a breath. "I should have... Where'd he come from?"

"The alley."

She glanced that direction. "I didn't even..."

He looked around, spied a bench across the street. "You need to sit."

A moment passed before she stood straight again. "I'm okay. I needed to breathe through it."

But he could tell by the look in her eyes she was hurting. "Why don't you sit, and I'll go get the pickup?"

She nodded forward. "Is that the restaurant?"

He saw the sign. "But you're—"

"I'm fine," she said. "They're only bruised."

"You didn't injure them more?"

"Nope." She smiled, though he knew it was forced. "Let's go. I'm hungry."

He walked beside her, one eye on her to make sure she was okay, until they reached the door. He pulled it open and let her step inside before him.

The benefit of eating such a late lunch—on a Monday—was that the place wasn't too busy. They were seated immediately on the covered patio that overlooked the harbor. They ordered drinks—water for both of them—and studied the menus silently. Silent was his normal, but not hers.

"Hurting?" he asked.

"Nothing I can't handle."

He went back to the menu, considered his choices.

Considered her injuries.

"How did you...?" He snapped his jaw shut. None of his business.

She set the menu down, met his eyes. Quirked one eyebrow.

He looked out at the water. A tugboat was chugging its way toward the sea. Beyond that, one of the bridges that led into Maine stood in stark contrast to the bright blue sky.

Yes. Focus on the scenery. Because there was something dangerously attractive about Angel Rossi.

When he looked back at her, he found her watching him with that quirked eyebrow, a half smile on her face. Waiting for him to finish his question.

Fine. "Tell me what happened."

"You've been dying to know, haven't you?"

He picked up his menu again. Annoying woman. He perused the choices. Mexican food. Seafood. Mexican seafood. He set it back down. "Did a boyfriend do that to you? Because you shouldn't let anybody treat you that way. You deserve..."

What? What did she deserve?

He focused on the menu again, but the words written there couldn't penetrate his confusion.

She folded her hands on the table. The smile and eyebrow thing were gone. Her expression was serious. Maybe she was waiting for him to make eye contact. He did, and he held it. He was a grown man. He could handle a simple conversation with a woman.

Just maybe not *this* woman.

The server delivered their waters. "You two know what you want?"

Angel rattled off her choice—lobster avocado salad—weird combo. He ordered the first thing that came to mind—fish tacos.

Angel didn't answer his question. Which should have been fine, except he wanted to know. Had someone she trusted done that to her?

The thought of it had Donovan's hands clenching into fists for the second time in thirty minutes. He hid them on his lap until the rage passed.

She sipped her water, set it down. "Not a boyfriend."

"Oh." Relief washed over him, coral and pink like a sunset after a clear day. Relief at what, though? Boyfriend or not, somebody'd hurt her.

"Who, then?"

"It's a long story."

"Why did he... What was he...?" Donovan didn't know how to phrase the question. He should let it drop. She obviously didn't want to talk about it.

She chuckled, though the sound died quickly. "He was hurting my friend. Had her pinned down and was..."

Was what?

She shook her head, looked away. "I walked in on them. Helped my friend escape."

Walked in where? She'd made it sound like it was an intimate moment she'd interrupted. Because the man was... what? She'd said he was hurting her friend. Had it been worse than that? And Angel had jumped into the fray? "You paid the price."

"It was a price worth paying."

"Was it your friend's boyfriend?"

She scoffed. "Just a slimy jerk with too much power."

"What kind of power?"

"Not important now." But the slight rise and dip of her shoulders didn't convince him the incident could be shrugged off.

Because it was important. Too important. Because she'd put herself in harm's way—in the way of a man with power—for the sake of a friend. The new information about Angel floated around his image of her, looking for a place to land. The picture in his head wasn't accurate, though. The Angel he'd held in his head all these years wasn't selfless. She wouldn't sacrifice anything for the sake of another.

His picture of her shifted, and the new information clicked into place.

This wasn't the same person who'd gotten Katie hooked on drugs.

He didn't know what to do with this woman. He didn't know what to do with the protectiveness that rose now, a deep green like the needles on the pines that circled like sentries around their world. "You're safe now," he said. "At least you got away from him before he could hurt you worse."

"Yup." Her lips popped on the P, and he had the distinct impression there was more to the story.

"You are safe, right? Is this guy going to show up at our house?" *Our* house? Why had he said that? That wasn't what he meant at all.

But she didn't react to the slip. "He has no idea where I am."

"Keep it that way."

He expected a smile, some reaction to his command, but she said nothing.

He wanted to question her and was considering how to do it but was waylaid when the wind blew his stray hairs into his face one time too many. With a huff, he gathered the strands, worked the hair into the stupid rubber band again.

She watched, amused. "I like your look."

"I hate it."

Her head tilted to the side. "Then why do you keep it like that?"

"Too busy to find a barber." Too wrapped up in himself to make conversation with another human being. To force himself to be nice. And yet, here he was, talking like a normal person.

Well, maybe not normal.

That authentic smile he was coming to love stretched across her face. "I ever tell you I went to cosmetology school?"

"You're messing with me."

"I can have that trimmed up for you tonight if you want."

Even if she was kidding, even if she had no idea what she was doing and would butcher it, at least the hair would be out of his face. "I'll think about that."

"So, tell me about your work. How did you end up with a painting at the Nightingale?"

He gave her the short version, but Angel's gift—one of many —was her ability to ask the right questions. Somehow, he'd let his guard down when he questioned her about her injuries. And he found himself unable to erect it again during lunch as he told her about the painting at the Nightingale and then about his other early works and where they were displayed now.

Angel smiled up at the server as the woman set their meals down. Angel's salad bowl overflowed with greens and reds and yellows, an explosion of color and texture. The scent of fish and roasted corn wafted from his plate, making his mouth water. He bit into the first of three tacos—crispy lettuce, flaky fish, spicy salsa. It was delicious.

While they ate, he told her about his years at college, his friends in Boston. He told her about the apartment he'd shared with Ian, the apartment where he still paid half the rent, even though he hadn't lived there since Katie's death.

"Do you miss the city?" she asked between bites of salad.

"Yes... and no. I miss..." What did he miss? "I miss my friends there. I miss being part of the art world."

She nodded as if she understood.

"But I don't miss the city. I thought I would, but..." But he'd become such a hermit, he didn't know what he missed and didn't, what he longed for and didn't. His grief had overwhelmed all of those emotions, tinged everything in a dull gray.

"Maybe you will again, someday. After you've had time to heal, things will look different to you. I don't think you can really know how you feel in the middle of all that sadness. It must permeate everything."

"Yes." She'd voiced exactly what he'd been thinking.

"I've never lost someone I loved like you loved Katie."

Love Katie. Present tense. Didn't matter that she was gone, the love remained.

"A grandfather, but he was sick and in a lot of pain." She picked at her salad, then pushed it across the table. "Still hungry?" She quirked a brow—that same sexy brow she'd lifted before—at his empty plate. "I'm done."

He eyed the salad, then speared a bite of lobster. Cold fish, tangy dressing. It was good. He traded it for his empty plate and dug in.

"So I don't know grief like you do," she said. "I do know regret, though. Soul-deep regret. I know how an emotion can affect everything else in life. Everything has to be filtered through it, and nothing comes out unscathed."

The food slipped down his throat while her words slipped somewhere else, somewhere deep. Because she understood something, had voiced something he'd never been able to put into words.

"It's not the same thing," she said. "Probably a stupid comparison."

"No." He wiped his mouth, sipped his drink. "That's exactly right. The problem is, it's hard to imagine a time when everything won't be sullied by grief."

She caught and held eye contact. "They say time heals all wounds. I don't think so, though. I think time passes, maybe dulls the hurt. But dulled pain is pain."

He swallowed, nodded.

"But God heals. I mean, He's healing my regret, helping me move past it, helping me believe I can be saved and forgiven. He must heal grief, too."

Her words were a lifeline of hope. Yes, things would get better. He wouldn't be mired in this grief forever. He'd be able to see clearly again.

Come to think of it, he was already seeing more clearly. Today, it was as if a layer of haze had been peeled back, allowing a bit of light to filter through.

And maybe the reason was the woman on the other side of the table.

The server returned with their check. "You guys need anything else?"

"We're good." Donovan snatched the bill. This wasn't a date, but... Well, he was buying, anyway, even if he couldn't come up with a suitable excuse.

But Angel wasn't arguing yet. She was focused on the server. "Any chance you're hiring?"

Hiring? Angel couldn't seriously be thinking of getting a job. She'd nearly passed out from pain when he'd pulled her out of the way earlier. She was in no condition to be carrying trays of drinks, bumping into customers. A place like this would be filled with tourists who drank too much and made passes. How could she protect herself?

"Matter of fact," the server said, "we are. Come on in when you're done, and I'll get you an application."

CHAPTER FOURTEEN

After the server had walked away, Angel tried to give Donovan cash for her half of the meal, but Donovan refused to take it. Sometimes, he looked at her with such loathing, it nearly burned her skin. Other times, he seemed interested in what she was saying, curious about her life.

She didn't understand. The man was a riddle she wanted to solve.

Not that her life had a lot of room for solving men's mysteries. Between Routhier, Opie, Anton, and Mason, she had enough men to contend with at the moment without adding another.

By the time they'd stopped at the paint store and returned to the house, the sun was setting. Donovan helped her from the pickup—concern for her injuries or gentlemanly manners, she didn't know—and then hefted the five-gallon buckets to the house as if they were filled with air, not paint. She held the door open for him, to make his life easier, of course. Not because she enjoyed watching him move.

Because that would be dangerous. Of all the things she was doing—conspiring with the police, working with the snake

Anton—she feared that spending time with Donovan was the most dangerous. Because those other things might steal her freedom or injure her body, but Donovan was gaining entry to her heart.

He passed her in the house and set the paint on the floor in the parlor. "Thanks."

She let the door close, then remembered... "Would you do me a favor?"

He turned to her, eyebrows lifted.

"My friend packed up my stuff. It's in a trash bag in the backseat of my car. I wanted to get it myself, but—"

"Is it unlocked?"

"I think so. I meant to ask you yesterday, but you were so..." Surly. She was trying to come up with a suitable way to finish her sentence when Donovan headed for the door.

A moment later, he returned with the trash bag Anton had left for her. "You want me to take it in your room or leave it at the door."

"Leave it on the bed. I'm hoping my tools are in there."

His eyes narrowed. "What kind of tools? I have—"

"Hairdressing tools." She glanced at the hair that had, once again, slipped from his ponytail.

He started to say something, then didn't. Instead, he carried the bag toward her room.

She followed and stopped in the hallway outside the door while Donovan dumped the bag on her bed. No reason for them both to be in the bedroom. Sharing a house was already intimate. She had to be careful not to let it become more so.

He hurried back out as if he might be caught.

"Thank you."

He nodded.

"I'll let you know if I find them. We can do it tonight. You have shaving cream?"

His eyes narrowed. "I can shave my own face."

She lifted her eyebrows, gave his whiskers a pointed look. "I believe you *can,* but that beard needs to be cleaned up. I might have some."

He rubbed a palm against his whiskers. "I don't... It's fine. Really. I'll just..."

But his words trailed off.

She stepped into the bedroom and dug through the contents of the trash bag until her hand felt the cool leather of her kit. She pulled it out, opened it, and smiled.

She turned, half expecting to see he'd left.

But he stood there in the hallway.

"I've got everything I need. Why don't you wash your hair and meet me in the kitchen?"

Again, he opened his mouth, then closed it and walked down the hall. From a few feet away, she heard him say, "Fine."

She stared after him, a little shocked he'd agreed. Shocked and pleased.

She grabbed the things she'd need, including her shaving cream from the shower—he'd love the lavender scent—and headed for the kitchen. The room was a good choice. He could look out the window at the view he loved, and she'd be able to sweep the tile easily. There were no suitable chairs, though. The barstools were too high.

She searched the downstairs, finally finding a side chair under a drop cloth in the dining room. It was heavier than she'd imagined, with carved legs and beautiful lines. She was in the process of dragging it to the kitchen when Donovan's footsteps sounded on the stairway overhead. A moment later, he appeared at her side smelling of soap and shampoo.

"Can you take this to the kitchen for me?" she asked.

He nodded and lifted the chair, then nodded for her to precede him.

All the nods. Mr. Silent was back.

She got him situated looking out the window, then draped her cloth over his shoulders.

"You weren't pulling my leg, I guess," he said.

She chuckled while she gathered the comb. "This was my job before."

She combed his hair. Wet, it skimmed his shoulders. "You know, if you gave it another month, you could put it in a pony-tail and it would stay."

"It's not like I was trying to grow it out. I just..."

But he didn't finish the sentence, and she thought maybe she understood. He'd been hiding here, and getting a haircut meant making a connection with someone. It meant having to talk, to make eye contact in a mirror, to be polite.

There was no mirror here. Maybe that would help him to feel more comfortable.

She brushed her fingers through his dark brown locks. It was thick and fine with very little curl. No sign of aging. All youthful and vibrant, like the man.

She dropped her hand and moved to face him. "How do you want it cut?"

He shrugged. "Just short."

That was helpful. "You have a picture of what you want it to look like? Or maybe an old photo of yourself I can use to compare?"

"Probably somewhere." But he didn't move to retrieve one.

"You're giving me carte blanche?"

"I don't care."

She ducked behind him again to hide the smile. If he didn't care, then that meant she could do what she wished with him. The idea was a little too tempting. She started snipping away. "Carte blanche. I've always wanted to try something... I think I'll shave the image of Tom Selleck on your scalp."

He growled, and she couldn't help the laugh. "You said—"

"A normal man's haircut."

She continued cutting. "Now, now. We already agreed you're not normal. Why should you pretend with a haircut?"

No reaction to that. Hopefully she hadn't offended him again. She moved in front of him to glance at his face. He didn't seem annoyed. A little nervous maybe. She hid a smile as she moved to the side again.

"If you're a hairdresser," he said, "why not get a job in a salon or something?"

"I need something that'll pay me now. It takes time to build up a hairdressing business."

"What happened to your last hairdressing job?"

She focused on his hair while she tried to formulate a good answer. And then she remembered her vow to be honest, always. Even when it was hard. "I got arrested. Then sent to rehab. All the clients I'd had found other hairdressers."

A few beats passed while she snipped away. "But serving will be hard, won't it? With your injuries?"

"I'll be fine. It's getting better every day. And anyway, hairdressing isn't exactly a sit-down job."

Donovan said nothing else. He was still, almost unnaturally so. His hands didn't fidget, his feet didn't move. Again, the image of a sculpture came to mind. Yes, he'd make a beautiful sculpture. A beautiful work of art.

She knew exactly the look he needed. A nice gentleman's haircut to match the gentleman he truly was. Because, as gruff as his exterior was right now, if her guess was correct, beneath that exterior lay a kind, sensitive man, a man hiding from the world, not because he didn't care but because he cared too much.

She snipped and snipped. He stayed silent, unmoving. When she was nearly finished, she crouched in front of him, checked the hair that would fall onto his forehead, snipped it to the proper length.

She got it how she wanted it, then combed it back and... My, but did he look good. The haircut was perfect. It highlighted his dark eyes...

His gaze met hers. Those eyes were smoldering.

When had she gotten so close? With everything in her, she wanted to lean closer, to lose herself in his eyes.

She stood, stepped back, bumped into the wall of windows. "I just, um... I have to shave the neck." She urged his head down. The buzzing of the electric razor had her raising her voice a little. "And then I thought I'd work on that beard, if you don't mind. It doesn't really go with the haircut now. I know you don't care, but..." She was babbling. She snapped her jaw shut.

He cleared his throat. "I'm going to shave it."

"Okay, then. I can help with that, too." She turned off the razor. "You're sure? About the beard?"

"I've been... preoccupied. I wasn't really going for the *Red Sox in the playoffs* look."

A joke. She hadn't known he was capable. She chuckled and took the electric razor to the beard. Had to get most of it off before she shaved him for real.

"I can take it from here."

"Could've fooled me."

She finished removing the bulk of his facial hair, then grabbed her shaving cream from the kitchen's island and shook it as she walked back around to his front.

His eyes narrowed. "What are we doing?"

"I'm going to give you a good shave."

He blinked. "With the electric razor, right?"

"Of course not." She reached behind him, grabbed the straight razor, and showed it to him.

His eyes widened. "Uh... I don't think so."

She tilted her head to the side. "Don't you trust me?"

His gaze flicked from the razor to her face. He licked his lips. "I don't... I mean, I don't think you'd *try* to kill me, but..."

Her short burst of laughter quieted him. "I promise, I won't hurt you. I used to work in a high-end shop. I did this all the time." Okay, *all the time* was an exaggeration, but she'd done it enough. At least once a week, anyway. "I've only sent a couple of men to the ER."

His Adam's apple bobbed.

"I'm kidding. You're too gullible." She covered her hands with the shaving cream. Then she held up her hands and met his gaze. "Seriously. You'll like it."

His look told her he wasn't convinced, but he didn't argue when she reached for his face.

While she shaved him, she chattered. Maybe to make him feel more comfortable. Maybe to keep her mind off the beautiful face she was discovering below all those whiskers.

"When I was in cosmetology school, we learned to do this by practicing on balloons," she said.

He didn't move a muscle.

"You can breathe, you know. It's not that delicate an operation."

He took a breath, and she tried not to smile.

"Anyway, one time when I was first learning, I'd covered my balloon with shaving cream and was running the razor over it when my instructor stepped into my field of vision. Now, you have to picture her. She always wore a skirt, a matching jacket, a pretty blouse, and a scarf. Her hair was always coiffed, her makeup always perfect. Usually, she wore high heels that clicked on the floors. I loved those heels because they warned me she was coming. That day, though, she'd worn flats with rubber soles. When she stepped into my field of vision, the razor slipped, and I popped the balloon. Shaving cream everywhere."

His lips trembled like he wanted to smile. Maybe he was afraid a smile might literally be the death of him as she ran the razor over his neck.

"It was so bad." She giggled, remembering. "You know how Wile E. Coyote looks after the Acme bomb explodes in his face? That's how she looked, except instead of dirt and grime, she was covered with shaving cream."

Now, Donovan couldn't stop the smile. He didn't speak, but she saw the amusement in his eyes.

"Fortunately, she laughed. In fact, the whole class got a kick out of it."

Angel finished the shave, snatched her towel, and rinsed it in warm water. She crouched in front of him and wiped the extra shaving cream away with the towel. Heavens, he was beautiful. The facial hair had hidden the chiseled jaw, the strong chin. Even his perfect lips had been overshadowed by that ugly mustache. This was a face that should never be covered.

An errant hair fell across his forehead. She brushed it back.

And met Donovan's eyes.

Oh, they were smoldering again.

She was too close.

But she couldn't seem to move. Her hand was still at his hairline.

He covered it with his own, held it to his chest, steadied her. His other hand reached for her, threaded in her hair.

His gaze held hers, then flicked to her lips.

She wanted him to kiss her like she'd never wanted anything. No work of art, no treasure, had ever brought her to this level of desire.

He leaned closer, close enough that she could feel his breath.

And then, his lips brushed hers. The slightest touch, so gentle it could have been a breeze. He did it again. And again.

And finally, he took her mouth, possessively, gently. Her lips parted, and he claimed the gift.

Beneath her fingertips, his heart pounded in rhythm with her own. She wanted more of this, more of him.

He dug his hand deeper into her hair, sending tingles of delight, of desire, over her skin to her very toes. The kiss lasted, but she feared it could never last long enough. She thought she could kiss him for the rest of her life.

And then, he pulled back. His fingers dropped from her hair.

She tipped and grabbed the leg of his chair to keep from toppling over. She should move, but she didn't know if her legs, in their weakened state, would lift her.

He swallowed. "I shouldn't have done that."

"We." She cleared her throat to make her high-pitched voice sound normal again. "I'm pretty sure I was involved."

He still held her hand to his chest. He looked at their joined hands now, and she did, too. He lifted them out toward her, an invitation to help her stand.

She did and stepped back. "It looks..."

Good. So good.

He touched the short hair. "Feels better."

"I bet." She could stare at him all day. Instead, she set to work cleaning up her things.

He carried the chair out of the room. As soon as he was gone, she leaned against the counter and held her hand against her heart and closed her eyes.

What was she doing? She shared a house with this man, and she'd let him kiss her? Would he expect more?

Did she want more?

Nope. She wasn't going to answer that question. Because it wasn't about what she wanted. She had to behave herself.

That kiss had brought some seriously unholy desires to mind.

"I apologize."

She jumped at the words. Her eyes opened to find Donovan leaning in the doorway.

"I have no excuse for my behavior," he said. "I promise it won't happen again."

With that, he turned and walked away.

AFTER ANGEL FINISHED SWEEPING the kitchen, she retreated to her bedroom and told herself not to think about that kiss.

As if that were possible.

But she had work to do, and she needed to keep her head in the game and not on the man who shared a house with her.

She should be nervous about that. The very thought of going near Anton made her skin crawl, and now she was living under the same roof with a man who'd kissed her. A man who, if her wires hadn't completely crossed, felt as much desire for her as she did for him.

But she wasn't afraid of Donovan. His gruff exterior hid a gentle, caring man. He would never hurt her. He would never force himself on her like...

The memory of Anton's hands, Anton's strength, pushed away the sweetness of the kiss she'd shared with Donovan. She hated Anton with renewed loathing.

She wasn't supposed to hate, though. Hate was the enemy. Along with greed and anger and fear and a whole host of other emotions that had once consumed her.

She shoved her hairdressing supplies in a drawer in the bathroom and dropped the towel and cape on her pile of dirty laundry. Back in the bedroom, she shoved all the things that had come out of that trash bag aside and sat on the edge of her bed.

Lord, my emotions are bouncing like fleas in a jar. I need Your help. She took a deep breath, tried to pull in God's peace. *Donovan isn't Anton, but that doesn't mean I should trust him.* And yet, for some reason, she did trust Donovan. *Should I be more guarded with him? Should I pull back?*

Of course she should. She was falling for a man who disliked her. Wanted her, no doubt, but also, sometimes, seemed to hate her. And she didn't know why. Maybe because she was alive and Katie wasn't. Maybe she reminded him too much of his sister. But it seemed more than that.

Why would she give her heart to a man who loathed her?

Why was she attracted to a man who'd been at turns gentlemanly, interested, and furious with her?

She lifted her face to the ceiling and begged the Lord for insight. She received nothing but the gentle reminder that Donovan was His, and Donovan was loved.

By You, she thought. *And if I'm not careful, by me, too.*

God had no response to that.

After she'd put away the things that Brittney had packed for her, Angel snatched her phone from the bureau. She'd left it in the bedroom, and when the screen came to life, she saw she'd missed a call from Routhier and a text from Anton.

Call now.

The text had come in an hour before. Good. Because she wanted to call now, and she would have had to wait at least an hour before doing so after that rude text. As if she'd ever obey his commands.

He answered on the third ring. "Where have you been?" His words were harsh.

She forced a casual tone, though his anger raised the hairs on the back of her neck. "Busy."

"When I contact you, I expect you to answer right away."

"You need to adjust your expectations."

She waited through a long pause. Finally, she heard an exhale. "You went to the Nightingale?"

"This afternoon. Two guards. One patrolled the east wing, including the Pisano room. The other patrolled the west wing. When I was in the Pisano room, he stayed with us."

"But if there were other people there..."

"I don't know what he would do," Angel said. "I assume, though, he'd focus mostly on the Pisano."

"And the security around it?"

"Plexiglass box, I assume. I didn't touch it. Couldn't tell if it was wired." And, honestly, she'd forgotten to look. Once she'd seen the sculpture, she'd forgotten why she was there, so enraptured with its beauty. Thank heaven she'd noticed the guard on her way out, or she wouldn't have realized he'd stayed in there with them.

"You'll have to go back, spend more time there. Figure out the guards' schedules. See what you can learn about the security system."

"When it's stolen, mine'll be the face they remember. When the cops ask if anybody's been hanging around—"

"You'll be fine," Anton said. "We won't get caught. I'll manufacture a great alibi for you."

"What kind of alibi?"

"I'm working on that. Somebody who'll swear you were with them at the time of the burglary. Assuming you even need the alibi."

"Get it in place. I want to know every aspect of this plan."

His short, humorless laugh told her what he thought of her demands.

"What's Mason learned?" she asked.

"He got the blueprints for the original building. He's looking for the ones for the addition. And he's digging around, trying to figure out what kind of security system they have."

"We need to know—"

"This isn't my first job," Anton said. "You're going to have to trust me."

She scoffed. "About as far as I can throw you... with bruised ribs."

Silence. A moment passed, then another. She wasn't about to fill it. She stared at the room she was coming to think of as home, then into the attached bathroom. She glimpsed that old, dingy vanity in the midst of all the beauty of the new fixtures. That's how she felt sometimes—old and dingy and out of place.

It wasn't true, though, that image. She was a new creation. She was the gleaming tub, not the dingy vanity.

Anton said, "Get over it."

"Kind of hard when my every move reminds me—"

"If you thought that was a beating"—his words were low and cold—"you have no idea what's waiting for you."

She held her breath. What was he saying?

"In prison, you'll get that and more all the time. So get over it, or I'll really show you what you missed out on that night. And then you'll land that tight little butt behind bars."

"Turn me in, and I'll return the favor."

He laughed. "Except they'll believe every word I say, and they'll call you a liar."

Not true, thanks to her deal with Routhier, but he didn't know that. She needed to act afraid of his threats.

Honestly, it wasn't that much of an act.

"I'll text you next week," he said. "When I do, I expect you to tell me the guards' schedule, the security around the Pisano, and your thoughts about the best time to pull off the job."

"That's not enough ti—"
"And don't make me wait next time."
He ended the connection.

CHAPTER FIFTEEN

onovan's thoughts would not be silenced. He'd drifted off early—miraculously—and then woken up a little after two. Now, he could hardly force his eyes to remain closed. It was the first time in days he couldn't sleep. Only instead of obsessing about Katie and all the things he should have done differently, he was obsessing about Angel and all the things he should have done differently.

He should have turned down her invitation to the Nightingale.

He should have refused to go to lunch with her.

He should have said no to her offer to cut his hair. The fact that his hair looked better than it ever had... The fact that he looked like himself again for the first time since the funeral, none of that was worth the cost.

He should have kept his mind occupied. He should have been thinking about something entirely *not* sexy when she'd had her hands in his hair, on his face. How hard was that, to focus the mind on something else? He could have thought about... about... wallpaper stripper. That wasn't sexy. And plaster that crumbled under too much pressure. And corned beef. There was nothing sexy about corned beef.

But none of those things had occurred to him. Because Angel had been touching him, her fingers on his face light and gentle, and his body had ignored his brain.

He turned over, punched his pillow, and worked to redirect his mind.

He tried to conjure images of Katie, something he rarely allowed himself to do, but even grief couldn't make all the feelings he'd stirred up tonight vanish. Because, God help him, he'd kissed Angel, and he could have kept on kissing her for eternity.

He tried to pray, but the images, the feelings, wouldn't leave him alone, and his prayers became nothing more than *Please help me sleep. I need to sleep.*

He was drifting away when a crash sounded, the sound of glass shattering.

Half awake, he lurched out of bed, pulled on a pair of sweatpants, and rushed down the stairs. Had someone broken a window? Was there an intruder?

Angel's attacker... Had he found her? Was she in danger?

Silent on bare feet, he ran down the hallway toward her room. He didn't want to warn anybody that he was coming. Better to catch the attacker off guard.

He burst into the room, braced for a fight.

And found Angel sitting on the floor next to the bed in the middle of shards of glass, which lay scattered all around her. Her eyes were wide, terrified.

He looked at the windows. Intact. Then toward the bathroom. No movement there. Then back to her. "Is someone else here?"

Her gaze darted around the room. "I don't... I don't think so."

He tried to calm himself with a deep breath. "What happened?"

"There was someone..." She rubbed her neck. Though the bruises were almost gone, he doubted the memory of what had happened to her would vanish that quickly. "I had a nightmare. At least, I think it was..." She gazed at the glass. Her eyes widened. "Oh. It's... it's that pretty glass vase that was sitting on the nightstand."

The vase had come with the house. Had been on the nightstand when he'd moved in.

And now it was in pieces.

"I'm sorry I broke it." Her eyes filled. "I was asleep."

She still was, if he were any judge. Or close to it.

"I was probably reaching for the lamp."

"It was only a vase."

She started to get up.

"Don't move. You'll cut yourself."

She picked glass out of her way and stood in the cleared space.

Stubborn woman. "Make sure there's no glass on your..." She wore a nightgown with skinny straps and a hem that barely skimmed the middle of her thighs. As if he needed more fodder for his fantasies. "Hop back into the bed. I'll clean this up."

She did as she was told. "If you'll toss me a pair of shoes—"

"Don't move. I'll be back."

He ran upstairs and slipped into flip-flops, then grabbed the broom, dustpan, and vacuum cleaner from the utility room.

When he returned to Angel's room, he found her sitting where he'd left her, except she'd pulled the blankets up to cover herself. Thank God.

"I can do it," she said.

"You cleaned up the hair." After sweeping up the bigger

pieces of glass, he turned on the vacuum. Glass rattled through the hose, filling the room with noise too loud to talk over.

Certain he'd gotten everything from the center of the hardwood floor, he removed the attachment and used another to get into the crevices, hearing a few pieces of glass get sucked up.

It took a good ten minutes. After he turned off the vacuum and set it in the hallway, he spied the shoes Angel wore around the house—white Converse sneakers—and set them beside the bed. "I might've missed some."

"I'm sorry I woke you. And I'm sorry about the vase. And I'm sorry about... about..." But she was crying. He didn't understand why.

"It wasn't my vase. It was your brother's. You can apologize to him."

"Oh. Right."

He stood beside her bed, concerned about those tears, berating himself for his concern. "Are you going to be all right?"

She shook her head. Nodded. "Yeah. Of course. Just..." She lifted her phone from the nightstand.

"What time is it?" he asked.

"Nearly five."

Morning. Or almost. And he sure as heck wasn't going back to sleep now.

"I'm going to paint."

She swallowed.

"You're welcome to come sleep in the sunroom, if you want."

Her gaze met his. "You're sure?"

He shrugged. "I haven't figured out how to stop you."

That got a smile, weak as it was. He spun, snatched the dustpan, broom, and vacuum from the hallway and carried them back to the utility room.

He got set up in the sunroom and waited for the sun to

brighten the view. It was too dark to paint yet, but in a few minutes, he'd begin.

Right now, he had to clear his mind. Between the kiss last night and now the image of her in that nightie, he wondered if he'd be able to get any work done.

Katie. He was doing this for Katie.

Katie, whom Angel had enticed into trying drugs. Katie, who was gone now. Because of Angel.

Problem was, he didn't believe that anymore. What if Angel had introduced his sister to drugs? She hadn't made Katie keep doing them. Angel hadn't gotten sucked into addiction, and it wasn't Angel's fault that Katie had.

Angel didn't seem to use drugs anymore. Katie could have made that choice. Yes, it was hard once a person got addicted. He understood that, but Katie'd had help. Their parents had poured thousands upon thousands of dollars into getting her healthy. And Katie had relapsed time after time.

None of that was Angel's fault. He had no right to hold anything against her.

But his parents did. As attracted as Donovan was to Angel— and here, with Katie's view in front of him, he could admit that attraction—she'd never be welcome in his family. He could never bring home to his parents the woman they blamed for Katie's addiction. Her death.

He needed to get his head straight, and soon. And maybe... He touched his short hair. She'd done a fine job. Maybe it was time to pay his parents a visit. He'd avoided them since the funeral, avoided everybody. Now, he felt stronger than he had in months.

Thanks to his houseguest. Angel's presence had been a healing balm.

And that was exactly the kind of thought he needed to banish. A trip to his parents' house would do the trick. They'd help him remember why Angel was off limits. They'd help him get his head straight.

He didn't turn but listened as Angel padded into the room, settled on the old sofa, and cozied under the blankets she'd left there.

For some reason, her presence calmed him, centered him.

The view outside had brightened enough.

He picked up his paintbrush and set to work.

DONOVAN PULLED UP OUTSIDE HIS PARENTS' house a little before noon that day. This wasn't the home he'd grown up in. That house, the pretty four-bedroom Colonial, had been sold, along with a lot of its contents, to pay for Katie's last stint in rehab. More loss. Senseless loss.

This small three-bedroom sat on a city-sized plot, which Dad insisted he preferred to the acre he'd had before. "Less to take care of. More time to relax."

There was nobody like Dad to put a good spin on a bad situation.

The front door opened, and Donovan's parents stepped onto the concrete front porch. Mom waved a hand in greeting. Dad climbed down the three steps and met Donovan in the driveway with a bear hug. "So glad you came, son."

"Glad to be here."

They walked up the steps, and Donovan hugged his mother. She backed up, touched his hairline, rubbed her hand against his cleanly shaven face. Tears shimmered in her eyes, and Donovan thought of Angel and all he owed her.

But he was here to get rid of thoughts like those.

"You look like yourself again." Mom's voice held tears, as it often had since Katie's overdose. "My sweet Donovan. I'm so happy to see you."

He kissed her cheek. She'd lost weight, though she'd had plenty to lose. Her skin looked healthier than it had last time he'd seen her. Maybe she'd spent some time in the sun.

She took his hand. "Come on. We're making your favorite."

Inside, the scent of roasting meat drew him to the kitchen. He lifted the lid on her Dutch oven and saw the roast inside. "Is that…?"

"Tenderloin, of course," Dad said. "Mom made me run to the butcher as soon as they opened."

"You shouldn't have gone to any trouble." But it smelled delicious.

"No trouble at all," Mom said. "Sit, sit. Water?"

They were treating him like an honored guest instead of like the selfish jerk he was. The person who'd avoided them because he couldn't handle their pain.

He understood how the prodigal son felt.

Mom buzzed about in the kitchen while Dad sat beside him, making small talk about his job and the house. "And tell us how your project is going? We'd love to come out and see that place sometime."

Dad had suggested it before, and Donovan had always rebuffed him. Now he said, "I'd like that." But he'd need notice so he could get Angel out of there. No sense throwing her in his parents' faces. "I'd like you to wait until I've finished a few more rooms, though. It's going to be beautiful."

"And do you think you'll stay there?" Mom asked.

"It's not my house."

"I know that, but you could buy it if you wanted," she said. "You could make a home there."

"It's not my home, either." Though it was beginning to feel like it.

Mom turned toward the stove.

Dad offered an apologetic smile.

"If it makes you feel any better," Donovan said, "Boston doesn't feel like home anymore, either."

She turned, a tremulous smile in place. "I'd be lying if I said I wasn't happy to hear that."

Mom had been in favor of Donovan going to the city for college, but when he'd decided to stay there, she'd been distraught. As if Boston weren't right down the road—less than an hour's drive.

When he'd lived in Boston, he'd thought he'd stay there forever, but now that he was back in New Hampshire, he liked it. He didn't want to live in Nashua, but the seacoast was beautiful, and Clearwater Lake in Nutfield felt as much like home as anywhere had since he'd lived with his family.

Mom set the roast in the center of the table. Dad carved it, and they dug in. Between the meat, which all but melted in his mouth, the creamy mashed potatoes, the roasted vegetables, and the crisp salad, Donovan planned to stuff himself.

"How goes the art?" Dad asked between bites.

Donovan didn't even try to suppress the sigh. "I don't know. Not well."

Dad's smile was kind, if not understanding. Dad was a practical sort, one who loved numbers and order. A financial planner, he spent his time with people and investment portfolios.

Donovan had gotten his artistic streak from Mom, who'd studied art when she was younger.

"You look good, Mom. What have you been up to?"

"You remember the McCormicks? They bought a new house, and I've been helping Nan decorate it."

"Back in the decorating business, then?"

"Just dipping my toe in."

"But you like it."

Her smile wobbled. "I have to do something or I'll go insane."

He knew exactly how she felt.

"I'm glad you're back at it," he said. "The activity will be good for you."

They ate a few bites in silence. Mom was better, but her grief was as obvious as the empty seat at the table.

"Time heals all wounds," Dad said. "We have to be patient."

Angel's words came back to him. "A friend said recently that time doesn't heal. She said time passes, maybe dulls pain. God heals it."

Dad nodded. "I like that."

Mom's eyes brightened. "*She?*"

Oh. Had he said that? "Nobody important. Someone I met recently."

"Are you dating this somebody?"

"No." He helped himself to another slice of meat and more potatoes. "Great meal. I need to come home more often."

Mom reached across the table and laid her hand on his. "I hope you will. We miss you. It feels like... like we lost you both."

"I wish I'd been...better." He flipped his hand over and held Mom's. "I wish I'd been more helpful. I'm going to try."

Dad said, "We're all grieving in our own way."

His guilt and anger had kept him holed up, but not anymore.

They finished their meals. Donovan tried to help with the dishes, but Mom shooed him away.

"Son, I could use your advice outside."

Donovan followed his father out the back door. They stepped onto the wooden deck large enough for a café table and the grill. Dad continued down the steps that led into the grassy yard. "There's a little rot here." With the toe of his loafer, he tapped one of the four-by-fours that supported the deck. "I'm not sure how to handle it."

"I'll replace it for you," Donovan said. "Maybe I'll come by next weekend."

"I can do it. Tell me what you recommend."

So Donovan explained how he'd tackle the project with Dad nodding as if he were enthralled. Which was Donovan's first clue that this had been a ruse to get him away from Mom. Because Dad had taught him everything he knew about home repair. And because Dad, despite the nodding, was only half listening.

Finally, Donovan put his hands on his hips. "What's going on?"

Dad lowered his voice. "Mom seems better, don't you think?"

Donovan glanced at the kitchen window and hoped she wasn't listening. "She does."

"I insisted she see somebody."

Dad had been trying for a long time, but Mom had refused. Of course, she'd refused to get out of bed for weeks after the funeral. "I'm glad."

"Between the counseling and the medication, she's healing."

He didn't like the idea of his mother taking drugs to get over her daughter's death from drugs—felt wrong, somehow—but legal, prescribed drugs were a far cry from the heroin that had killed Katie. "It's working, so I say keep it up."

"I wondered... You look better, but maybe you could consider—"

"I'm fine, Dad." His voice had come out too loud, so he lowered it. "I'm not like Mom was. I get out of bed every day. I work hard. I keep busy."

"You got a haircut. That's something."

Donovan touched his head again. He sure didn't miss that

stupid ponytail. The thought of it made him ask... "You remember that I'm living in Jack Rossi's house?"

"Of course. You said it's coming along—"

"His sister is staying there right now. Angel."

"Oh." Dad glanced again at the house. "I thought she'd... gone away."

"Been sent to prison, you mean?"

Dad shrugged. "I wasn't sure exactly what happened."

"It's a long story, and I don't know it all." And suddenly he remembered what Jack had said when he'd first brought Angel to the house, that her presence needed to remain quiet. "I'm not supposed to say anything about it, so don't tell anybody I mentioned it. Including her parents. And especially Mom."

"I won't tell her. She still harbors resentment toward Angel."

Resentment. Another of Dad's euphemisms.

"Seems fair that she does," Donovan said, "considering Angel introduced Katie to drugs."

Dad shoved his hands deep in his pockets and jingled the change there. "Thing is, I don't think she did. Mom... It's easier for her to have someone to blame, and when Angel started getting in trouble—shoplifting, I think it was—Mom decided that, since they'd been friends, Angel must have played a part in Katie's drug use. The problem with her logic is that, when Katie started using, their friendship fell apart. You know, their dad is one of my clients, and he told me a little about what was going on with her over the years. He was always honest about his kids and their struggles. When Katie was struggling with addiction, he sympathized, but he never indicated he'd gone through anything similar with his kids." Dad shook his head. "I don't think Angel even did drugs."

And when she was an adult, she was caught with drugs but insisted she wasn't an addict. Donovan believed that. He'd seen addicts, and Angel had none of the characteristics. She was honest and forthright. She ate healthy food. She kept normal hours and spent most of her spare time at the house. She'd been injured a week prior and probably could have gotten painkillers, but hadn't.

Donovan had no reason to believe she was using drugs.

So... what did that mean?

"You're saying you don't think Angel had anything to do with Katie's drug use?" Donovan clarified.

"I don't think so, but there's no sense arguing with Mom when she gets an idea into her head. I'm hoping the counselor will help her move past that resentment, move into forgiveness, so she can find healing, too." Dad frowned. "Truth is, your mother blames herself."

"It's not her fault Katie started using drugs."

Dad met his eyes. "It's not your fault either, son. And it's not mine. We loved her as best we could. The Lord saw fit to take her home."

"You believe that? You believe she's in heaven?" He reached for the light of those words, hoped desperately for them to be true.

Dad smiled. "With all my heart. In fact..." He swallowed, blinked a couple of times. "After she died, I had a dream about her. She was sitting at a table. You know how, in dreams, you know stuff about the situation?"

Donovan wasn't exactly sure what his dad was getting at, but he nodded anyway.

"In this dream, I knew Katie was lying on the hospital bed after her overdose, but while she hovered on the edge of life and death, in my dream, she was sitting at a table with Jesus. They were holding hands and laughing. They were friends." He looked away, wiped his eyes.

Donovan used the moment to wipe his own.

"It wasn't a dream or a hope," Dad said. "It was a gift from God. Your sister is in heaven, free of pain, free of her addiction." He grabbed Donovan's forearm. "We're grieving her, and that's normal and natural, but we also need to remember the girl she used to be and the free woman she is today. We need to celebrate the life we have. Your mother is working on it. I need to know you are, too."

"I am." He could hardly get the words out. "I will."

After the visit, Donovan drove home with a renewed sense of peace. Dad believed Katie had truly been saved. When Donovan wanted to argue, he felt the Lord's whisper. *Your sister is at peace. You should be, too.*

And, at that moment, he was. He felt more at peace than he had since Katie's overdose.

Not only with himself, but with the warring emotions he'd had toward Angel since she'd moved in. Katie's addiction wasn't Angel's fault. Which meant Donovan's feelings for her weren't wrong.

Could he open himself up to her, let himself trust her?

He didn't know for sure, but he was willing to try.

CHAPTER SIXTEEN

Angel completed the paperwork at her new job and started her first training shift. The menu wasn't complicated, and she had no doubt she could memorize it and pass the test they promised to give her the following day. The issue was the physical aspect.

Donovan was right. She wasn't ready for this. By the time her short shift was over, her ribs ached. Somehow, the exertion, which hadn't been much, exhausted her. Unfortunately, she had one more stop to make before she could head home.

She drove to the Nightingale and parked in the little lot out front.

Mary Lynn called a welcome from the entry room on the right, and Angel stepped in, relieved to see her there.

"It's you again," the curator said.

"I wanted to thank you for the lunch recommendation yesterday."

"You and the hottie have a good date?"

She'd love to see Donovan's reaction at being referred to as *the hottie.* "We're only friends." The memory of their kiss warmed her cheeks, but that kiss hadn't changed anything. If

Donovan's reaction were any indication, they wouldn't be kissing again. Which was all the same to Angel.

Mary Lynn laughed. "Sure you are."

Angel was usually better at hiding her thoughts. Though it would be good if Mary Lynn believed her easy to read. "Okay, fine. Maybe I think he's a little hot."

"A little," Mary Lynn said. "Like, the ocean is a little big."

Angel giggled. "Yeah, like that."

"I'm glad you enjoyed the restaurant."

"Loved it enough that I got a job there. Maybe I'll see you sometimes."

"Wow. Good for you."

She lifted one shoulder. It was only a waitressing job, after all. Nothing special.

And there she went again, downplaying a perfectly honorable job because it wasn't exciting or adventurous. Downplaying it because it was *normal*.

Right now, her life was far from normal. Which brought her to the real reason for her visit. "I can't stop thinking about that Pisano."

"I wish I had his talent." Mary Lynn's voice got wistful. "It gets under your skin, doesn't it?"

"I think I'll pay it another visit."

Mary Lynn looked around. The museum seemed empty, again. "Go ahead."

An offer to see it without purchasing a ticket. Which gave Angel the perfect opportunity to show herself to be a moral, upstanding citizen. "I insist on paying. Actually, since I'm going to be in town a lot, maybe I'll buy a membership."

Mary Lynn explained the different levels, Angel plopped down the fee, and just like that, she could come back whenever she wanted.

She moved through the museum again. She liked Mary

Lynn, thought the two of them could be friends. If not for the fact that Angel was using her to get information.

Without Donovan at her side, she was better able to scan for cameras and observe the guards' movements. Like the day before, there was only one guard in the east galleries. He wandered among the rooms but stayed in the Pisano room with her when she was there. She met his eyes, smiled at him.

He nodded back. He was an older guy, maybe sixties. Dedicated to his job. She couldn't imagine a scenario where she, Anton, and Mason could steal the sculpture during business hours. Maybe if they created a diversion, but the museum would need to be much more crowded, and it wasn't as if she could conjure visitors. And anyway, they were trying to steal the most valuable thing in the museum. The guard would likely focus on it, regardless of what else was going on.

Angel turned her attention to the sculpture. And, like the day before, she was enraptured by the Pisano. Amazed both by the workmanship and the grace the image portrayed. She wasn't there to contemplate her undeserved salvation, though. She was there to figure out how to steal the thing.

She circled the sculpture, feeling the eyes of the guard on her. She studied the Pisano from all angles and, with quick glances, the small case that surrounded it. She saw no screws, but at the corners, the plexiglass was thicker and opaque. She assumed the box was screwed into the stand from beneath. She resisted the urge to run her fingers beneath it to feel for the hardware.

With her back to the guard, she looked for any signs that the box was wired. As far as she could tell, there was no alarm on it.

Could it really be that simple?

She'd gotten as much information as she could on this visit. As she wandered throughout the rest of the gallery, noting the cameras and chatting with the other guard, she considered the problem. If she were in charge, how would she do it? Angel's real skills came in her ability to befriend people, make them trust her. She wasn't a snatch-and-grab thief. No, she gained people's trust until they either gave her what she wanted or would never have suspected her of having been the culprit. Unfortunately, there was no way to con the statue out of this building.

If they could get past the alarm, they could break in at night, snatch the sculpture, and be long gone before anybody knew anything.

Would there be a night watchman? She needed to figure that out.

There'd be lights on in the museum twenty-four hours a day, of course, for security. The wings that had been added to the original house had no windows, but the old house did. Maybe she'd be able to see movement through the glass.

A night grab would be best.

Or maybe she just didn't want to do it when Mary Lynn was working. She didn't want Mary Lynn held responsible.

She wandered through the galleries, finally coming to a stop in the room that featured local artists. She studied Donovan's painting.

It was magnificent.

The curators had displayed it prominently, as well they should have. It put the rest of the paintings in the room to shame.

The lines, the colors were masterful. The canvases Donovan had done at the house were good. They displayed his technical abilities, his artistic eye, his years of training.

But this painting had heart.

Beyond that, she didn't know how to describe the difference. She knew Donovan was seeking something every morning at his easel. He had to be seeking this... this depth of emotion, this fearless pouring of his heart onto the canvas.

He hadn't found it yet, but maybe... Maybe she could help him with that. She'd seen a difference in him. She'd been with him less than a week, but in that time, she could already see him opening up. To a degree.

He'd need to heal even more if he wanted to create like this again.

She touched her lips, remembered their kiss. For a moment, she'd gotten a glimpse of the Donovan beneath the mask. She'd liked it.

When he'd come to her rescue the night before... She wasn't sure what had happened. She'd been dreaming of Donovan, dreaming of their kiss. But Donovan had morphed into Anton, and Anton's hands had wrapped around her neck. Cutting off her oxygen. She'd grabbed something to hit him with.

And knocked the vase over.

She had no idea how she'd gotten on the floor.

She'd sat in the middle of all that broken glass, confused, until Donovan barged into her room wearing nothing but joggers. She'd stared at him, at that beautiful chest. Amazed that he'd come running to her rescue.

He'd been cold to her after that, erecting his walls. By the time they ate breakfast together, he'd hardly spoken. That he regretted the kiss was obvious, but not because he felt nothing for her. No, she was convinced he regretted it because it had awakened feelings he'd been trying to bury. Because if he felt something for Angel, then he'd have to feel the weight of his feelings for his sister, those feelings he was trying to push away.

It had to be the reason his work suffered. He refused to let himself feel, but Angel was breaking through. And it would be hard, she knew, when he really had to deal with his grief. That would be the beginning of his recovery.

She was determined to do what she could for Donovan. If nothing else, he was her old friend's brother. He'd been kind to her. He'd run to save her that morning. If she were honest, though, she'd admit that none of those excuses was her true motivation. She'd try to help him, to draw him out, because she cared for him. She cared too much.

And he was coming to care for her, too. Maybe he didn't want to admit it. Maybe the feelings frightened him, but they were there. She hadn't imagined that. This thing with Donovan, it could be like nothing she'd ever experienced. She'd had boyfriends, idiot boyfriends who'd used her for her looks or her abilities. And she'd been no better than they had, driven not by love but by greed and a quest for adventure.

Donovan was different. Everything about him was different. And, God help her, she wanted more of it.

Which meant she would have to keep her plans regarding the Nightingale a secret. Because if he ever got wind of what she was plotting...

It would ruin the tenuous trust he'd put in her, and there'd be no repairing the damage.

Angel reached the house that evening wondering which Donovan would greet her. The kind man who'd had lunch with her? The brooding man who'd kissed her? The hero who'd barged into her room to rescue her?

She'd take any of those Donovans. It was only the angry Donovan, the one who loathed her, she never wanted to see again.

The scent of paint greeted her when she stepped inside. She found Donovan in the parlor, crouched on the floor with a tiny paintbrush, dabbing at the wall where it met the baseboards.

The walls were a pretty soft gray, the transformation in the room remarkable. "Looks great."

He turned to face her. "Where you been?"

"I started training for that job."

"Are you going to be able to carry trays with your injuries?"

"I managed a few today. They won't start me on my own for a couple of days. I'll have more time to heal."

He regarded her through narrowed eyes. "You look tired."

"Gee, thanks."

He smiled, shook his head. "You always look beautiful, but I can't say that every time I see you. Wouldn't want to give you the big head."

Beautiful? Had he complimented her?

Was he *flirting* with her?

Oh, she liked this Donovan. A lot.

She was a bit worried that maybe aliens had invaded his body, but she wasn't going to say so. Instead, she said, "Good save."

He shrugged. "I can be charming, if I have to." He focused on his work again.

"You hungry? I'm going to warm up some of that cacciatore."

"Ate a huge lunch with my parents. They like the haircut, by the way. Thanks again for that."

"Okay, then. I haven't eaten." She spoke to his back while she watched him work.

"I'll be in in a bit," he said. "Thought we could watch a movie or something. I mean, if you want."

A movie? Together? Like a date?

He'd definitely been abducted by aliens. "What'd you have in mind?"

"I don't care. Pick something out."

In her room, she pulled out the small notebook she'd picked

up on her way home and sat on the bed, where she noted everything she'd learned about the Nightingale. Not enough, but she'd gather more in the days and nights to come. When she'd recorded everything, she shoved the notebook into the top drawer of her bureau beneath her underwear. Not that Donovan ever went into her room, but even if he did, he certainly wouldn't look through her private things.

After a quick meal, she scrolled through the selections on Netflix. Finally, she found something she'd like to watch. Donovan had told her to pick something out, hadn't he?

So maybe he hadn't been expecting what she's chosen, but she'd get to see how the man rolled with the punches.

He came in a little while later, freshly showered and smelling of pine-scented soap. "You need anything before I sit?"

Her water glass was full. She shook her head.

He went to the kitchen and returned a few minutes later with a steaming bowl of popcorn and his own glass of water. He sat beside her.

Not in the chair across the room, but right beside her.

Those walls he'd erected had definitely come down. She prayed they'd stay that way.

He tipped the bowl her way.

"Thanks." She was full but took a handful anyway and ate a few bites. "It's good."

"I made it myself. An old family recipe passed down from Orville Redenbacher."

She smiled as she found the movie, then peeked to see his reaction.

"'Singin' in the Rain'?" His eyebrows were hiked when he looked her way.

"Ever seen it?

"Uh... No."

"Well, then, you're in for a treat."

He groaned, and she giggled as they settled in to watch. She cackled at the funny parts, and he laughed with her. Or maybe at her. She didn't care which, because he was laughing.

Laughing!

And it was one of the most beautiful sounds she'd ever heard.

The sound of a baby cooing.

The sound of voices lifted in praise to God.

And the sound of Donovan laughing.

Somehow, during the movie, they drifted closer together. Her attention shifted from Gene Kelly and Debbie Reynolds to the man beside her. The man whose arm was warm against hers. The man whose scent mingled with those of soap and buttery popcorn and made her mouth water. And not for the salty treat.

There was a shift in the atmosphere. Though the movie continued, it felt like background noise instead of the evening's entertainment. The arm that had been pressed against her slipped around her shoulders.

She snuggled against him.

And then, he turned to face her. Took her face in his hands. Leaned in for a kiss.

Gene was singing in the rain.

Angel was glorying in Donovan's touch.

They made out like a couple of teenagers in the back row of a theater.

He was sweet and gentle, and everything about him drew her. Then his touch went from sweet to something else. Something more urgent. He trailed kisses down her neck.

She couldn't help but respond. Her head tilted back. Her hands slid up his shoulders, broad and strong. She weaved her fingers in the soft hair at his nape. She loved the feel of his skin, hot and smooth, against her palms.

He pulled her closer, tipped her back until she was nearly reclining on the sofa.

Suddenly, he pulled away. Scooted to the far side.

Oh, no. What had she done wrong? She shouldn't have let the kiss get so... stirring. Her cheeks burned, and she looked away.

He'd build those walls again now. He'd stomp off, resume his brooding. Stupid. She should have pushed him away before he pushed her away. She should have protected herself from his rejection. She should have done...

Something.

The movie continued. Talking, not music, but she couldn't focus on the words.

She couldn't sit there staring at her knees for the rest of the night. She'd faced his rejection before. She could face it again. She lifted her gaze to his, bracing herself. And found him...

Smiling?

"I did it again, didn't I?" he said.

"The kiss? Like yesterday, I did it, too."

He glanced at the movie, but it didn't hold his focus. "Maybe next time we should choose something a little less..."

"Romantic?"

He chuckled. "I was going to say boring, but whatever."

She dropped her jaw in mock surprise. "Boring? I'll have you know this movie is a classic."

"'Jaws' is a classic. This is a bunch of people singing and dancing."

"I thought you, as an artist, would see the beauty in it."

His smile faded. "I see beauty." But he wasn't talking about the movie anymore. He inched closer, ran his fingers along a lock of her hair, sending chills down her spine. "I see plenty of beauty."

She leaned into his touch, closed her eyes.

He groaned. "Any chance there's corned beef in the fridge?"

Her eyes opened. "Huh?"

"Never mind." He stood, looked around as if he'd forgotten where he was. He walked to the chair on the far side of the room and sat again. "You're very tempting. And this is your brother's house. And I don't think he'd appreciate... And I mean... We have to be careful about... You know."

She did know, but his words... his words told her something she was almost afraid to hope for. "Careful, as in..."

"Maybe no kissing in the house. I should say no kissing at all, but... maybe no kissing in the house. Or no kissing after dark."

"Right. Because nothing could happen in the daytime."

He ran his hands through his hair. "I should stay somewhere else."

"You'd be here all the time, though. Literally from dawn to dusk, right?"

He looked toward his studio. "Yeah."

She didn't want to, not even a little, but she said, "I could find somewhere else to stay."

His gaze snapped back to hers. "You're safe here. And after what happened with that guy, I want you where I can protect you."

"He doesn't know where I am."

"Perfect reason to stay. We're both adults. We can do this."

She gazed out the windows that looked over the dark grounds. Truth was, though being in Donovan's arms was wonderful, the night before, their kiss had brought memories of the attack too close. She wasn't sure if she could go farther with Donovan if she wanted to.

Those memories were insistent now.

Which, maybe, was good.

But... She turned back to Donovan. "What changed? I

mean, yesterday when you kissed me, you acted like it was a big mistake. Like you deserved to be flogged for having considered it. Today..."

He stood, snatched the remote, and turned down the TV until she could barely hear it. She'd guess he was ignoring her question if not for the ticking of his jaw. She loved that he was no longer hiding his emotions behind that ugly beard.

"I thought... My mother always thought..." His words trailed.

Angel remembered Mrs. Gilcreast. The woman had been nice to her when she and Katie were friends. After that, the few times she'd seen her, it seemed as if Katie's mom had hated her. She'd never understood why.

Maybe she was about to learn. "She thought what?"

"That you were the one who introduced Katie to drugs."

Angel stood. "Me? Why would she think that?"

Donovan shrugged. "I never knew why, but she seemed sure."

"And your sister died of an overdose, so..."

"It wasn't fair, but I blamed you. Mom blamed you, and I thought she knew what she was talking about."

"I've never done drugs. Ever. Katie tried to get me to. I refused. That's when our friendship ended."

He nodded as if he accepted that. "I'm sorry."

"It's not..." She looked at the screen again, at the dancing couples, the pretty costumes. She turned back to him. "I've done a lot of bad stuff in my life, Donovan. I was no... angel. I didn't stay away from drugs because I was better than Katie. Drugs were common, and drugs ruined people's abilities to think. Even in high school, I was perfecting my ability to lie. To con people. And drugs would only make me weak. Don't think for a second that I'm judging Katie or thinking I'm better than she was. I'm guilty of a lot of stuff, but I'm not guilty of that."

"I know."

"You know? How, all of a sudden, do you know?"

"When I mentioned you to my dad today, he explained that Mom needed someone to blame, and you were an easy target. He never argued with Mom or tried to correct her, but he doesn't agree with her. I've observed you this week. You don't use drugs. Your brother brought you those Tylenol PMs, and you haven't even been taking them. Even though you're not sleeping well, you haven't had a single one."

"You counted them?"

He looked away, nodded.

Okay, then. She didn't know what to think of any of that. The man was hard to keep up with.

"The thing is," Donovan said, "all that stuff you did before—stealing and... whatever else—that was the old Angel. Now you're new. You're saved and redeemed. If you had gotten Katie into drugs—"

"I didn't."

"I know. Even if you had, you're not that person anymore. You're a new creation. How can I hold your past against you when you're working hard to get free of it?"

Easy. Lots of other people did.

"Maybe I would have, before." Donovan looked at the floor. A moment passed, and then he gazed at her. His expression had shifted. This wasn't defensive Donovan or angry Donovan or even brooding Donovan. This was true, raw, unguarded Donovan.

That he would show himself to her like this had her swallowing. Did she deserve the trust he was putting in her?

She'd never deserved anyone's trust.

"If what my dad believes is true," he said, "if what I feel like the Lord is telling me is true, then Katie has been forgiven and is in heaven with God. If God can forgive her for everything, then

He can forgive all of us. And who am I to hold a grudge where He doesn't?"

She wasn't sure what to say about that.

"And in this case, there's no grudge to hold." Grief flitted across his face. With grief came something else. Something generous in the corners of his mouth that almost lifted into a smile. Something kind in the eyes that held hers. He stood and took her hands in his. "You aren't even the tiniest bit responsible for Katie's death. I hope you can forgive me for thinking you were."

His hands felt sure around hers. Gentle and strong. The affection in his eyes pulled her up short.

Here was a man who loved with his whole heart. She knew that, had known it since she'd first discovered who he was and realized the depth of pain he felt at his sister's death.

Donovan didn't give his affection away easily. It had to be earned. And somehow she'd earned it.

He cared for her, and now that he'd allowed himself to admit it to himself, he wasn't afraid to admit it to her.

He'd slid his heart out onto his muscular arm, where she could take it, nurture it, see what else was there.

Angel had won him over, but was this her charm at work, or did he really care for her, the real her? She didn't know. She'd been good at winning people's affection for her own gain all her life. Could she trust this? Could she trust his heart?

Could she trust hers?

And what would happen if Donovan ever learned the truth about her? Because if he ever got wind of what she was up to with Anton, the heart he'd confidently offered her would break. And it would be her fault.

Forget the pain she'd experience. That would be pain well deserved.

But Donovan only deserved truth.

And she'd been lying to him since she'd met him. Lying when all she wanted was to be honest and truthful. All she wanted was to put her deceitful past behind her.

She should back off, encourage him to erect his walls again. Because she could only hurt him, hurt him like she'd hurt everyone she'd ever cared about. Her parents. Her sister and brother.

Even Katie, way back when. Rather than encourage her to get help, even tell her parents she was on that bad road, Angel had backed away. Found new friends. Left Katie to fall deeper into her addiction.

And ultimately, overdose.

It wasn't Angel's fault, but if she'd cared more, she might have helped to prevent the years of addiction that followed.

And here was Katie's brother, his heart hanging there like an unguarded treasure.

If she had half a brain, she'd tell him to put it away.

Instead, she leaned forward and kissed his cheek. And she lied to herself, saying that, as long as he never found out about the robbery she was planning to commit, everything would be fine.

It had been one of the best weeks of Angel's life. She and Donovan had settled into a routine that was both predictable and exciting. She was sleeping better and had only crept in to watch him paint a couple of days. Every morning, she woke early enough to join him for breakfast. Then he'd get to work, and she would head to the restaurant or the museum. When she wasn't working an evening shift, they'd have dinner together, turn on the TV, and kiss.

And when the desire became too much, one or the other or both would put a stop to it.

Her dreams featured more of Donovan and less of Anton every night. The only problem was that being with Donovan made her long to tell him everything, to come clean about what she was up to with Anton and the Nightingale. Of course, if she did and if anybody got wind of it, she'd forfeit her deal with the DA's office and Routhier. Her freedom would be snatched away, and she'd lose everything, including Donovan.

The only bad spots on the previous week were the late-night treks to Portsmouth to observe the Nightingale, where she'd park, watch, and take notes on what she was learning.

If only she'd met Donovan when she was truly free.

But God knew what He was doing. And this was almost over. Soon enough, Anton would be behind bars and she'd be done with the lies.

Dread had Angel's pulse racing as she parked outside the warehouse the following Wednesday evening. As before, Anton's car was already there. As before, she didn't want to go inside until she knew Mason had arrived.

This time, it was Mason who jogged out to her car. He tapped on her window and opened her door, wearing a wide smile, seemingly unconcerned about the seriousness of what they were doing. "You really don't like our partner, do you?"

She grabbed her purse and stepped out. "That, my friend, is the understatement of the century."

Mason's smile faded. "He do something to you?"

She studied the younger man, whose gaze flicked from her to the door to the warehouse, where Anton stood in the opening, watching her.

A shudder slid down her back. "It's not important now. As long as he keeps his distance."

"Should I... I mean, you need me to do anything? If he, like, does anything, you tell me, and I'll make him sorry."

She squeezed Mason's arm. "That's very sweet. I'll let you know." Maybe Mason could protect her from Anton, but she was pretty sure Anton wouldn't do anything to Angel with the other man present. No, he'd wait until he got her alone.

Which was why they never would be alone, not if she had any say.

Angel waited at the doorway for them to walk inside. Mason did, but Anton kept his spot. It would be petty to refuse to walk past him, though she feared having her back to him. She forced herself through the door, not meeting his eyes.

"Nice to see you again, Angel."

His voice rumbled too close and had her swallowing a rise of panic.

Inside, they gathered around the table, where the men had already spread out blueprints. She focused on Mason, trying to pretend Anton wasn't there. "You got them?"

Mason's chest puffed a little. "For the house and the additional wings."

Together, they studied the museum layout. Angel showed them where the Pisano was, where the cameras were located, and where the guards generally stood.

"I've been watching the place at night. Looks like they have one guard who's there from close to open. There's one guy who works Monday through Friday and another who works the weekend shifts. The weekend guy is more vigilant, patrolling the museum all hours. The weeknight guy, though... He seems to move around more early in his shift, but after midnight, he sets up shop in the office in the front." She pointed at the room. "I saw no movement at all between two and four-thirty."

"What's he doing?" Anton asked.

"No idea. Sleeping? Watching Netflix on his phone?"

Anton focused on Mason. "And what have you learned?"

"I figured out how to hack into their system. I've been poking around to see if they'd know I was there. They're totally clueless."

"That's dangerous," Anton said. "If they find you, they could tighten security."

Angel waited for Mason to apologize, but he didn't. Instead, he turned to Anton, shoulders back. "If they tighten security, I'll get past it again. You brought me in because I'm good at what I do. Don't question it."

"You'll do what I say."

"And you said to test their security. That's what I'm doing. Back off."

She had no desire to witness a staring contest. She turned back to the blueprints. "So when are we thinking?"

She didn't see who blinked first. She hoped it wasn't Mason.

"Next week," Anton said. "We need to get it done and get out. Afterwards"—he focused on Angel—"you'll keep visiting like you have been, act as if nothing's different."

"You have an alibi in place for me?" she asked.

"I will by then."

"I'm not doing anything until I've confirmed it myself."

Anton stepped closer, looked down at her.

She told herself to stand her ground, but her fear was louder than her rational thought. She stepped back, bumped the wall behind her. Went to sidestep, but Anton stuck out his leg, which blocked her on one side. He grabbed her opposite forearm and squeezed. "You'll do what I tell you to do."

"Dude, let her go."

Anton ignored Mason, leaned closer until she could feel his breath on her cheek. "If you get arrested, Angel"—her name dripped with sarcasm—"you'll give me up, and I don't plan on going to prison. It's in my best interest that you not be caught. You're going to have to trust me."

She had no answer. No words. She might have screamed if she could have gotten anything past the terror clogging her throat.

Mason grabbed Anton's shoulder and yanked him away. "I said, back off."

Anton rounded on the younger man. "You have no idea who you're dealing with."

"I won't put up with one of my *teammates* threatening another. Either you treat Angel with respect, or I'm outta here. And you can't do this without me."

While the men got into another staring contest, Angel turned, held onto the table for balance. She wanted to rub her arm where he'd hurt her, but she didn't. She wouldn't show him any more fear.

She hadn't wanted to show any at all, but she had. Anton had seen her terror, and he'd loved it.

He'd reveled in it.

Lord, help me do this. Help me bring this man to justice, and protect me in the process.

She hated that, in bringing Anton down, she'd probably be sending Mason to prison. She didn't know what to do about that, but she had no choice now.

No choice. She might not be in prison, but she was a prisoner of her own stupidity, her own past. Would she ever be free of it?

Anton cleared his throat. "Forgive me, Angel, if I overstepped." His words were kind, in direct opposition to his threatening stare.

"Forgive me if I don't believe anything that comes out of your mouth."

He chuckled and focused on Mason. "Let's make a plan."

CHAPTER SEVENTEEN

Donovan leaned against the sunroom doorjamb as Ian set out the canvases to analyze them.

"If you'd warned me you were coming today," Donovan said, "I'd have been ready."

Ian's only response was a distracted, "Mmm-hmm," as he propped three canvases on the back of the sofa so they were leaning against the wall.

Clouds had moved in. If it had been brighter outside, the sunroom would've been dimmer in contrast, and it would have been harder to see the paintings—and the fact that they weren't very good. Of course, Ian had a good enough eye. He'd notice the lack regardless of the light.

When he had all the paintings spread out, he stood back and gazed at them, one after another. Many were propped on the floor, others on window ledges. Twenty-two paintings. All completed—if Donovan had a mind to sell them at a kiosk at the mall.

But to hang in a gallery?

Ian finished his first scan, then started again at the beginning, moving more slowly. Studying each one.

Seeing their deficiency.

Donovan wanted to throw up. At least it would be an excuse to leave the room.

In the back of his mind, way back in places he didn't like to acknowledge, he'd hoped that this new thing he had going with Angel might have helped him get his magic back. But he'd done what Ian was doing right now. Though he hadn't spread them all out—because surrounding himself with his failure was never high on his list of things to do—he'd looked at the canvases, tried to figure out what was wrong with them. What was missing.

But he'd failed.

It was one thing to fail all by himself. It was entirely different to have witnesses.

Donovan's best friend—and, until now, biggest advocate—continued his slow perusal, one painting to the next.

Ian said nothing, but his thoughts might as well have been written in one of those cartoon-clouds over his head.

Not good. Not good enough. Not even close.

The room took on a reddish-orange tinge until everything was colored in failure. His failure. To protect Katie. To support his parents. To create beauty.

Finally, Ian turned to him, a plastic smile in place. "I think I've got a handle on where we are."

Donovan nodded once, spun on his heel, and headed for the kitchen. "Something to drink?"

He heard Ian follow but didn't turn. Couldn't look at the man.

"I could use a beer."

"If I'd known you were coming..." He turned at the fridge. "I have coffee, soda, and water."

Ian's eyebrows lifted. "Still not drinking?"

"Nope." Donovan had done enough drinking in college to last the rest of his life. He'd given it up when he'd become a

Christian. Starting again would have been foolish. Because alcohol was a depressant, and he'd been depressed enough. Because his sister had died of her addiction. And because his parents didn't need to worry about losing their only surviving child to substance abuse. Truth was, Donovan had been afraid he'd open a bottle and dive right in and never figure out how to climb back out.

"You're really taking this whole Christian thing seriously, aren't you, mate?"

"My faith is the only thing that's kept me alive."

Ian let the remark go without comment. "Right, then. I have to drive back, anyway." Ian gazed around the kitchen at Donovan's handiwork. "It's beautiful."

Donovan poured his friend a Sprite, got himself a glass of water, and joined Ian at the windows overlooking the lake. Ian hadn't changed a bit, which made sense. Ian had inherited his skin color and hair from his black father and his hazel eyes from his white mother. His hair was short, his beard trimmed. As usual, he wore a button-down shirt—this one royal blue—and a tie along with his pressed slacks. Donovan figured there was a suit coat in the car. The clothes, the accent, the charm... Ian had never lacked female companionship.

Donovan handed Ian the drink and gazed at the view. "I know they're missing something."

"What, though?"

He blew out a breath. If he knew that, whatever *it* was would no longer be missing. "I'll figure it out."

Ian sipped the Sprite.

The front door creaked open and then clicked closed. Angel. Donovan wasn't sure whether he should be happy or not she was there. He could use her support, but did he need her taking part in the whole *Donovan's a total failure* conversation?

"Who's that? I thought you'd been rambling about this big house alone."

"The owner's sister lives here, too."

Ian looked at him, one eyebrow raised. "A sister, eh?"

Before Donovan could shoot a response—and maybe a warning to keep his distance—Angel stepped into the room. "Oh. There you are."

"Well, well, well, aren't you lovely?" Ian stepped forward, hand outstretched. "I'm Ian Hawkins, friend of Donovan's."

She offered him the pretty smile that usually made Donovan's heart do funny things. It was doing funny things now, but they were tinged in green.

"Angel Rossi." She shook his hand. "What kind of accent is that?"

"Australian. Family's from Brisbane. You ever been?"

Angel shook her head. "I'd love to go sometime."

"Ah, its beauty pales in comparison to yours."

Angel blushed, and Donovan groaned.

Ian shot him a look and backed up a step. "And who are you to Donovan?"

"Not that it's any of your business," Donovan said, "but she's the owner's sister and my friend."

"Another friend, eh?" He kept his gaze on Angel. "Then we have something in common already."

The urge to shove Ian out the closest window was strong. Donovan squelched it. Ian was a flirt by nature, but Angel was no fool. She'd see right through him.

He believed that despite the smile she aimed Ian's way, which stretched wider. "I see you two were busy staring at the view."

"I am now," Ian said, gaze not leaving Angel.

She glanced at Donovan. "A charmer, I see."

Donovan might actually punch Ian. That would not be a good career move.

Though, considering the state of the canvases in the sunroom, his career might be over anyway.

"Ian runs the gallery that was supposed to display my paintings this fall," Donovan said.

Ian turned to him, *charming* smile gone. "Still the plan, mate."

"They're not ready. You said it yourself."

"They will be," Ian said. "They have to be."

"I'll leave you to it, then." Angel spun toward the door.

"Perhaps Angel can help us," Ian said.

Donovan squelched another groan. "She has other things to do." He leveled a look at Angel. "Right?"

She shrugged, either not picking up his hint or purposely ignoring it. "Nothing important."

Of course not. She'd already put in her shift at work. If it were a normal night, she'd get something ready for them to eat while he finished up whatever project he was working on. They'd eat together, he'd do the dishes, and they'd sit on the sofa, pretend to watch movies, and make out.

Ian set the Sprite on the bar, placed his hand on the small of her back, and guided her toward the sunroom. "Tell me, what do you know about art?"

Donovan followed, jealousy and failure mixing with rage and tinting everything in a muddy swirl of color.

"Not much." When they reached the sunroom, Angel deftly stepped away from Ian's hand and turned to face him. "I know what I like."

"Don't let her fool you," Donovan said. "She has a great eye."

Her gaze flicked to his. "That means a lot coming from you."

"Let's set the mutual admiration society on hold for a

moment." Ian scanned the canvases, finally choosing *Winter Morning*. He lifted it for her to see. It pictured a cabin in a snowy forest, smoke rising from a little chimney. "What do you think of this?"

She studied the piece. "It's beautiful, of course. I love the snow, the way it's rounded on top of the porch railing."

Ian said nothing.

"The way the light is filtered through the trees... It's masterful, that use of light."

"What else?" Ian asked.

She took her lip between her teeth, looked Donovan's direction.

"Go ahead," he said. "I know it needs work."

She swallowed. "It's just... It lacks... something."

That was helpful. Everybody knew it sucked. Nobody knew why.

He started to speak, to let Angel off the hook, but Ian held out a hand to silence him.

Again, her gaze flicked to Donovan, back to the canvas. "It's just... there's no feeling in it. It's... it lacks heart."

Another *very helpful* comment.

But Ian was nodding. He set the painting down, turned to Donovan. She did, too.

"Hold on a sec." Donovan snatched a brush from the table beside his easel. "Let me just add some heart."

She blinked, back straightening.

"I'm sorry." He tossed the brush back down. He was a being a jerk.

"I'm not trying to hurt you," Angel said. "I want to help."

Ian looked from her to him and back. He gave Donovan that one-eyebrow-up look again.

Donovan turned his back on both of them and stared at the canvas on the easel, Katie's painting. It was the largest, and it wasn't bad. He knew how to paint. He'd studied it all his life, and he had no idea how to add *heart* to a painting? Had he done that before? What was missing—from his life, from his art, from his heart?

He didn't know. And painting Katie's view hadn't brought *it* back, whatever *it* was.

Maybe it was gone forever.

Maybe he should stick to painting walls and skip trying to create art.

The kitchen he'd redone looked good. Maybe he could pour his *talent,* whatever was left of it, into remodeling houses. That was satisfying work. It paid well enough. And anyway, he had enough money from the paintings he'd sold in the past to last him a good long while. He could invest it, start a contracting company.

Nobody accused contractors of lacking heart in their work.

Wouldn't that be an easy fix?

Behind him, Angel sighed. He heard the sound of the canvas being set back on the floor.

He was blocking their exit. Otherwise, he was sure they'd have both abandoned him by now. And he'd be alone again. He should have never opened his heart to Angel. It hadn't helped him with anything. It had only exposed his vulnerability. And now he'd exposed his failure to her as well.

"I have an idea."

He swiveled at Angel's words.

"I looked you up after our trip to the gallery." She blinked, gazed at Ian.

She looked nervous. Though Donovan's anger was self-directed, his glare was aimed at her. He tried to soften his expression.

"All your best work has people in it," she said. "They're not in the foreground. They're often like the painting at the Nightingale—"

"I love that one," Ian said.

She smiled at him, seemed to gain some courage when she looked away from Donovan. And wasn't that a nice thought. "Me, too," she said. "It's beautiful, but what makes it unique are those two silhouettes."

"A man and a boy," Ian said.

"Father and son," Donovan said.

They looked at him, and he shrugged. "They're not random images. They're real." Didn't they see that? *Boston Light at Dawn*—he remembered the people in that painting as if they were old friends. "He's a laborer in the city, works dawn to dusk most days in order to feed his family. On his days off, he takes his son out on the little boat." The man had scrimped and saved for that boat. The two would motor to the Boston Light to do some fishing. Not because the man couldn't have used the sleep. Not because the man couldn't have spent a leisurely morning at home with his wife, but because he loved his son enough to sacrifice for him.

So maybe, in real life, it didn't make a lot of sense. In real life, the guy might take his son to a pier close to home, not out to a lighthouse in Boston Harbor. But it was Donovan's story, his painting. They were his people—even if they were pretend.

Ian was looking at him as if he were crazy.

Angel, though. What was that look? Awe?

He focused on her. "It helps if I know them."

Her eyes lit up, and a cheerful yellow filled the drab sunroom. "The heart in your paintings comes from the people you place there."

Donovan said, "That doesn't even—"

"That's it." Ian slapped his thigh and focused on Angel. "You're a genius. A gorgeous genius."

"It's only a thought."

"It's a brilliant thought!" Ian turned to Donovan. "Try that —add people to your paintings. It'll work. I know it. We should celebrate. Is that seafood place down the street any good? I'm buying."

Donovan was not going to eat with Ian. He was too furious to eat.

Except Angel ran to change clothes, promising to be ready in fifteen minutes.

Donovan put the canvases back where Ian had found them, fuming at the turn of events. They'd looked at his paintings— paintings he'd been laboring and worrying over for months—and *solved* his problem. As if it were nothing. As if it were *obvious* what was wrong with him.

Adding people was not going to give him back his heart, whatever the heck that meant.

When his sunroom was back to how he wanted it, he stomped into the living room, passed Ian, who was on the phone, and up the stairs. Because as little as he wanted to spend another second with Ian and Angel tonight, there was no chance on the planet he was letting them go to dinner without him.

DONOVAN GLANCED AT ANGEL, who snuggled on the old battered couch in the sunroom, eyes closed. She wasn't asleep yet, though. Her breathing hadn't evened out, and the hand he could see gripped the blanket tightly.

The last week, she'd hardly been joining him during his painting time in the mornings. In fact, they'd both been sleeping better this week. But she'd padded in to the sunroom seconds after him and fallen onto the couch with a single word of explanation.

"Nightmare."

He wished he could dig, find out what terrors haunted her in her sleep. Likely the same man who'd left those bruises on her body. If Donovan ever got his hands on him, that man wouldn't be hurting Angel or anyone else, ever again.

He forced his attention away from Angel and onto the canvas in front of him. The sun wasn't out yet, but that was okay because he wasn't working on Katie's painting today. Instead, he'd pulled out the one Angel had remarked on the day before. The cabin in the snowy woods.

He stared at the image. There was nothing wrong with it. He had enough confidence in his abilities to know that his technique was sound. Better than sound, in fact. Yet Angel and Ian were right. The painting lacked heart.

The pride in him refused to believe they could solve his problem with hardly a glance after he'd been laboring over the issue for months. Still, it would be ridiculous, stubborn beyond reason, not to at least try.

The problem was, there was no place in the painting for people.

No. That didn't make sense at all. Smoke poured from the chimney. There were people there. Where were they?

He closed his eyes, let the cabin come alive.

The world was silent, all sounds muffled by the inches of powdery snow outside. Little wind had accompanied the snowfall. It had been a peaceful storm. No footprints marred the blanket of white. So, whoever was inside was at rest. They'd gotten up... Yes, they. A man and a woman. Husband and wife. They'd stayed up late to watch the snow fall. He'd woken early to light the fire—or stoke it—for heat, and to make her happy.

As a surprise, she'd brought the things to make a big breakfast to their little cabin hideaway. Pancakes and eggs and bacon. No, sausage.

After the man had stoked the fire, he'd gotten back in bed. When he'd fallen to sleep, the wife had sneaked to the kitchen. Today was the perfect day for her surprise.

And there she was, in the window. Donovan dipped his paintbrush and dabbed the canvas, working furiously as if she might move away at any moment. The *scratch-scratch* of the paintbrush on the canvas created a rhythm to his work.

When the woman was immortalized on canvas, he saw the whole scene differently. Clean paintbrush, new colors... He dabbed here and there, adding light, adding *birth*, even though that made no sense at all.

When he'd gotten it right, he set the paintbrush down, stared at it.

The woman... She was the heart of the picture. He'd done it. He'd actually done it.

He glanced at Katie's painting. Not yet. He wasn't ready yet. He walked to the window and stared at the lake, which was beginning to brighten in the dawn. The echoes of Katie's laughter seemed to rise up from the glassy surface. If only she were really here. *Oh, Katie.*

What he wouldn't give to pull his sister into his arms and tell her now what he should have told her before. That he was sorry for being too busy for her, for avoiding her, for judging her. That he loved her, no matter what. Addiction or no addiction, she was his sister, and he adored her. That he'd give anything to have her back, anything to see her healthy and happy again.

Tears streamed down his face, but he didn't bother to wipe them. Katie was worth his tears. Katie, with her joy for life, her quick smile and easy laughter. She was worth this grief, this pain.

There it was again, that echoing laughter, as if she were

right there, splashing in the lake. Maybe... maybe the laughter was more than an echo from the past. Maybe Katie was just across the veil, in the arms of the God who'd given everything for her. Katie wasn't tormented anymore by her addiction. She was at peace.

She'd want Donovan to be at peace, too.

He breathed in the truth, blew out the remnants of guilt and shame, and felt freer than he had since her death.

A rustling behind him warned him Angel was waking. He wiped his tears, cleared his throat, and tried to pull himself together.

"It's breathtaking."

He turned as Angel stood. She approached the canvas propped on the easel. "Donovan, it's... She's pregnant, isn't she?"

He tore his gaze away from the disheveled woman behind him and back to the woman he'd drawn. Her face was cast in shadow, but the curly hair was unmistakable. He hadn't meant to imagine Angel in the picture, but there she was.

One hand caressing her abdomen.

"She's about to tell her husband."

"You found it," she said. "The heart is in the stories you tell."

She was right. Of course she was. Angel saw deeper into his soul than ever had.

"I have you to thank."

"You did it. I just..."

Her hair was a mess. Her cheeks bore imprints of the pillow. And she was the most beautiful thing he'd ever seen. He wrapped his arms around her back, lowering his head for a good-morning kiss.

He could feel her warmth through the thin fabric of her nightgown.

She pressed her hands against his chest, then slid them up to his neck, his hairline.

He could stay here for the rest of his life. Except not here.

He imagined his painting, the people in it. The man waiting for his wife in that king-size bed.

There were beds in this house...

She stilled. Backed up.

With every ounce of strength he possessed, he dropped his arms and let her move away.

She swallowed. "I should..."

"Definitely."

As she inched past him, he caught a glimpse of something he hadn't noticed before. He caught her hand, turned her wrist.

Bruises. Fresh bruises on her arm.

The imprint of a man's hand.

Her eyes widened, and she tried to pull away, but he held fast.

She yanked. "Let me go."

"Who did that to you?"

"It's not important."

Crimson. Everything turned crimson. "Did someone at the restaurant—"

"No. It's nothing..." She yanked the blanket off the sofa and wrapped it around herself.

"Who did it, Angel?"

"It doesn't matter."

"Some man grabbed you. Some man..." The same man, of course. The one who'd hurt her the week before. "Is it a boyfriend? You're seeing—"

"No. I told you—"

"You told me it was someone who was attacking your friend. Was that a lie?"

She swallowed. "I have never lied to you."

"Then..." He had to think. "Was it the same person who hurt you last week?" The one she'd called a slimy jerk with too much power?

She tried to meet his eyes, failed. Stared at the floor. Took a breath. "It's not your concern."

"What power does he have over you?"

It seemed to take all her strength to meet his eyes. "I like you, Donovan. You're a nice guy, and I've really enjoyed getting to know you, but there are aspects of my life that I have to keep to myself. This is one of them. I'm sorry, but I won't explain further."

She brushed past him and left the room.

DONOVAN FIXED breakfast for them both, but Angel never came. He was buttering toast when he heard the front door open and slam.

She didn't have to work until ten-thirty. It was barely seven a.m. He had no idea where she'd gone, and he tried not to care. Failed, though. Because all he could see were those fresh bruises.

Why? Why would she spend time with a man who'd hurt her? A dangerous man? He didn't understand, but he desperately wanted to. Because Angel had opened his eyes to what was missing in his paintings, and in his life.

He'd closed himself off to all human connection, even to the point of not putting it in his paintings.

No, not *human connection.*

Was he really so far gone he couldn't use the word?

Love. Love had been missing.

And then Angel had come along, and she'd awakened that feeling. Since she'd come, he'd remembered that he used to care about things. He'd visited his parents. He'd poured love into his work.

He'd opened his heart to her.

And she'd slammed hers shut.

He ate his breakfast, barely tasting it, and was cleaning up when the doorbell rang.

Angel?

No. Of course not. She had a key. She'd come right in.

He made his way to the front door and yanked it open. A man in coveralls stood there. Behind him, a truck idled.

"Got a delivery for you."

"What is it?"

"Bathroom vanity and a slab of marble."

The vanity for Angel's bathroom. "Wish you'd warned me it was coming today."

"I deliver 'em. You can call the store if you have a complaint. Where you want 'em?"

The cabinet he could move himself, but the slab would need to go into her bathroom. It would be hard enough getting it in place without having to haul it down the hall first. "Follow me."

The man was joined by another, and they hefted the vanity from the back of the truck, into the house, and down the hallway to Angel's bedroom. He hated to enter without her permission, but it wasn't as if he were snooping. They left the vanity in the bedroom and the marble leaning against the claw-foot tub.

When the men were gone, Donovan dialed Jack. "I'm going to need help with the marble in the master bath."

"Is it ready to install now?" Jack asked.

He glanced at the old built-in. "It'll take me a couple of hours to get the new one in place."

"I can be there about one. How's my sister?"

Beautiful. Infuriating. "Recovering well."

"You two getting along all right?"

"Oh, yeah. Fine."

"Good, good," Jack said. "I'll be there this afternoon."

Donovan hung up, eager to get started. Because there was nothing better for frustration than demolition work. And Angel had given him plenty to be frustrated about.

He was halfway to the bathroom with his tools when he realized he should let her know what he was up to. He started to text, then had second thoughts.

He needed to hear her voice. Needed to know she was all right.

But the call went to voicemail.

"It's me. I was calling to let you know I'll be working on your bathroom today. I hope that's okay."

And then he tossed the phone on her bed and went into the bathroom and collected her things to set on her bureau. Hairbrush, comb, blow dryer. Makeup. A spiral-bound notebook and pen.

Odd.

He was on his way to the bedroom with the items when a word on the notebook caught his eye. *Guard.*

He glanced down and read it again.

Single guard, 9p to 9a.

What in the world? He set the other things on her bureau and studied more on the page.

Flipped through it, saw more about guards. Alarms. Cameras.

Flipped back further, all the way to the first page. One word caught his eye.

Nightingale.

She was studying the museum.

No. She was *casing* the museum.

She'd taken him with her to the museum to case it. To steal from it.

His image of Angel changed. Pieces he'd thought he had in place crumbled. New pieces took their place, distorting her face until it was ugly, hideous.

She had lied to him. She'd been lying to him all along. About everything.

All her talk of repentance—lies.

All her talk of her newfound faith—lies.

And how she felt about him...

Lies.

All of it.

This was what he got for trusting her. For opening his heart again. She'd played him for a fool.

CHAPTER EIGHTEEN

Angel had worked the lunch shift, had been sent home at three, but the day had started early. She hadn't planned to leave the house at seven, but Donovan had been so angry when he'd seen the bruises that she'd almost broken down and told him the truth—about Anton, about the museum job, about the deal.

But if she did that, she'd lose the freedom she'd been fighting for. Rather than risk a stupid decision, she'd gone to Portsmouth and watched the museum. Unfortunately, she'd left her notebook at the house. Anton had called her that morning while she'd been getting ready, asking for details on the number and locations of cameras.

One more week and it would all be over. Until then, she needed to placate Donovan and his fears. All day, she'd contemplated stories she could tell him to explain the bruises. Lies, good lies that would make him feel better and tamp down his suspicions. But she couldn't do it. She wouldn't lie to him. She'd have to ask him to trust her. Hopefully, his anger had drained in the hours since she'd left.

Inside the house, she glanced around at the common rooms

but saw no signs of him. He'd painted the parlor, the library, and the other small room off the front hallway. He'd begun the hall, and she'd figured it would be completed by the time she returned home, but it didn't look as if he'd worked at all.

She checked the back of the house, but he wasn't in the kitchen, dining room, living room, or sunroom.

She glanced out the utility room window and saw his truck. Maybe he was upstairs. She headed down the hallway toward her bedroom and saw that her bedroom light was on.

Her heartbeat quickened. Why would he be in her room? He must have had a good reason.

Worry had acid filling her stomach. She couldn't put her finger on the source of her rising anxiety, but it was there, thumping with her pulse.

She stepped into the room, saw her things scattered on her bureau.

Something rattled in the bathroom, and she stepped into the space.

She gasped at the sight of the vanity.

Dark wood, carved legs, and curved lines. The white marble countertop accented the colors in the room beautifully.

Donovan's back was to her, his head beneath the sink. She watched him work, not wanting to startle him. Not wanting to rush into the conversation she knew they were about to have.

After a minute, he backed out and turned to her, seemingly not a bit surprised to see her there.

"It's stunning."

He made no indication he'd heard. Instead, he stood and turned on the water, testing each faucet.

Satisfied, he gathered his tools and tossed them into his toolbox.

She reached for some bits of trash lying on the floor.

"I got it," he said.

"I don't mind—"

"I got it."

Definitely angry.

Fine, then. She dropped the trash back on the floor and walked out—of the bathroom, of her bedroom. She wandered to the kitchen, grabbed a handful of peanuts, and stood there while she munched them, staring at nothing.

This was ridiculous.

She headed back to her bedroom. It was, after all, *her* room. She had every right to be in there. And she and Donovan needed to talk.

She sat on the bed. A moment later, Donovan stepped out of the bathroom. "I need to clean it."

"I'll do it."

"It's my job. I'll take care of it."

She started to protest, but the look on his face had the words clogging her throat. This was more than anger or frustration. He was furious.

"I'm not seeing anybody."

He laughed, though the sound was far from amused. He turned, snatched something from her bureau and tossed it to her.

The notebook.

Oh, no.

He crossed his arms, waited.

"I..." But she had no idea what to say. Couldn't tell him the truth. Wouldn't lie to him. "It's hard to explain."

"No. Not hard to explain. Hard to excuse."

"It's not what you think."

"What I *think* is that you're planning to steal something from the Nightingale. The Pisano? I bet that would claim a pretty penny on the black market."

"I can't talk—"

"I assume you're in this with your boyfriend."

"He is not my boyfriend."

Another hard chuckle. "Lover. Whatever."

She hated that he was looming over her and stood. That hardly helped at all. "Listen, Donovan, I can't explain this, but you're going to have to trust me."

"I don't have to do anything with you or for you. And I sure as"—the silent curse word floated between them—"don't have to trust you."

"Please, let me..." But she couldn't explain.

"Come up with another lie? No, thank you."

She stepped forward, into his space, but he didn't back away. She tapped his chest with her finger. "I have never lied to you." Her voice was low. She put as much heart into it as she could when she added, "Never." This man had no right to judge.

Except he did. Because her whole life was built on lies. Lies upon lies.

A flimsy foundation.

"I'm calling the police," he said.

She sat back on the bed, looked out the window. "I haven't broken any laws."

"You're obviously planning—"

"Planning isn't illegal." She didn't look at him. Couldn't.

"Fine. I'll call the Nightingale."

That would be bad. Very bad. She couldn't have that, and she couldn't tell him the truth.

Maybe if she asked Routhier for permission to tell Donovan...

But if she did, and if Routhier didn't grant it, she'd be in a bigger pickle. Because Routhier didn't trust her at all. He'd assume she'd told Donovan already, and if he questioned Donovan, Donovan would tell Routhier he'd discovered that she was planning a museum job, and Routhier wouldn't care that it had been an accident. Angel was supposed to keep it secret. He'd use her stupidity against her. She'd lose her deal.

This was her fault. She'd been distracted by the argument with Donovan that morning. She'd been diligent to keep the notebook hidden, but she'd simply forgotten that morning after Anton's call.

Forgotten the most important thing she had to do.

Routhier wouldn't care about her excuses. And he wouldn't grant her permission to tell him anyway. There was no point in contacting him.

She could call her lawyer. Maybe Ms. Laurent could help.

But nothing was going to change Donovan's mind. And ultimately, that was what Angel wanted.

No. She had to think straight. Donovan wasn't the goal here. She needed for him not to call the Nightingale.

That was of primary importance.

She turned to face him. He was leaning against her bureau, arms crossed, fury rolling off him in waves.

"If you really want to have me thrown in prison," she said, "you should contact the Manchester PD. Tell them you think I've been conspiring with known criminals. Tell them what you suspect. I'm on probation. They'll take you seriously."

His eyes narrowed. "If I do that, you could go to jail."

She shrugged. She thought Routhier would protect her, if for no other reason than to protect the job, but she wasn't certain. She'd never been a CI before. She had no idea what would happen. She'd rather see that than see the whole operation blown because she'd been too stupid to put her notebook away.

That was her problem. She'd let herself get comfortable here. She'd let her guard down.

She wouldn't be dumb enough to do it again. "I can give you the name of my probation officer if you want."

A muscle ticked in his jaw. "Why would you do that?"

"Because…" She stopped, forced away the emotion that was building behind her eyes. "Because I'm not doing anything wrong, but you don't trust me. I wish I could demand your trust. I wish I could believe I deserved it, but I don't. If you want to call, then call. I'll deal with the consequences."

He stared, didn't move.

She stood. "Whatever you decide to do"—she waved toward the door—"do it out there. I have to pack."

That muscle ticked again, but he said nothing as he pushed off the bureau and stormed out. He slammed the door behind him.

CHAPTER NINETEEN

Donovan stomped through the house, out the back door, and onto the overgrown lawn.

He'd wanted Angel to explain. As angry as he'd been all afternoon, he'd been sure there'd be some reasonable explanation for that notebook. He'd been convinced she would tell him something... even if it was a lie.

Not that he'd wanted to be lied to, but that was what he'd expected.

But she hadn't lied. And she hadn't explained. Which meant... what? That she truly was planning to rip off a museum? That she was working with a cruel man to get it done, a man who'd hurt her twice?

She was playing a dangerous game with violent people and high stakes. But why?

Why would she risk her freedom, risk her future, to rip off an art museum? For the money? Was it that simple? Was she that greedy for gain?

But she didn't seem greedy.

Right. She *seemed* sweet and gentle and honest, but he'd

known from the start that she wasn't. She was a thief and a con. Had been for years.

Donovan was a fool.

He lifted his gaze to the cloudy skies. *If You have any insight for me, I'll take it now.*

She was going to leave. Any minute now, he'd hear her car start, hear the tires on the driveway. And she'd be gone. Maybe not for long. Maybe she'd cry to her brother, and Jack would kick Donovan out. It would seem fair enough to Jack, but only because Angel's brother didn't know the truth.

Donovan could tell him.

That would really ingratiate him with Jack. And probably ruin Angel's relationship with her brother. Which wasn't his goal. He didn't want to ruin Angel.

What did he want?

He looked up, begged for help, for insight.

But none came.

Fine, then. She could leave, and then he'd be free of her. Angel wasn't his problem.

Like Katie wasn't your problem.

Katie. He'd washed his hands of his sister, too. When her addiction had become unmanageable, when she'd blown through their parents' money and still hadn't gotten free, he'd turned his back on her.

He should have tried harder to reach her.

His final image of his sister filled his mind. She'd overdosed. He'd gotten the call, met his parents at the hospital, where they'd sat at her bedside. She was alive when he got there, but not for long. Because the damage to her heart was too extensive. They couldn't make it pump normally again.

He'd watched his sister's life drain out of her in front of his eyes. Watched his mother's spirit drift away too. Watched his father's tears drip from his chin. His father, who'd never cried in front of him. His father, who could put a good spin on anything, had wept at his daughter's bedside.

The three of them had clung to each other, waiting for someone to come in and tell them it had all been some big colossal joke. Because girls like Katie didn't die of heroin overdoses. Girls from good families, girls who'd been raised in church. Girls who loved big and laughed loud and embraced life.

Girls like Katie were supposed to get married and have a houseful of kids and teach Sunday school and play with grandchildren.

They weren't supposed to be buried at twenty-four.

Donovan blinked, tried to focus on the yard, the house, the lake. Everything blurred as tears streamed down his face. He made no effort to wipe them. He missed his sister. He'd been a fool not to try harder. Maybe he couldn't have saved her. Maybe he'd have reached out and she'd have rejected him, but at least he wouldn't carry this burden of guilt.

The image of his sister's body morphed until it was Angel lying on that hospital bed. Angel's face drained of color and life.

Angel, gone forever.

No.

No. He couldn't let that happen. He wouldn't let another person he cared for rush headlong into danger and not do... something.

But what, Lord?

The answer was a simple whisper in the breeze. *Love her.*

DONOVAN WAS ROUNDING the house when the front door opened. He jogged to the bottom of the porch steps as Angel hefted her bag onto the porch, wincing with the effort.

She glanced at him but didn't hold eye contact. "I have to get the rest."

"Just... Can we talk for a second?"

"Nothing else to talk about." She stepped into the house, but he followed, snatched her hand as it swung behind her.

"Please?"

She rounded on him, yanked her hand back. Opened her mouth, snapped it shut. Stared at him a moment. "There's nothing else to say." Her eyes were rimmed in red, her cheeks blotchy, the makeup gone.

"I think there is."

"Fine." She crossed her arms. "I'm in a hurry. Get to it."

"I don't want you to leave."

She scoffed, shook her head. "Don't worry. I'm not going to get you kicked out. You and Jack have a good arrangement. I have no intention of—"

"That's not why." He ran his hands through his short hair. Sometimes, when he was frustrated, he missed the length. It was easier to grab and yank when it was long. He tried to get his thoughts in order. "I care for you."

Her angry burst of laughter made her feelings on that clear. "You care for me, but you don't trust me. I get it. I don't deserve your trust. Not that I've ever lied to you. Ever."

She kept saying that. "You told me you wanted to see the Nightingale—"

"Which I did. I wanted to see it. I needed to see it. I didn't lie to you."

"You didn't tell me why."

"You didn't ask."

He started to argue. Stopped. "It's a lie of omission."

She sighed. "Everything I've never told you could be considered a lie?"

"No. Of course not, but in that case..."

"If you'd asked, I'd have told you I was working on a project, which I am. It's not a lie. And for your information, not every aspect of my life is your business."

"You're planning to steal a work of art. I'd say that's someone's business."

"You have no idea what I'm planning."

"Then tell me."

She swiveled, headed for her room.

He should let her go.

Like he'd let Katie go.

Love her.

Fine.

He followed. "I don't want you to leave."

She kept walking. "I'm not obligated to do what you tell me, Donovan."

"I know that. I'm just..."

She entered her room and slammed the door.

He leaned against the wall. This was ridiculous. He should give up.

But love didn't give up. And maybe he didn't love her like... like he'd thought he might someday. Like he'd imagined when he'd painted the woman in his picture that morning. But he could love her like a sister in Christ. That's what God was asking him to do.

The door swung open, and Angel dragged a trash bag into the hallway.

He reached for it. "At least let me help."

She glared at him, then handed him the bag. "Whatever gets you through the night."

She started down the hall, but he stepped into her room and set the bag on the bed.

She stomped back. "What are you doing?"

"I don't want you to leave."

"So you said."

He held his ground.

"You're going to hold my stuff hostage? Is that your big plan?"

He had no big plan. He only knew she needed to stay.

"Why?" The single word was a demand. "Why do you want me to stay?"

"I care about you."

"You say you care about me. But you threatened to call the police and the museum you think I'm planning to rip off. I'm having trouble figuring out which remark is accurate."

"Both. I care about you, and I don't want you to go to prison. I want to do something that'll keep you from that. That'll stop you from doing this stupid, reckless thing."

"You have no idea..." But her words trailed off. She leaned against the doorjamb. "I can't explain it. I wish I could, but I can't. If you would trust me..."

He walked across the room, took her arm, and pushed the sleeve of her shirt back to reveal the bruises. They'd darkened since that morning. "Can you tell me who did this?"

She shook her head.

"Is he part of your... project?"

She didn't look at him, but her head tipped down, then up. A nod.

"How do you intend to protect yourself from him?"

"I don't..."

"A handgun?"

"Not legal for me to carry a gun."

Right. Because she was a felon. "Pepper spray?"

She shrugged. "It's a bruise. It'll fade."

She wasn't going to tell him anything. She was probably planning a big criminal scheme with her boyfriend, and when it was over she'd either disappear or end up in prison. At that point, she wouldn't be his problem anymore.

But right now... right now, he wanted her here, where she was at least safe when she was home. Where he could know, every night, that she'd made it through another day. If she left, he'd lose contact with her. And he'd never know.

And if she were here, then he could figure out what was going on with her. If he couldn't convince her to stop whatever she was planning, he could at least find the guy who'd left those bruises.

If Angel wouldn't protect herself, then Donovan would have to do it.

He wanted to take her hands, to pull her into his arms, but that aspect of their relationship needed to end, now. There'd be no more movies, no more kissing, no more intimacy until he knew what was going on. Still, they could eat together. They could talk. And he could protect her when she was home.

"Will you stay? Please? I won't ask any more questions. And I won't call anybody. I'll do my best to trust you, even though it makes no sense."

A long moment passed before she nodded once. "I'll stay."

CHAPTER TWENTY

"We're going to make it simple," Anton said.

Angel had gone to church that morning—alone, again. She and Donovan had mostly avoided each other the previous day. She'd peeked into the empty sunroom and seen a different canvas on his easel. He'd added another person to another painting and, once again, found that missing ingredient that made the painting come alive. The scene was a rocky coastline being battered by a turbulent sea. Overhead, storm clouds threatened. Donovan had added a man standing on the edge of the cliff, hands in his pockets, shoulders hunched, focus on the rocks below.

Donovan had conjured desperation and despair in a simple, stark image of a man.

Even now, the memory of it felt burned into her brain.

"You with us?" Anton asked.

"Of course." She snapped her gaze to Anton across the table and scrambled to remember what he'd said. "The simpler the plan, the better."

Mason stood by her side. Anton had kept his distance,

enabling her to focus without worrying about Anton's propensity to hurt her for the sheer joy of it.

Not that that wasn't a tremendous worry, but one thing at a time.

"Mason, you'll disable the alarm at precisely three twenty-seven."

"Dude, seriously?" Mason's eyebrows lifted. He gave Angel a can-you-believe-this-guy look.

"Precision!" Anton's shout got Mason's attention. "The most important thing is precision. You understand that?"

"You're the captain," Mason said. "Three twenty-seven, alarm goes down."

"What about the cameras?" Angel asked.

"I'm gonna have 'em playing on a loop while you're in there," Mason said.

"You can do that?" she asked.

"No problem. I already recorded the footage. It's uploaded to their file. Gotta tap into the video stream—"

"We don't need the details," Anton said. "You'll be doing all that from the car. You'll keep your eyes open for anything unusual. Cars that pull up, cars that leave, people walking on the street. Everything."

"Lookout," Mason said. "Got it."

"We'll be on a three-way call, and we'll use headphones to communicate. Angel, you and I will go in through the door here." He pointed at the emergency exit door in the room—they assumed it was a warehouse—behind the wide gallery on the far end. "You're confident you can pick the lock?"

"Far as I can tell," she said, "it's a standard panic door. Not a problem."

"And if it's dead-bolted?"

"It shouldn't be," she said. "The guards go in and out that

door when they change shifts. I've never seen any evidence that the guard goes to unlock it before his replacement comes."

"Idiots." Anton shook his head almost as if he were disappointed it wasn't going to be harder. "How long will it take you to pick it?"

"Plan on two minutes. If it's dead-bolted, it could take up to four."

"That works." He tapped into his phone where he was making notes. "I'll carry a screwdriver kit to manage the case."

"A simple snatch and grab," she said.

"It's not very elegant," Anton said. "We won't have much time. I'll unscrew while you keep watch. When we're ready, you'll open the bag—"

"What bag exactly?" she asked.

"We're obviously not going to run out with the statue in our hands. I'll have a backpack. You'll open it, I'll snatch the statue and shove it in."

"It'll be heavy."

"I'm aware."

"And then get out of there," Angel said. "We'll be going opposite the guard, so even if he hears us, he shouldn't see our faces if we move fast enough."

"We'll need masks, just in case," Anton said. "If the guard comes, we'll have to take him out."

She glared across the table. "What do you—?"

"Whoa, man." Mason stepped away from the table. "I'm not interested in going down for murder."

Anton shook his head as if they were both morons for thinking it. "I'm not gonna *kill* him."

Except he had once before. He'd murdered that cop in Boston.

"How will you take him out?" Angel asked.

Anton glared at her.

Mason waited for an answer.

"Pepper spray." Angel tossed the idea out, silently thanking Donovan for mentioning it Friday. "It sprays far, it'll keep him from being able to see, but it won't do any permanent damage."

Anton blew out a long breath. "Buy some."

"Good idea," Mason said. "Unless you had a better plan."

Anton shrugged. "I was gonna punch him."

Sure he was. Angel didn't believe that for a second. Anton was too arrogant for his own good.

No, if she knew him, and she was pretty sure she did, she figured Anton's plan was to shoot the guard if they were discovered. Which meant he'd be carrying a weapon.

The thought of it made her shudder.

What had she gotten herself into?

"We get the Pisano," Anton said, "and we get out. No wasting time on anything else. Right?" He looked at her as if she might argue.

"There's nothing else worth risking our freedom for." Though in her eyes, Donovan's painting was priceless.

"Then what?" Mason asked. "When I see you guys come out, I turn the alarm back on and drive away?"

"You go nowhere until I reach you," Anton said. "I'll hand you the bag."

"Me?" Mason's eyes widened.

"We'll split up. We can't all get caught. Angel and I will run to our own cars, and we'll all meet back here."

Here? Not where he kept the rest of his artwork? "Do you think that's wise?" she asked. "We've all been coming and going from this place. If the cops are watching any of us, they'll know to look for us here."

"The cops watching you, Angel?" Anton asked.

"Not me, but I don't know about you two."

"I'm clean," Mason said.

"Nobody suspects me of anything," Anton said.

How wrong he was.

She didn't care, not really. It was the principal, though. And the fact that he needed to believe she did care. "It's unwise to meet here," she said. "Another location, any location..."

His smile was condescending. "Don't worry about it. I've got it figured out."

"But—"

"We meet here." Anton's voice was hard. "You have a problem with that?"

She glared across the table. "I have a problem with going to prison."

"If there are further instructions, I'll give them to you that day." He focused on Mason. "You take off with it, you don't show up, I'll be very upset."

"Dude, I'm not gonna—"

"I know where your pretty little girlfriend lives. She'll be the one to pay for it."

Mason's eyes narrowed, and he pushed both hands on the table and leaned toward Anton. "You touch my girlfriend and I'll kill you."

Another staring contest. Excellent.

Angel sighed. "As long as everyone does their part, nobody will get hurt." Anton messed with his phone and focused on Angel. "I got your alibi worked out. I'm texting you his contact info... now."

Her phone dinged in her pocket.

She snatched it. "John Jones? Feels like a fake name."

"It's his real name. He's an old friend. About thirty, chubby and balding. He's going to swear you two were on your first date, went back to his place, and were going at it hot and heavy at the time of the robbery."

She stifled her shudder. "You're disgusting."

"Just trying to keep your pretty little tail out of prison, sweetheart."

Prison. No matter what happened to Angel, at least Anton would end up there. "As long as I don't have to admit to sleeping with *you*, it's no problem."

Mason laughed. "Chubby bald guy beat you, dude."

Anton ignored Mason and glared at her. "You'd better learn to keep that mouth shut."

"Or what?"

His leer answered her question. The memory of his hand on her neck sent a shudder she couldn't hide down her back.

"I think you know," he said.

She tried to come up with a biting remark, but panic lodged in her throat.

Mason said, "Cut it out. We're on the same team."

Anton's amused laughter did nothing to assuage her fear. "I'm messing with you guys. We're all good, then, right?"

Mason looked from Angel to Anton and back. "You okay?"

"Fine." She glared at Anton across the table. "This is it. We do this, and you have nothing on me, and I have nothing on you. Right?"

"Of course." But the way his eyes danced belied his words. He had something in store for her, and it definitely had nothing to do with her freedom.

At least she knew where she stood. She turned to Mason. "I'm good."

Anton walked them through a few more details, and they ended the meeting. They wouldn't see each other again until the wee hours of Saturday morning.

And then it would all be over.

After Angel pulled onto the highway, she dialed the number Anton had forwarded. A man picked up on the second ring.

"John Jones speaking."

"Hi, John. This is Angelica Rossi. We have a mutual friend—"

"Ah, yes. Angel. I've been waiting for your call." His voice was high-pitched for a man, and he sounded a little too eager.

She said, "I understand we have a date Friday night."

"Absolutely. I thought I'd take you to the Olive Garden over by the mall. They have that great buy-one-take-one special. We can each get two. That way, we'll have a late-night snack for later."

An Italian meal for a snack after dinner?

"I'll order the spaghetti with meat sauce," he said.

"Okay, uh... Don't they have a good chicken marsala?"

"Marsala. Good choice. Then, I'll take you to my favorite gelato place. It's not too far from there. You'll love it."

Two Italian dinners and ice cream? How big was this guy?

"And then," his voice lowered, "we'll go back to my place, get to know each other a little better."

She forced a lighthearted tone. "You know this is all pretend, right?"

"Yeah, yeah." His voice squeaked, and he cleared his throat. "But, you know, we need to have a good story. In fact, I think we should meet, get a feel for each other, in case something goes wrong."

A feel for each other. Right. "I'm not sure that'll be necessary, John." The last thing this guy wanted was for them to meet. If the police got wind that he was willing to lie about her whereabouts, he'd be as guilty as the rest of them. She'd rather not have a face to put with his name, in case it ever came to that. "You don't seem like the kiss-and-tell type. If the police contact you, tell them we were together. I was delightful, of course." She laughed to put him at ease. "And you'll skim over the more, shall we say, intimate details of the evening."

She heard his sigh through the phone. "If you think that's best."

"It'll be safer this way."

"Just in case, though, we should text each other this week, don't you think? You know, as a paper trail. I mean, not paper, but..." He seemed flustered, embarrassed.

"Sure, that's a great idea."

"And maybe you could send me your picture?"

"I'll think about that." And decide against it. "I really appreciate your help, John. Thank you."

When the call ended, Angel considered Anton's plan. It seemed like it could work—on paper, anyway. The guard would be three rooms away, assuming he wasn't patrolling. If he was, he'd catch them for sure. The place simply wasn't that big. If he heard them, he'd try to trip the alarm. When that didn't work, he'd likely call 911, and they'd have to leave without the sculpture. Or, if he heard them and came running, they'd have to incapacitate him. At least Anton had left that to her. She could use pepper spray, and then Anton could... what? They should have some way to bind the man, if it came to that.

She didn't want it to come to that. She didn't want to hurt anybody.

Honestly, she didn't want to do any of this. She and the curator, Mary Lynn, had become friends during Angel's visits to the museum. What would Mary Lynn think when she learned Angel had been using her for information? Would it matter that she'd been working with the police? No, because whether for the cops or for the robbers, she'd used Mary Lynn either way.

Lord, I don't want to do this.

He knew her heart. He knew she was doing this for her

freedom and to put Anton away, and if she was hearing Him right, He'd encouraged her to go forward with this plan.

The plan felt shaky, though.

There were issues that needed to be dealt with, like the fact that Anton didn't intend to take them back to where he'd hidden the rest of his stolen artwork. His lair, as she'd been thinking of it. Of course he wouldn't show them that. He didn't trust her or Mason any more than they trusted him.

She'd told Routhier that would be a problem. What if the detective called the whole thing off? Would Angel get her deal? Or would it all be off the table?

No. Her contract was binding. No matter how it played out, as long as Angel did her part and kept the detective informed, she'd be cleared of her charges.

But she wanted more than that. She wanted Anton to go down, not only for robbery but for murdering that cop. After what he'd done to Brittney, he deserved to rot in prison forever.

When she got home, she stepped inside and listened for Donovan. The house was silent. He wasn't painting the hall-way, which was where she'd expected to find him. The downstairs bath was dark.

The man hardly ever left the house, but it seemed he had that day. She was glad. Glad he'd done something besides handi-work and painting. It was good he was entering the real world again. Maybe, if nothing else, Angel'd had a hand in that. Even though she'd lost his respect and his affection, maybe she'd been good for him. And maybe, God willing, she'd be able to win those other things back, too.

She longed for things to go back to how they'd been before Donovan had found her notebook. She longed to feel his arms around her, for the comfort and protection she found in his presence.

She went to her bedroom and grabbed her second cell

phone. Good thing Donovan hadn't found it on Friday. That would've added more fuel to his fury.

She saw a text from Routhier.

Meet ASAP at usual place. Text when you're on your way.

What in the world?

She texted, *What's up?*

The three dots danced immediately. *Meet you there. Now.*

Something was wrong. She grabbed her things and hurried to her car.

Less than thirty minutes later, she parked in her usual spot in the parking garage feeling more exposed than normal because it was nearly empty on this Sunday afternoon.

Routhier and Opie joined her at her car. Opie—O'Donnell—looked sympathetic, but Routhier looked furious.

"What happened?"

Routhier said, "You were followed."

"What?" She looked behind her as if Anton might be there.

"Not now," he said. "Earlier. When you went to the warehouse."

"Wait... How do you know—?"

"You told us about the meeting," Opie said. "Remember?"

"I didn't know you were watching me."

Routhier glanced at his partner. "We're trying to keep an eye on you when you're with Anton, after the... you know."

"After he beat the crap out of me? Nice of you to care."

Routhier smirked.

"I was there." Opie's kind eyes held her gaze. "Nobody deserves what he did to you. I have a particular loathing for men who hurt women."

He was serious. He did care. That was... unexpected.

Opie wasn't a complete jerk, even if his partner was.

Not Opie. O'Donnell. She'd think of him that way from now on. "Thank you, Detective. I appreciate that." To Routhier, she said, "What are you saying? Someone followed me home? Anton?"

"To the warehouse."

"Nobody knew about the meeting but you."

"He drives a pickup truck, black," Routhier said. "We ran the plates, and the truck is registered to a"—he glanced at his phone—"Donovan Gilcreast."

She closed her eyes at the sound of the name.

"You know him?" O'Donnell asked.

"He's my... He lives in the house where I live."

"You're living with him?" Routhier asked.

She shook her head. "My brother owns the house."

"That huge house is owned by your brother?" O'Donnell asked.

"You've seen it?" She glared at the man she'd been starting to trust. "You followed me?"

Routhier said, "We tracked the phone we gave you. It's not a big deal."

Not a big deal, but he hadn't planned to tell her that. Because, of course, he didn't trust her.

Join the club, mister.

"Whatever." She focused on O'Donnell. "We're not living together in the... the Biblical sense. He's living there while he fixes up the house. Jack is letting me stay there, too."

O'Donnell said, "So you and Gilcreast are...?"

"Friends."

"Nothing else?" Routhier asked.

"What difference does it make?"

"Come on, Angel," he said, "use your brain. The man *followed* you today. You're either sleeping with him or he's a crazy stalker who wants you to sleep with him."

"You've got a dirty mind, Routhier, you know that? Not all

men are pigs." She turned to O'Donnell. "Why did you go to the warehouse today?"

"I wanted to make sure you were safe."

She glared at Routhier. "Not a crazy stalker. Maybe Donovan also wants to make sure I'm safe."

"Right." Routhier sneered. "I always follow women when I'm worried about them. That makes perfect sense."

"He's... protective. That's all." When Routhier and O'Donnell shared a glance, she said, "It won't happen again. I'll make sure he backs off."

"Tell us what you told him," Routhier said.

She hadn't *told him* anything. He'd guessed, but she hadn't confirmed or denied his guesses. So... "Nothing."

Routhier started to say something, but O'Donnell spoke first. "I don't understand. Why would he follow you? If he knows nothing, why—"

"Anton hurt me again last week." She pushed up the sleeve of her T-shirt. The bruises were fading, but they were there. "Donovan saw them. He questioned me, but of course I couldn't explain. My guess is that he followed me to find out who keeps hurting me."

O'Donnell said, "That makes sense."

Routhier scoffed. "Maybe you should move out."

She'd have to make Donovan back off—for his own good. "You have a place for me to stay, Routhier? Maybe your wife'll let me crash on her couch."

He jerked back. "Not a chance I'm telling *you* where I live."

"I guess I could stay at a homeless shelter. You guys know of any?"

Opie... O'Donnell shook his head. "I don't have room for you, or I'd let you stay with me."

He would? The young detective surprised her again.

"What about your brother?" O'Donnell asked.

"No." She took a deep breath. "No, Anton could find me there. Jack doesn't need that. His wife is pregnant."

Routhier said, "Seems you're safe where you are, as long as you can get your boyfriend—"

"He's not my—"

"—to back off." Routhier opened the little notebook he kept in his breast pocket. "What's the plan?"

She told them everything Anton, Mason, and she had decided. When he was finished taking copious notes, he slid the notebook back into his pocket.

"You're meeting back at the warehouse?" he asked. "That is odd."

That bothered her, too. "He said something about how that was the plan for now, and if he changed it, he'd let us know. We'll probably get an updated plan the day of the robbery. If we do—"

"You'll let us know," Routhier said.

"Problem is, I won't have the phone you gave me with me after I leave the house. I might not be able to."

"You have to take it," Routhier said.

"Bad idea," she said. "If he finds it—"

"Leave it locked in your glove box," O'Donnell said. "When you get back in the car, you can text the new address then. We'll be close by. We won't need a lot of notice."

Routhier nodded. "Good plan. Or text us from your regular cell. At that point, we'll be closing in."

"You plan to arrest him that night?"

"Not until he leads us to where he keeps the rest of his stolen goods. We'll simply follow the sculpture."

"He claims he's going to give it to Mason."

"Makes sense," Routhier said. "But he'll get it when he meets back up with you guys. He won't want to hang onto it for long. We'll be watching."

"He owns a lot of properties," O'Donnell said. "The sober living houses, his personal home, rental properties. Even that warehouse you've been meeting in belongs to him. He'll lead us to the right one, and we'll get a warrant."

It all sounded too optimistic. There were no guarantees, and while they waited, Anton would be free. She'd have to stay out of his grasp. Which meant, no matter where Anton, Mason, and she were supposed to meet that night, she wouldn't be there. She'd come up with an excuse for why she couldn't make it. Car died. She got pulled over. Something. Another lie, but for good reason.

She'd stay away from Anton, keep her distance until he was arrested. That was the only way to stay alive.

She started to share that with the detectives, but then didn't. They might talk her out of it, insist she go through with all of it. No, they'd get the same lie Anton did. She had to protect herself, and she wouldn't trust Routhier or even O'Donnell to put her safety over their desire to make their arrest. *Is that okay, Lord?*

There was no quick answer, but He'd given her the go-ahead to do this. Surely He didn't want her to die in the process.

"Okay, then," she said. "It's a plan."

Routhier's dark brows lowered. "The only thing that can screw it up at this point is Donovan Gilcreast. Make sure he backs off, or he's going to blow this whole thing. If he knows what's going on, then it's off to prison with you."

"That wasn't the deal," she said. "I haven't told Donovan anything."

Routhier shrugged. "Read the contract. It's your responsibility to make sure nobody knows. Do what you have to do."

CHAPTER TWENTY-ONE

onovan climbed the ladder in the hallway, paint roller in hand, and worked on the area below the tall ceiling.

He'd been painting since he'd returned from following Angel. He hadn't planned to follow her, but when she'd rushed home after church, then rushed back out again, he'd had the strongest feeling he needed to keep an eye on her. At the time, it had felt like the Lord's leading. Now... maybe his fear for her had spurred the decision.

Either way, he was glad he'd done it.

The abandoned brick warehouse, complete with broken windows and fading paint on the trim, was exactly the kind of place he'd imagined an art heist would be planned. He'd parked on the far side of the building next door, then crept through overgrown shrubs, across the gravel lot, and to one of the unbroken windows to peek inside.

The room was huge and nearly empty. Angel stood at a folding table with two men. The one beside her looked young, and, if her body language was to be believed, she didn't see him as a threat.

The one across from them was older with trimmed brown hair and glasses. If Donovan hadn't witnessed the meeting, he'd have guessed the man was mild-mannered, laid back. Gentle even.

Though he couldn't hear their voices through the glass, he'd had no trouble discerning the guy's aggressive nature.

Donovan would bet the house that was the guy who'd hurt Angel.

He hoped someday to return the favor, blow for blow.

Not that Donovan was a violent man, not even close, but her bruises, the way she winced when she moved too fast...

The guy had it coming and more.

Donovan hadn't lingered. He'd stayed for about five minutes, then taken a photo of the license plate on the car parked beside Angel's—a black Audi—and crept back to the neighboring building. He'd watched the lot until the three emerged from the building. The younger guy walked Angel to her car. After Angel left, the two men talked for about ten minutes. Then, the older guy drove away, and the younger one walked to the street and turned toward the main road.

Donovan had been surprised when he'd gotten home to find Angel wasn't yet home. He'd been working ever since. Working and agonizing over what he'd seen.

They'd definitely been planning something. And whatever it was, Angel was in deep.

Donovan couldn't reconcile what he knew about the woman he'd come to care for with the image today. Was she a sweet, gentle soul who'd given her life to Christ?

Or was she a con artist and a thief?

There was evidence for both. It didn't make sense.

The front door slammed open.

He climbed down while Angel stalked down the hallway.

He set the paint roller in the tray as she stopped in front of him, glaring. "You followed me?"

"Oh. Uh…" How did she know? Had she seen him through the window? He hadn't thought so, but—

"You were seen."

"What? No way. Nobody even glanced my way. You three were too busy plotting to notice me."

"How did you…?" Her eyes widened. "You looked inside?"

He was confused now. He took a breath, told himself not to meet her rage with his own. "I peeked in the window, that's all."

"What is wrong with you?" Her voice was loud and reverberated off the high walls. "How dare you!"

"I wanted to make sure you were safe, that's all." He worked to keep his tone reasonable. "I knew you didn't have to work today, and when you—"

Fury blazed in her eyes. "How?"

"You told me. Last week, before"—he gestured down the hallway toward her bedroom—"when we were friends. You told me your schedule."

She stepped back. "I should have lied."

"No, I'm glad you didn't. I'm glad—"

"You have no idea what you've done."

"I don't know how anybody saw me. There was nobody else there."

"The place was being watched. The people watching it are better than you are at staying out of sight."

He hadn't thought of that.

Wait. Why was he the one on the defensive? He hadn't done anything wrong. She was the one plotting to rip off a museum. "You've got a lot of nerve questioning me."

"You're the one sticking your nose where it doesn't belong, causing trouble."

"The only trouble is that you're a thief!" As soon as the words were out, he regretted them. True, maybe, but the shouting, the accusations... He ran his hand through his hair. "I'm not trying to cause trouble. I'm worried about you. Between the bruises and the notebook... I wanted to figure out what you were up to."

She crossed her arms. Anger, or self-protection? "And what did you learn?"

"It was the older guy, wasn't it? He's the one who beat you up."

Her eyes widened. "That's none of your business."

He'd guessed right. "What's his name?"

"It doesn't matter."

"He could hurt you again."

"I'm handling it."

"You think that skinny kid's going to protect you?"

Her arms fell to her sides, fists clenched. She stepped closer, glared up at him. As if he'd be intimidated by her tiny frame. "Whether he does or not, it's not your concern. My life is none of your business. You'd better keep your distance, unless you want to land yourself in prison."

He swallowed hard at that.

She angled around him and the painting supplies.

"After you left," Donovan said, "those men stood outside and talked for a good long while."

She froze, turned her head toward him. "Doesn't matter." Except her eyes widened just enough to show nervousness.

"Does matter," he said. "Maybe they're up to something and keeping you out of it."

"You have no idea what you're talking about." She glanced at the paint, the walls, before glaring at him again. "Stick to what you know, Donovan. Unless you're trying to get me killed, you'd better stay out of my life."

She stalked down the hallway. A moment later, her door slammed shut.

He didn't follow. Couldn't make his feet move. Because her words reverberated.

Get me killed.

That was the last thing he wanted, but somebody had to look out for her. Those two men she was working with were the problem, not the solution.

And whoever had seen Donovan that day had likely threatened her as well.

Lord, did I make a big mistake today? Have I made things worse for her? And what am I supposed to do now?

There was no answer, but the Lord's words from two days before reverberated. *Love her.*

He hadn't done a good job loving Katie when he'd left her to her own devices. So, he'd continue to keep an eye on Angel. He'd have to be more careful next time.

Donovan crouched in front of the new vanity in the tiny downstairs half bath and considered the week. It was Friday afternoon, and Angel was at work. He'd been trying to draw her out since their argument on Sunday. Maybe he shouldn't have. Maybe he should've left her alone, left her to her foolishness and her crime, but the Lord's command had never drifted far from his mind.

Love her.

Like a friend, right? Surely that's what God meant, that Donovan should love Angel like a friend would. Maybe like God loved her. A friend would keep reaching out, regardless of how many times he was rebuffed. That's what unconditional love was, to give and expect nothing in return.

Except the more Donovan tried to love Angel like God would, the more his own feelings for her grew. Not brotherly feelings. Not even friendly feelings.

Over-the-top and head-over-heels feelings.

It was crazy. She was a thief. And his heart was in no way prepared for love. A few weeks before, he'd barely been able to get himself to leave the house. He was better now.

Better because of Angel.

Back in college, when alcohol flowed like the Charles River and sexy coeds moved through frat parties like schools of tropical fish, Donovan had enjoyed his share of women. He'd even thought himself in love with a few. In lust, more like.

To his shame, those women blended together in his memory —curvy bodies and flowing hair, all painted in the scarlet shades of passion and desire. The lust had revealed his true colors. What were theirs? What colors were loneliness and pain and a desire to be loved?

Angel... He could close his eyes and see every nuance of her face. Angel wasn't swathed in a single color. No, she was simply Angel, awash in God's beauty. In his mind's eye, she was surrounded by an aura of peaceful blue, cheerful yellow, royal purple... and that deep green, that life-giving hue, that had driven him to follow her on Sunday.

God, what are You asking of me here? How can I fall in love with a thief? Surely that's not what You want for me.

God shared no insights.

Donovan yawned and thought of all he'd accomplished that week, especially considering how little sleep he'd gotten. If Angel and her accomplices didn't pull off the job soon, Donovan would die of exhaustion.

He'd completed painting all the front rooms and the first-floor hallway. Yesterday, the new half bath's vanity and toilet had been delivered, and today he was installing those. Unfortunately, plumbing, like painting and wallpaper stripping, didn't require much concentration. Which meant he had plenty of time to obsess about Angel.

And pray for her.

He'd been praying for her almost constantly since she'd yelled at him on Sunday afternoon. At night, he prayed. All day while he worked, he prayed. When he ate his breakfast and his dinner alone—because apparently, ever since Sunday, Angel had decided not to eat at mealtimes—he prayed.

He'd never understood the command to *pray without ceasing* until this week. And whenever he wondered if it would have made a difference if he'd prayed for Katie that way, he forced the question aside.

Katie was gone. He'd never get her back, and that was all right. She was in God's hands, in a place where she didn't have to fight her addiction anymore. She was free and happy and alive in the presence of the Lord.

Donovan had to forgive himself for his failures. He had to let Katie go, had to embrace the future God had for him.

Whatever that was.

This week, while Donovan had pulled canvas after canvas from the stacks and let himself feel the moments, see the people in them, he'd opened up more and more. He'd walled his heart after Katie's death, but with every brushstroke, another piece of that wall crumbled.

His heart was exposed more now than it had ever been.

And every day that week, he'd laid himself out for Angel, and she'd rejected him.

Not in so many words, of course. She was, deep down, a kind person. She'd always had viable excuses.

When he'd invited her to eat with him Monday night, she'd claimed exhaustion. By the dark rims around her eyes, he didn't doubt it was true.

When he'd prepared sandwiches for them both on Tuesday before her shift at work, she'd claimed she had an appointment.

Both Wednesday and Thursday, he'd invited her to watch a movie with him after dinner, and both nights, she'd simply said she needed her rest. As if eight p.m. were her normal bedtime. He wondered if she realized he could hear her moving around back in her room. Probably not.

Every morning that week while he'd worked in the sunroom, he'd listened for the sound of her footsteps, but each time he glanced at the ugly couch, it had been empty.

If she wouldn't be his friend, if she wouldn't confide in him or even take comfort in his presence as she'd done before, then praying was the only thing he could do.

While he tightened the nut behind the toilet, he reminded himself of one great truth. Maybe prayer was all Donovan had left, but it was also all he needed.

God was with her.

Donovan could hope for no better Protector.

The front door opened and closed, and Donovan stood, brushed dust and debris off his jeans, and met Angel in the hallway. "How was work?"

"Friday lunches are always busy, and it's pretty out there today. Every table was full."

That was the most conversation he'd gotten out of her all week. "Leaves are starting to change."

She shifted on her feet.

They were chatting in the hallway like strangers who lived in the same building. Except he could imagine the feel of her in his arms. The taste of her on his lips.

"Will you start working on Katie's painting again soon?" she asked.

"Another day or two."

She nodded, peered beyond him. Then, her face lit up. "It's beautiful."

He turned to gaze at the bathroom. He'd added wainscoting and a chair rail a couple of weeks back. Rather than make this room gray like the rest of the downstairs, Jack had opted for a dark purple, the color of royalty. The color of triumph.

The gilded mirror over the sink added to the aura of wealth, as did the ornate light fixture Donovan had installed.

He moved out of the way, and Angel stepped inside and looked around. "You do beautiful work." She didn't see his shrug, instead studying the mirror. "Where did this come from?"

"I found it in one of the upstairs bedrooms."

She touched the edges. "Have you had it appraised?"

"Your brother doesn't want to sell it."

She turned to face him. "This place is going to be stunning when you're finished." Her voice sounded breathy, wistful.

"You want to stay." He should have phrased it like a question, but he felt sure he was right.

Her chuckle was short. "I'm pretty sure Jack has better things to do with it than to give it to his wayward baby sister. And I couldn't exactly afford the rent."

Donovan couldn't respond because something clicked into place.

He hadn't given much thought to what he would do when the house was completed. He hadn't even started on the second floor, and there was a third floor beyond that. And the living room, and the grounds...

In the back of his mind, he'd imagined moving back to Boston, but as he let that idea come forward, he rejected it.

He didn't want to go back to the city.

Like Angel, he wanted to stay in this house forever.

Which was ridiculous. Even if he could afford it...

Well, he could afford it. If this place were turned into a bed-and-breakfast, it would provide income, pay for itself after a time.

He could see it in his mind. He and Angel could run this place themselves. He'd be the crazy artist who worked in the attic and did maintenance work when he wasn't painting.

She'd be the friendly face guests would long to come back to see.

They'd be a team, together, forever...

Insane.

Utterly...

Perfect.

Except for the whole *Angel was about to go to prison* thing.

And yet, the image didn't dissolve and float away as it should have. Because the dream was right and true.

Lord...?

Love her.

He did. God help him, Donovan did love her.

He swallowed the thought, the sudden desire to pull her into his arms. She'd reject him, push him away. Not because she didn't feel anything for him, but because...

Because she was a thief and a liar.

He should call the police.

But he couldn't. He'd promised, and... And, somehow, it wasn't the right thing to do. Which didn't even make sense, because of course telling the police about a crime would be the right thing. Except this was Angel, and he couldn't believe all the things he kept trying to convince himself about her.

"I need to..." She nodded toward the hallway beyond him.

"Sorry." He stepped out of her way, and she walked out of the bathroom and down the hallway, her rubber-soled shoes quiet on the hardwood. "Um, Angel?"

She turned. "Yeah?"

"How 'bout I throw a frozen pizza in the oven, and we can watch a movie together?"

He waited for the rejection, knowing it would come.

Instead, she smiled. "I'll make us dinner instead."

He was too surprised to answer before she continued down the hall and into her bedroom.

He'd cleaned up the bathroom and was halfway down the stairs after his shower when the scent of grilling chicken reached him.

In the kitchen, she stood at the industrial stove lifting a pot of pasta. She glanced his way. "Perfect timing. I was afraid I was going to have to keep it warm for us." She dumped the pasta in a colander in the sink.

"What're we having?"

"My mom always called it chicken and bowties. You'll like it."

He watched while she added chopped grilled chicken, Parmesan cheese, sun-dried tomatoes, pecans, and some kind of salad dressing to the steaming mixture. She mixed it with a big spoon and set the bowl on the bar between the two dinner settings. Then, she snatched a loaf of bread from the oven.

He peered at the mixture. It smelled... heavenly. "What's in the dressing?"

"Balsamic vinegar, olive oil, and basil."

"You like to cook, huh?"

"I love it. I especially love cooking for others. In the sober living house, I made a lot of meals for the women. It was... rewarding, I guess, to see them enjoy what I'd prepared. Good food leads to good conversation, you know? To... camaraderie."

He was nodding, seeing that same image he'd seen earlier. She could run this place. She would be good at it. Excellent at it.

She took out a little bowl, added some vinegar and oil, and set it by their plates. "You need a drink?"

He got himself a glass of water and refilled hers, and they sat together at the table. She reached for her fork, but he took her hand, stilling her.

Stilling him, too, because it was the first time they'd touched in more than a week, and the feeling of her skin against his overwhelmed him.

He uttered a quick prayer and let her go.

Silently, they dug into the food. It was delicious. How did this woman turn a handful of everyday ingredients into... this?

She was a marvel.

And a thief, he reminded himself.

But the words had no effect.

As they settled in to watch TV—her on the sofa, him on the chair—he could hardly keep his eyes off her.

She was fidgety. Hardly seemed to see the movie.

Nervous.

Because of him?

But the truth hit him as if it had been another word from the Lord. And maybe it had.

She'd agreed to dinner, made it, cleaned up—even though he'd offered—and was now watching TV to keep her mind occupied. Because whatever she was planning, it was going down tonight.

The image of that man who'd hurt her was burned into his brain. She'd be with him tonight.

Donovan wouldn't let her get hurt again. Maybe she was right, and maybe following her could land him in trouble with the law. At that moment, it didn't matter.

He was going to protect the woman he loved, whether she wanted his protection or not.

CHAPTER TWENTY-TWO

Angel hadn't slept, had hardly forced her eyes closed, not that she'd thought she would. After dinner and the movie, she'd gone to bed as if it were a normal night. Except nothing about this night had been normal.

On a normal night, she and Donovan would have shared laughs along with the meal.

On a normal night, they'd have cuddled on the couch side-by-side, not watched from opposite sides of the room.

On a normal night, she wouldn't have been dreading each tick of the clock. If she were a normal person with a normal life, she'd have gone to bed free and woken up free.

She wasn't either.

She'd prayed for hours, prayed that God would get her out of this. If only... If only she weren't the person she was, she wouldn't be in this predicament.

If only she could go back to eighth grade and never steal that first tube of lipstick. The lipstick had run out, and it hadn't looked good on her anyway. It had led to more stealing, and more. And then more elaborate cons. She'd never sunk to stealing from old people or children. But she'd stolen her share of goods, conned her share of trusting people out of cash.

If only she could start over, do her life differently. She'd do anything, anything to be free. To not have to go through with this.

A phrase filled her mind. *Forgetting what is behind...*

It seemed familiar, that phrase. She pulled out her phone and typed the words in the search box. A verse from Philippians came up. *But one thing I do: Forgetting what is behind and straining toward what is ahead, I press on toward the goal to win the prize for which God has called me heavenward in Christ Jesus.*

The prize? What was the prize in this case? Not the Pisano, that was for sure. She, Anton, and Mason were about to steal a statue that depicted grace, the free gift of salvation. She was sure neither Mason nor Anton saw the irony in it.

That wasn't what jumped out at her in the verse. Angel was a believer now. She was supposed to forget her past. Maybe not literally, but maybe she was supposed to not let it determine her future. Instead, it seemed God was telling her to press on.

Press on with tonight's plan.

Then, press on into freedom.

Perhaps, someday, she could press on into a relationship with the man she'd come to care for. She hardly dared to hope.

Even if Donovan wasn't part of her future, at least freedom would be.

She could do this. She could press on tonight, do what she'd agreed to do. She closed her eyes, breathed *Thank You.* She was ready. As ready as she'd ever be, anyway.

At two a.m., Angel dressed in black jeans, a black T-shirt, a black jacket, and the black rubber-soled sneakers she wore for work. Once she'd pulled her dark hair into a ponytail, she grabbed everything she'd need and crept out of her room.

The house was silent, but Donovan was as bad a sleeper as she was. In this creaky house, she could wake him if she weren't careful. And then there'd be an ugly confrontation. He'd try to stop her from going through with her plan. She'd have to insist he mind his own business. She imagined she might have to resort to cruelty to shock him into letting her leave.

The last thing she wanted was to hurt Donovan.

Please, let him sleep.

She eased out the front door and hurried to her car. The moon was barely a sliver, hardly offering any light through the trees as they shimmied in the light breeze. It was silent outside, chilly enough to see her breath. She glanced toward the side of the house where Donovan parked the pickup, but of course she couldn't see it from here.

When she reached the road that rimmed the lake, she blew out a relieved breath. First hurdle managed.

Twenty minutes later, she passed the street the Nightingale was on. She saw a beat-up sedan parked where Anton had directed Mason to be. Must be him.

No sign of Anton's big Audi, but there were plenty of places he could've parked. This part of town was a maze of narrow roads and alleys. The old houses had tiny or nonexistent driveways, which meant there were plenty of cars parked along the street. The thought of Anton set her hands to trembling. If he had any idea she was working with the cops, he'd kill her.

He couldn't know. Her job tonight would be to go along with whatever he said. Be agreeable, make him feel confident and in charge. She could do this.

And anyway, she wasn't alone.

She swung her gaze in the opposite direction of the gallery. Routhier and O'Donnell were there somewhere, watching. The plan was for one to keep an eye on her while the other followed the statue.

O'Donnell seemed to have her best interests at heart, but Routhier didn't like her and didn't trust her. And the feeling was mutual. If she ever did this again...

Nope. No chance she'd ever get herself into any foolishness like this again.

Right now, her greatest desire was to see Anton behind bars. And to not get killed.

No reason to think this would end in her death, but her stomach churned on the idea anyway. Because Anton loathed her. And he wasn't exactly the kind of guy who tolerated enemies. He'd said it himself—nobody suspected him of anything. He was wrong, but he was certain.

And she could cast doubts about him. She could damage his reputation and worse if she went to the police.

Maybe she wasn't entirely nuts to worry that he might kill her.

Maybe that was exactly his plan.

This would be okay. Routhier and O'Donnell would protect her. Anton wouldn't kill her in public, not with Mason close by. Anton had every reason to believe she'd show up at the warehouse later. He'd wait until then, wait until they were alone.

She wouldn't give him the opportunity. After they pulled this off, she wouldn't see him again until she testified against him in court.

That day couldn't come soon enough.

Two blocks from the museum, she backed onto a narrow side street lined on both sides with old houses that had been built so close together that there was hardly room between them. She parked facing the main road. From here, at this time of night, she could be on I-95 in five minutes.

Her heart thumped, and she pressed her hand against her chest. She wasn't about to break the law. It felt like she was, her body was responding as if she were, but she wasn't.

She was in this with the police. She wasn't doing anything wrong.

Right, Father?

The only answer was a hint of peace. She breathed it in. She could do this.

The words of the Psalm she read the night before came like a promise. *I am continually with you. I have taken hold of your right hand. With My counsel, I will guide you.*

He was with her in this, in all of it.

She pushed her earphones into her ears and shoved her phone and keys deep into her pockets. She checked her jacket pockets for the lock-picking kit and pepper spray. Her outside jacket pocket held a small square of chamois, leather gloves, and a black ski mask.

When her phone rang in her ears and vibrated against her hip, she tapped the earphone, and Anton's voice came through. "Ready?"

"Ready," she said.

"Let's do it," Mason said.

Angel got out of her car and walked between two houses as if she belonged. The narrow alley led to the street behind the museum.

She met Anton in an alley across the street from the back entrance of the Nightingale. They barely looked at each other and didn't speak.

He studied his Apple Watch. She watched her own cheap digital.

The instant it read 3:27, Mason said, "Done."

They crossed the street and pulled on their ski masks and gloves, and Angel set to work on the lock. Amazingly, her fingers weren't trembling. *Thank You, Lord.* It took her less than ninety seconds.

She faced Anton. He nodded once, and she pulled the back entrance open.

They paused, waiting for the blare of an alarm, but the night was silent.

Inside, the room was dark. They hadn't known what to expect here. A dim overhead light glowed, offering little more than the outline of the room's contents. There were file cabinets, a desk, a coffee maker, and a small refrigerator. It was more of an office/break room than a warehouse.

Anton leaned forward, whispered in her ear, "You have the pepper spray?"

She nodded.

"Give it to me."

"Why?"

He searched her jacket pockets. His hands on her had her wanting to punch, to push him away, but she needed to remain silent. She tensed as he patted her down, forced herself not to move.

He took the pepper spray from her jacket pocket. "If he comes, you tell me. I'll handle it. I'm afraid he'll overpower you before you can manage it."

Anton crossed to the door that led to the galleries. It was closed, of course. This was a risky part of the operation because the door could make noise when it opened, and that noise could reach the guard.

Slowly, Anton pulled the door open. There was a click, and they froze. No sounds came. No footsteps, no creaking of chairs. Anton peered into the gallery and then slipped through the doorway.

As they'd planned, Angel shoved the chamois between the door latch and the jamb to muffle the closing click.

She'd expected the rooms to be as bright as they were when she visited, but only the dim glow from the exit signs lit the spaces. They crept through the first gallery, keeping to the edges and out of sight of the openings between the rooms. When she looked, she could see all the way to the front, to the desk where the guard was sitting. That room was brightly lit. Most of the guard's body was out of sight. Only his feet were in her line of sight where he'd propped them on the desk. Suddenly, he shifted, and one foot disappeared from her view.

Just before Anton started through the next gallery, she grabbed his wrist, and he froze. She nodded toward the guard, and they stood beside the opening and watched.

A moment later, the guard shifted his feet, placing his other foot on the bottom.

She let go of Anton's wrist. That she'd touched him made her want to wipe her hands with disinfectant.

They made it into the Pisano room, and Angel crept to the door that led toward the guard. A low rumble of conversation came from the front. Probably the TV.

The sound of a laugh track confirmed her suspicion.

She glanced behind her. Anton was deftly and silently unscrewing the plexiglass case. With the mask in place, he looked every bit the villain she knew him to be.

Of course, at this moment, she did, too.

She focused on the guard again, counting seconds, then glanced at her watch. They'd been inside three and a half minutes. Mason had told them he thought they had about seven to get the Pisano and get out before the alarm-monitoring company would call to alert the guard it was down. If it went back up within those seven minutes, the company wouldn't call.

They'd assume a glitch. Especially since Mason had been "glitching" the system for a week.

Through the earphone, Mason whispered, "Car just passed. Late model SUV."

She tapped the earphone so he'd know they'd heard.

Probably nothing to worry about.

The faint pat on her shoulder came sooner than she'd expected. She turned to see Anton taking off his backpack. He pulled an empty canvas bag from inside and handed it to her. It was a drawstring backpack identical to the one on his back.

Odd that he'd have two.

Then, he pulled two more canvas bags out. These didn't look empty, though.

What in the world?

Anton must've seen the question in her eyes, because he gave her a stern look through his mask and set the bags on the floor.

She'd worry about that later. She opened the bag he'd handed her and held it to allow him to access it easily.

He focused on the plexiglass box, took a deep breath, and lifted it.

No alarm blared. She glanced toward the guard, but his feet remained propped on the desk.

Anton grabbed the Pisano and put it in the bag. When she got her hand under it, he let it go.

She'd known it would be heavy but was unprepared for the weight of it. Ten pounds, maybe more.

She'd barely processed it when he snatched the bag from her, grabbed the others off the floor, and rushed toward their exit.

She couldn't believe it. This was going to work. Except... why all the bags? Anton was up to something he'd told her nothing about. Maybe that was what he and Mason had been talking about outside the warehouse when Donovan had watched them. Maybe they were conspiring against her.

Too late to worry about any of that now.

Anton opened the door, careful to keep the chamois in place, and hurried through.

She closed the door softly, then followed him.

When they were almost to the rear exit, he handed her one of the canvas bags. There was something inside, but not the Pisano. It wasn't nearly heavy enough to be the statue.

Each bag had been prepared. What was he up to?

"Take off your mask," Anton whispered, "put it in the bag, and slip the bag on your back."

She did, and he did the same with one of his bags. When they were ready, he pushed open the door, and they stepped outside.

The door closed behind them.

Anton started across the street, and she followed. "Engage alarm and wait."

"Done," Mason said.

They'd actually pulled it off! She couldn't...

Tires screeched as a black SUV screamed around the corner, barreling toward them.

Angel hurried to the sidewalk, fearing the car would hit her. What in the—?

It braked inches from Anton.

She half expected to see cops surrounding them, but aside from the SUV, the night was quiet.

Its passenger window was down, and Anton shoved one of the bags through it. Before she could process what had happened, the car was gone.

Through the earphones, Mason shouted, "Who was that? What—?"

"Shut up." Anton grabbed her wrist and dragged her down the street.

She didn't protest. She should have, but she was focused on watching where the SUV had gone.

This was bad. This was very bad.

Routhier or O'Donnell or both would follow the statue. Assuming that bag had held the statue. The bag on Anton's back didn't sag enough to account for the weight of the Pisano.

But he had another in his hand. It was impossible to know where the statue was.

The plan had been for them to split up. She tried to shake off Anton, but he tightened his grip and dragged her forward. "It's okay. You have to trust me."

If she could have gotten breath, she might have laughed.

Mason was parked on the next block, windows down.

Anton rushed to an open window and tossed the black bag in. "Go, go!"

Mason peeled off.

Would someone follow him? Even if Routhier and O'Donnell were in separate cars, it was likely the one who hadn't followed the SUV would now follow Mason.

The whereabouts of the statue didn't matter to her. What mattered was the man who gripped her wrist.

Angel tried to wrench her arm from Anton's hand. "Let me go. I'll take this and run to my car."

But Anton ignored her, pulling off the wider road and onto a narrow path lined on one side with houses, the other with overgrown shrubs. While he ran, he yanked his phone from his pocket and hit a button.

In her ear, the phone beeped, proving he'd ended their three-way call. She'd forgotten they were on the call. She should have told Mason what was going on. Should have begged him for help.

Not that he would have turned around, but she could have tried. Now Mason was gone, her only possibility for help gone with him.

And whatever happened next, Anton didn't want Mason to hear.

Panic rose in her throat. The pepper spray... He'd taken it, not to use against the guard, but to keep her from using it against him.

She had to get away. She could hardly keep her feet, he was pulling her, keeping her off balance. He was much stronger, and she could do little but stumble along with him. She could fall, refuse to move further. But then, whatever he planned to do to her, he'd just do here in this empty alley.

She forced a scream, but she was out of breath and panicky, and the sound was low and scratchy and seemed to be absorbed by the night air. They were almost to the street. Anton's Audi was parked at the curb. She would scream again when they weren't hidden. Maybe there'd be somebody...

But before they reached the street, before she could draw a full breath, Anton spun and backhanded her.

The pain barely registered in her panic. She stumbled back, lost her balance.

He flipped her around, shoved her face-first against the building beside her. Her forehead bounced off the brick. She blinked to regain her focus, ignored the pain. She had to think.

She tried to push off the building, but Anton shoved against her back. His hands squeezed her shoulders, and he whispered in her ear, "If only we had more time."

Then, he slipped her phone from her back pocket, shoved his hand in her front pockets. Another wave of panic had her trying to get away, to get his hands off her. He was too big, too strong.

He pulled her keys out of her pocket. He grabbed her wrist

and, before she could even try to get away, he yanked her onto the sidewalk.

She was off-balance. Always a step behind.

The trunk of his car opened.

He shoved her toward it. Pushed her inside.

Far away, a man shouted, "Hey!"

She tried to get out, to keep the lid open.

Anton punched her in the head, pushed her down. Then, the trunk lid trapped her in the dark space.

CHAPTER TWENTY-THREE

onovan sprinted to his pickup, heart pounding, frantic prayers flying.

He'd been here long before Angel. He'd crept out of the house around midnight and driven to the Nightingale, parked a few blocks away where he could see the back of the building, and watched. For a couple of hours, nothing happened. And then, a newer sedan parked along one street. Some kind of older car parked a block from the museum.

A black Audi had passed him and turned into a side street. Donovan recognized the license plate number. It was the guy from the warehouse Sunday. The guy who'd hurt Angel. Donovan could take him out right now. Beat the crap out of him, foil all their plans.

But would that put Angel in danger? Would it make things worse for her? Without knowing her plan, without knowing why she was doing what she was doing, Donovan could do nothing but watch.

Because he had all sorts of theories about why she was doing this. Maybe she worked for an insurance company and was testing the museum's security.

Maybe she was working for the cops.

He didn't know. All he knew was that the Angel he'd gotten to know these last couple of weeks wasn't a thief.

She'd shown up around three.

Her car passed him, and she, too, pulled onto a side street and out of sight. He didn't know where she'd parked, but he was more concerned with the Audi. That was the car he'd keep his eye on. Whatever happened now, when it was over, Donovan and that man were going to have a talk.

Maybe more than a talk.

A few minutes later, Donovan saw Angel, dressed entirely in black, walking toward the museum. The leader came from the other direction.

Should Donovan sit there and watch? No. He had to find the Audi.

When Angel and the man had disappeared between two buildings, Donovan pulled onto the street and turned in the direction he'd seen the leader walking from. He couldn't have parked far. Donovan weaved along the streets until, finally, he spotted the Audi. He parked his truck a few car lengths behind, climbed out, and jogged toward the Nightingale.

He was going to observe, make sure she was all right. Then he'd follow the guy, confront him. Hopefully, the guy would take a swing at him, and Donovan would have a good reason to punch him. One way or another, he'd convince the guy never to touch Angel again.

Then he'd go home, and Angel would never know he'd been there.

From the opening of a dark alley a few blocks from the museum, he'd seen the back door of the museum open and Angel and the man step out. Then, that SUV had flown around the corner. Angel had looked shocked.

The leader'd tossed a bag through the open window.

When the SUV was gone, Donovan had watched as the man dragged Angel down the street. It'd taken every ounce of self-control not to bolt in her direction and rescue her. She wouldn't thank him for that, though. So he waited.

The man gave another bag to the guy in the beat-up car a block farther away, and that one drove off.

Behind Donovan, a car pulled from the curb. Who was that? How were they involved?

But he had no time to contemplate it, because the creep dragged Angel out of sight.

Donovan ran down the narrow road parallel to them, saw them come out, cross the street, and rush down another alley.

The creep was taking her to the Audi.

Donovan bolted down the alley nearest him. He'd meet them on the other side. But when he reached the next street, they weren't there.

They were taking too long.

Donovan started in that direction. He was a few blocks away, but if he ran...

Then, the Audi's trunk opened, the man dragged Angel toward it and shoved her inside.

"Hey!"

The shout had been an instinct. A stupid instinct.

The creep saw him, then rushed to the door of his sedan and climbed inside. No way Donovan could catch him before he locked that door. And then, he drove away.

While Donovan climbed in his pickup, he dialed 911, then started his truck and threw it into gear.

The operator answered as the call switched to Bluetooth. "What's your em—?"

"A man shoved a woman into the trunk of his car." *Where did they go? Where were they?*

"Where are you, sir?"

He peered at road signs as he careened around a corner. *There!* "They're on Pleasant Street."

"What city?"

"Portsmouth!" He shouted the word. "It's Marcy Street now. Wait..." He'd lost them. The road turned. Another car shifted onto the road in front of him, and he slammed on his brakes. Almost zero traffic, and then this jerk.

"Describe the car."

"I got the license plate. It's here..." He drove, tapping his phone and praying God would keep him from hitting anything —or anyone. He found the photo he'd taken of the plate number and rattled it off.

"Good. Headed in what direction?" the operator asked.

"Uh... North. Going north on..." He glimpsed the Audi. "Wait. He's turning... Hold up."

After a moment, the operator said, "Do you see the car?"

"Not right... I think he turned."

He couldn't see it. He stifled a curse, pausing at a large, empty intersection. Where were they?

He peered in every direction. *Please, God, please...*

"Sir?"

He'd blown it. He'd been there to protect her, but he'd been too far away. Too far away to do anything but shout and alert the man to his presence. Which had only made things worse. "They're gone. I can't... They're gone."

"It's okay, sir. Every officer in the city will be looking for the car. They won't get far. We'll catch him."

But would they catch him in time? By the time they caught up with the man Angel had worked with, would they arrest him for kidnapping... or murder?

CHAPTER TWENTY-FOUR

Angel stifled a scream. There was no point in that now. It would only make her head pound worse.

She was lying on her side in the hard and bumpy trunk, feeling around in the pitch-dark space. She yanked off her gloves to get a better feel. There had to be an emergency release. There had to be a way to open this trunk.

The car turned sharply, and she braced herself to keep from smashing her head against the trunk wall. Her body slid against whatever was beneath her. Something slick. She examined it with her fingertips. A tarp of some kind. There to protect his carpet from...

Don't think about that.

She had to focus.

She closed her eyes and imagined her own car. The latch was yellow, plastic, and in the center near the edge of the trunk lid. She ran her hands along where she thought it should be.

The car whipped into another turn. She wasn't fast enough to brace herself, and her head smacked against the side.

She shook off the pain. *Focus, Angel. Focus.*

She found a hole in the metal, but no latch. She shoved her fingers inside, felt the raggedy edge of plastic. This was it, but it had been cut. She tried to grab it with her finger and thumb, but when she pulled, her grip slipped.

She wiped her fingertips on her jeans to get the sweat off, then shoved her fingers in the hole again, tried again. Failed again.

Another turn had her bracing herself.

Anton had disabled it. He'd planned this from the beginning. He'd never intended to let her get away tonight.

What would he do next?

God, help! I need…

Desperately. And He knew exactly what she needed.

She rested, breathed. Something dug into her shoulder. The backpack. She pulled it off, shoved her hand inside. It was too dark to see anything, but she felt around. There was the mask. Some other item. She pulled it out, examined it with her fingers. Felt plastic. A solid plastic… something. Maybe a statue. Probably about the same size as the Pisano, but not anywhere near the same weight. A decoy.

She tossed the statue and bag to the back of the trunk, forced herself to take a deep breath. She had to think. How else could she get out? Not through the trunk door, but another opening…

The taillights. Maybe she could push one out and signal a car behind her. She pulled the tarp out of the way, searched in the dark for an edge to the thin carpet beneath it. Found it, yanked it up, then touched where she thought the lights should be. There was something there… Cold, metal.

The car rolled into a slow right turn, then up a hill.

The sound beneath her changed. She froze, concentrated.

They were crossing a bridge. She imagined the city. Bridges

everywhere. They weren't going fast enough to be on the interstate. Too many options to guess which one.

She dug at what she hoped was the taillight, though she couldn't see it. She tried to find a way to pull it out, push it out, but it was fastened too tightly.

The sound beneath her changed again. Back to solid ground.

Forget the taillight. A weapon. She searched for where the jack and lug wrench were hidden. Had to shove the tarp away again. Somewhere on the side...

The car slowed, and Anton took a sharp left turn.

He didn't speed up again. Wherever Anton planned to take her, they were almost there.

She found a plastic latch, pulled on it, felt around inside.

Empty.

Empty.

Out of ideas, she stilled and closed her eyes.

It was over. Her life had come to... exactly what she deserved. Nothing.

Except... except did she believe in God, or didn't she?

Whatever happens next, I'm Yours, Lord. Please, let my family know I was free. Maybe not legally, but in You I found freedom. Don't leave them wondering and worrying about my salvation. Let them believe, despite the circumstances of my death, that my faith was in You.

Her eyes burned as her regrets, all her bad choices, came to the forefront of her mind. *Oh, Father, I've made so many mistakes. I've done so little to deserve You.* She pictured the statue she'd risked everything to steal. The grace it depicted spoke to her even now. *Thank You for reaching down to save me.*

And then Donovan's face came to mind. She loved him. Maybe it was a new and fresh little sprig of love, but it was there. If only they'd had time, it would have grown into a strong and steady oak. Together, they could have built a life, raised children. They could have been happy, she and Donovan. If she could have ever been good enough for him, they could have been happy.

Protect his heart, Lord. Let him understand why I did this. Let him learn the truth about me and not think I died as a thief. Somehow, tell him I loved him.

Tears were flowing now. She didn't want to die, not when she was only now learning how to live. Whatever happened next, she knew who she was. She knew Whose she was.

All she could do now was wait for the trunk to open, wait for Anton to kill her.

She closed her eyes for one last prayer. *Lord, let it be quick. And don't let him touch me.*

Fight back.

The thought was loud enough that it was as though someone had spoken it. With what could she fight, though? Anton was much stronger than she. She had no chance against him. What would be the point?

As if from far away, a memory filled her mind. Karen, the waitress she'd worked with, had said, *You know what your problem is? You think everyone is worth fighting for except yourself.*

Angel was fighting for her freedom, though, wasn't she?

Yes, but also, no. She'd agreed to this crazy scheme to nail Anton for what he'd done to Brittney. This fight had been for Brittney's sake, not her own.

Was Angel worth fighting for?

I think you're worth dying for.

The words brought fresh tears. *Oh, Lord, could it be true? Am I worth it?*

The Lord's only answer was an overflow of peace. And a sudden idea.

It wouldn't work, but she had to do something. Maybe if she did her part, the Lord would bring a miracle. Either way, she wasn't going to let Anton kill her without a fight.

CHAPTER TWENTY-FIVE

"Sir, are you there?" The 911 operator's voice was detached and calm.

Donovan floored the gas as soon as his tires hit the Memorial Bridge. There were taillights disappearing on the other side. Whether they belonged to the Audi or not, he didn't know. At four a.m., there wasn't a lot of traffic. It was the only moving car he'd seen since the one that had cut him off earlier.

It had to be her.

Please, God.

"Sir?" the 911 operator said.

"Yeah. I'm here," he said. "I might have them." He told her where he was as he peered into the distance. The taillights... Were they still there?

He made it across the bridge, slowed down. *Where'd you go, Angel?*

Lord, direct me.

But the car was gone.

"Sir, the police are nearby. If you see the car, please tell me immediately."

"Yup." There were buildings on both sides, hotels or houses, he didn't know. He was looking for the red glow of taillights. The car'd disappeared. The road was straight and flat, though. If they'd remained on it, he shouldn't have lost them. Meaning, they'd pulled off.

To where?

Assuming it was even Angel and the creep and not some random someone.

He scanned the buildings and the cars on each side. Nothing.

He was passing a street when a flash of red on his left caught his eye. He braked, turned around, and headed back. "I might have them."

"Where are you?"

There was no street sign on the road where he'd seen them. "The road past it heading east is Island Road. This is across the street, heading west."

The woman said, "Okay..." Then... "I have it. It's a dead end. Park where you are. Police are on the way."

"Not a chance."

"Sir, the abductor could be armed."

That's what Donovan was afraid of. He crept along the road. Flipped off his headlights.

It was dark, but he could see enough to continue.

"Sir, are you parked? Looks like police are seven minutes out."

"Looking for them."

"It's not your responsibility to rescue this woman. Let us—"

"I'm in love with her." They felt like the truest words he'd ever spoken, and he was glad he'd said them aloud, even if only to this stranger he'd never speak to again.

"I didn't realize you knew her," the operator said.

Irrelevant information at the time.

He peered into the darkness, followed the curve of the road.

There, beside a building. Ahead maybe fifty yards. Tail-lights. The car was creeping slowly forward. "I got 'em," he said. "End of the road. There's a big building. Too big to be a house, maybe—"

"It's a business," she said. "I'm sending the address to the officers en route now."

The police were coming. If nothing else, the man wouldn't get away with it.

Donovan parked in front of the building out of the sight line of the Audi, turned off his car, and opened his door.

The call switched from Bluetooth to his phone, and the operator's voice sounded tinny and far away. "What are you—?"

"Quiet." He whispered the word. "I'll leave the line open. I'm getting closer, but you need to be quiet or you're gonna get me killed."

"Sir," she whispered, "you should..."

Her voice faded as he crept to the side of the building and peered around it. The car had stopped near a long dock. The man stepped out and walked toward the trunk.

Definitely the same man.

Donovan silently jogged toward him, hoping to catch him off guard.

The trunk opened a few inches. Angel's captor tried to lift it.

It didn't rise higher. Angel must have been holding it from the bottom.

Something came out from the opening.

She shoved something hard into the creep's groin. He grunted, bent, tried to slam the trunk. The item, whatever it was, was wedged between the lid and the car, keeping the lid from closing.

He stepped back, one hand on his groin, the other holding the trunk lid down. There was something black in that hand.

A gun.

He stepped back, aimed at the trunk.

"No!" Donovan sprinted the last few paces and barreled into him.

The gun went off, splitting the silence, as the two of them tumbled toward the ground.

The creep fell onto his side, cushioning much of Donovan's fall. Donovan aimed a blow at his head.

He ducked away, shifted his right hand. His gun hand.

Donovan squeezed the wrist with his left hand, punched the creep in the side of his head with his right.

He saw movement behind him. Angel.

He shouted, "Run!"

The man used the distraction, kneed Donovan in the ribs.

Donovan punched him in the head again. He needed more leverage. Needed to back up, get a good blow.

Another knee to the ribs, but Donovan kept his weight on his gun hand, levered himself higher. Punched him in the face.

His head snapped to the side. "Oof."

The sound barely registered as Donovan punched him again.

Angel came into his line of sight, tore the gun from the creep's hand, and stepped back. "I think he's out."

Donovan peered at his face. Sure enough, the eyes were closed. Donovan wasn't convinced, though. "You've got the gun?"

"Aimed at his head."

Donovan climbed off him. Only then did the sound of sirens reach him. They were getting closer.

Beside him, Angel staggered. He put his arm around her, steadied her, studied her features. "You all right?"

"I think so. Thanks to—"

The man shoved himself up from the ground.

Donovan pushed Angel away an instant before the guy barreled into him.

He threw Donovan to the ground, straddled his chest, and squeezed. "You're a dead man!"

Donovan gasped for breath, tried to push the hands off his neck. But the creep had all the leverage now. Donovan wanted to yell at Angel to run, but he couldn't get enough air. He was going to pass out, and then she'd be trapped with him. Would she use the gun? Would she be able to protect herself?

Father, protect her.

And then, a heavy *thunk.*

The man collapsed on top of him.

Angel stood over them both, the gun gripped in her hand like a club. She'd hit him. Hard.

Donovan rolled the unconscious body aside, pulled in a deep breath of cool, salty air, and stood. He approached her. "You got him."

She nodded, didn't take her eyes off the creep.

Donovan reached out, and she placed the gun in his waiting hand. He opened his arms, and she stepped into them.

Her knees gave way, and he held her against his chest. "I've got you."

She pressed her face against Donovan's chest, shuddering, gasping.

Time seemed to stop.

She was solid and warm and breathing. Alive and safe.

They were safe now.

Thank God. Thank God.

Thank You, Father.

CHAPTER TWENTY-SIX

Angel shook her head to clear it, which only made things worse. Between Anton's fists and the battering the car had given her, she'd taken too many blows to the skull to think straight.

Donovan made her sit on the ground. Apparently, she'd looked like she was about to drop. Felt like it, too. He stood over Anton, the gun aimed at him. Anton seemed unconscious, but after what just happened Donovan wasn't taking any chances.

The sirens were closing in. She looked around to get her bearings.

They were behind a building she'd never seen before, beside a long dock. If not for Donovan's help, she'd have likely been at the bottom of the harbor by now. How long before someone would have found her washed up on the shore?

Would her parents have had to identify her bloated body?

Nausea roiled in her stomach, and she held her hands against it, willed it down.

There was a bridge over the harbor and, beyond that, the city of Portsmouth. Which meant they were... where? Which bridge was that?

It was the one she could see from the restaurant. Memorial Bridge.

They were in Kittery, Maine.

Leaving the state of New Hampshire was a violation of her probation.

Was that what was bothering her?

No. Surely a judge would be lenient, considering she'd been trapped in the trunk of a car against her will. But...

Something was wrong.

She needed to focus.

The sirens were getting louder. She had to think. Something was... not okay. *Lord, help me...*

Donovan.

She stood, and he glanced her way. "Please sit. You're in shock."

He was right. She was freezing, and she hadn't noticed. Now that she did, her teeth chattered.

He shrugged off his jacket and handed it to her, quickly aiming the gun at Anton again.

She wrapped his jacket over her own. Better. That was warmer.

A siren blared as it closed in, then abruptly shut off. The first police car screeched to a halt in the lot in front of the building.

She squeezed Donovan's arm. She needed to tell him... something.

Behind her, a man shouted, "Drop the gun!"

Donovan stepped in front of her. He lifted his hands high and tossed the gun toward the cop. "It's his." He nodded back toward Anton.

The police closed in.

Ambulances followed.

Within seconds, both she and Donovan were wrapped in

blankets. She was seated on a gurney while a paramedic examined her and asked her questions.

She answered, feeling a need to do, to say... something.

Donovan leaned against the back of the ambulance between the open doors, insisting he was fine.

He was here. He'd saved her life.

That niggling worry... As she warmed up, her brain seemed to come back to life.

The flash of red and blue lights caught her eyes. They were coming over the bridge. The bridge from New Hampshire. Probably Portsmouth police...

That was it.

They'd be here any minute.

She pushed the EMT away, stood on shaky feet, and walked toward Donovan. "Did you follow me?"

He reached out, took her hand. "Honey, you need to—"

"How did you find me?"

"I saw him throw you in the trunk, but I was too far—"

"No, I mean... Why were you in Portsmouth?"

He looked away, brows lowered. "Long story."

She turned to the paramedic who'd trailed her. "Can we have a minute, please?"

The young guy gave her a stern look. "Ma'am, you need to sit down."

"One minute." She gave him a *go away* look, aimed another one at the cop who'd been asking Donovan questions. "He saved my life. I'd like to thank him—in private—if you don't mind."

The paramedic shrugged, the cop backed off. They saw her and Donovan as victims, but the police coming from Portsmouth would see them as criminals. And they'd be here any minute.

Donovan opened his arms, she stepped into them, and she almost forgot what she needed to say. She was too fuzzy-headed. "How were you there?"

He glanced behind her, lowered his voice. "I got to Portsmouth about midnight. I thought maybe tonight was the night."

Midnight. Three hours before she'd arrived.

She closed her eyes. That was bad. She grabbed his hand. "You have to listen to me."

He pushed off the back of the ambulance, lifted her as if she weighed nothing, and set her on the metal floor of the emergency vehicle.

He was right. Sitting was better.

He said, "I think you should—"

"You were there before me. That means you had prior knowledge of a crime. Unless you reported it—"

"I would never do that to you." He angled away. "I'm only glad you're—"

"Listen. They might have seen you."

He scowled. "Who are—?"

"If they saw you there before the robbery... They know who you are, Donovan. You followed me Sunday. They won't believe it was a coincidence you were there. You'll be arrested."

His eyes narrowed. "I saved your life."

"I know." Tears prickled her eyes. "Thank God you were here. Thank God..." She owed this man everything, everything. Which meant she couldn't get emotional now, couldn't get distracted. "They'll try to take you down to hurt me."

"What are you—?"

"I can't explain. You have to trust me."

He studied her face, and she tried to put all the emotions she didn't have words for into her eyes. The love she felt for him, the urgency that he hear her.

"I trust you," he said.

"These cops are treating us like victims." She glanced at the bridge. The police cars she'd seen coming over had disappeared.

They'd be here any second. "The ones coming from Portsmouth will see us as criminals."

"But I didn't—"

"You're an accessory. If you knew and didn't report it—"

"I didn't know. I suspected. I hoped I was wrong. I thought maybe—"

"Get a lawyer. Tell him what you hoped. Tell the police nothing." She squeezed his hands. "Nothing."

"I don't understand."

"Will you do it? Trust me, please? And have your lawyer contact mine." She gave him her attorney's name. "There's a lot you don't know."

He smirked. "Apparently."

She squeezed her eyes closed. If only she could tell him everything. Even though the job was over, her contract was in place. She couldn't say any more, not if she wanted to earn her freedom.

If she'd told him before, and if he'd known she wasn't breaking the law, then he wouldn't be an accessory, just a protective boyfriend.

That was the only way to get him out of this. After everything she'd done...after being beaten up, shoved in a car. After seeing the barrel of that handgun that could easily have killed her. After almost being murdered... After all of that, she'd still end up in prison.

But Donovan would be free.

In order to make it happen, she'd have to lie. And she'd have to get him to lie, too.

What should I do?

"Whatever it is you're not telling me, I don't care." He wrapped her in his arms, and she rested her head against his chest, praying for wisdom, taking comfort in the steady beat of his heart.

When would she hug him again? Would she ever?

Lord?

If she told Donovan the truth now, then... then he'd still be an accessory because he hadn't known before. She didn't want to lie. She didn't want him to lie, but she couldn't let him go down for a robbery he'd had nothing to do with.

Lord, should I tell him? Should I encourage him to lie?

Trust Me.

Just like she'd asked Donovan to do. Trust.

And trusting God meant obeying Him. Obeying Him meant not lying.

It's in Your hands now, Lord. Protect Donovan. Whatever else happens, protect him.

"Angelica Rossi!" Routhier's raised voice sent a jerk of fear down her spine.

Donovan was yanked away by a uniformed cop. His eyes held hers as he was pulled from her side.

"Don't say anything," she called.

Routhier stepped between them. "Giving your boyfriend legal advice?"

She took a deep breath. She had to be smart now. She turned what she hoped was a hateful gaze toward the detective. "You were supposed to protect me."

"If you'd told me the whole plan—"

"I told you everything I knew."

"What did you think?" Routhier said. "They'd hide it, you'd get your freedom, and then you'd get your piece of the pie for that, too?"

"What are you talking about?"

"The fourth partner. Why didn't you—?"

"I didn't know." Her raised voice sent her head pounding. She pressed her hands against her skull, willed it to stop.

"In case you weren't sure," Routhier said, "you're going to prison."

Maybe that was true, and maybe not. Either way, Routhier wasn't in charge of her future. She knew exactly Whose she was, and He was a lot more powerful than this hateful, small-minded detective.

His eyes narrowed, and the little vein on his forehead bulged. "I'm going to make it my personal mission to see you behind bars. And your boyfriend, too."

Her focus was fading again. She peered past Routhier to where Donovan was standing beside O'Donnell. *Lord, please let him take my advice and get a lawyer. Please don't let him incriminate himself. Or me.*

Routhier said something, but his words seemed far away. She watched Donovan being helped into the back of a police car. No cuffs, but they wouldn't arrest him yet. They'd make him feel comfortable, try to get him to talk.

Lord, are You there?

She leaned back on the ambulance floor. She'd lost her ability to think. She'd lost Donovan. She'd lost her freedom.

A different voice, a man's voice, reached her. "Detective, you need to back off."

A moment later, hands pulled Angel up. Her head pounded as men on both sides half-walked, half-carried her to the gurney. They laid her down, pointed a flashlight in her eyes. Asked questions. She tried to answer honestly. She wasn't a liar.

She wasn't.

Not anymore.

Lord?

The detective's voice came as if from far away. "Who was the fourth partner, Angel?"

She needed to take the advice she'd given Donovan. What was it? Oh, right... "Lawyer."

CHAPTER TWENTY-SEVEN

When Donovan arrived at the police station in Portsmouth, he called Angel's attorney's office and left a message with the answering service telling them what was going on and asking them to send someone to represent him. Then he'd been left in a tiny, windowless room for hours. The cops probably thought the time alone and trapped would break him, but Donovan had used the time to pray, at one point getting on his knees on the dusty wood floor to beg God for wisdom, for guidance. For miracles.

For Angel.

When the door opened, Donovan stood and brushed off his knees, feeling stronger than he had before. God was there. He'd filled Donovan with peace, and He would direct this conversation.

Whatever happened now, God was in it.

A man about six inches shorter than Donovan stepped in. "Marty Franklin. Cassandra Laurent's office called me about representing you."

Donovan shook the man's hand. What he lacked in height,

the attorney made up for with his sharp suit and confidence. Franklin sat across the table from him and pulled out a small notebook and a pen. "How did you know about the robbery last night?"

"I didn't," he said.

"Did Angelica Rossi tell you what she was planning?"

"Not a word."

He sighed. "You found out somehow."

He explained about the notebook he'd found in her bathroom.

"And when you confronted her," Franklin said, "did she tell you—?"

"She told me to mind my own business."

"And what did you think was going on?"

Donovan shrugged. "I had no idea. I couldn't imagine her pulling off some big criminal act. I thought maybe she was working for an insurance company, maybe testing a security system. Or working with the cops."

"You guessed that?"

Another shrug. "I didn't know. I honestly didn't care that much. Which... I get that I should have. I mean, I have a painting at the Nightingale, but that wasn't my problem. I figured they knew how to protect their property. Is she okay?"

"We need to focus on you."

"What do I need to say to keep Angel out of trouble?"

"You need to focus on keeping yourself out of trouble."

"I don't care—"

"Listen, Donovan." Franklin gave him a stern look. "You can't help her. She's got to deal with her stuff. You've got to deal with yours. What you need to do is tell the truth. Why didn't you contact the authorities?"

"And tell them what?"

"What you saw in that notebook."

"I saw a couple of words. Not enough to prove anything. What would I have told them? Somebody might be trying to steal something from a museum at some point in the future? How would that have been helpful?"

Franklin took a deep breath. "You had prior knowledge of a felony—"

"I didn't have knowledge of anything!" He pushed away from the table. "I had no idea—"

"You knew when it was going to happen, Donovan. You were there."

"And thank God I was, or Angel would be dead."

The man blinked, and his head tilted to the side. "I didn't hear that part of the story."

Donovan sat and explained what happened that morning while the lawyer scrawled notes. Recalling the events had Donovan's hands trembling. She was okay. He had to keep reminding himself that she was okay.

When he was done, Franklin whistled. "That's a heckuva story. You saved her life, and they want to throw you in prison." He smirked. "It doesn't change the fact that you were at the museum where the job took place, watching, and you didn't call the police."

True. That was all true. "I didn't know what was going on."

"What did you guess?"

Donovan looked away, didn't want to say. Because he'd guessed they were breaking in. He hadn't thought it through, and it hadn't occurred to him to call the police. "I wanted to protect her."

The man drummed his fingers on the table, impatient. "You were there... what? As a lookout?"

"I wasn't involved."

"You knew where the break-in was taking place. You knew the day. You knew the time."

"No. I didn't."

"You're saying you just happened to be in Portsmouth in front of the museum at the exact time—?"

"No. I'm not... I was there every night this week."

Franklin's fingers froze. "Every night?"

"I didn't have any idea what was going on, but I knew who she was working with." He considered keeping this part quiet but then remembered what Angel had said. *You were seen... The place was being watched.*

If Donovan's guess was correct, that warehouse had been watched by the police. Which tracked with the words Angel had let slip hours before when she'd confronted him at the back of the ambulance. *If they saw you there before the robbery... They know who you are... You'll be arrested.*

The only thing that made sense was that Angel had been working with the police. If that was the case, then what he had to say now wasn't going to come as any surprise to them. And if he was wrong... There was no crime against following a woman.

Okay, well, stalker laws... But he wasn't a stalker. Maybe an overprotective fool, but not a stalker.

"Last week," he said, "I followed her to a warehouse in Manchester." He explained what he'd seen and what he thought about the man she'd met. "I was sure he was the guy who'd hurt her before." At Franklin's raised eyebrows, he had to back up and share that story.

When Donovan was done, Franklin lowered his pen and nodded. "You had nothing to do with the break-in."

"Nothing."

"No interest in the museum and what it held? What they were going to steal."

"I didn't know anything about any of that. I knew something was going on, and I knew she was in it with a guy who'd hurt her."

Franklin nodded slowly, then shrugged. "I doubt it'll make a difference to the cops, but it'll play well with a jury."

CHAPTER TWENTY-EIGHT

The paramedics had wanted to take Angel to the hospital, but she'd refused. A couple of Tylenol and her headache was better already. Now that she was warm and the shock had worn off, she could think again. And she'd had plenty of time for that in the hours since she'd been tossed into this tiny room in the Portsmouth PD.

Her lawyer, Cassandra Laurent, arrived a couple of hours later. She was a good ten inches taller than Angel and attractive enough that she could've been a model in a younger life. In fact, if Angel's memory served, she may have been a model. Or maybe a beauty queen back before college and law school.

The expression on her face as she tossed her briefcase on the table wouldn't have won her any contests that day. "You told your boyfriend?"

"Not a word," Angel said. "I wouldn't risk my freedom, this whole deal—"

"Then how did he find out?" She pulled a pen and yellow legal pad from her briefcase.

While Angel explained what happened, Ms. Laurent made

notes. "You're saying he was snooping and discovered the information on his own."

"He wasn't snooping. He's redoing the house. The new vanity came in, and he called to let me know he'd be installing it, but I was at work and didn't answer the phone and didn't get the message. My brother was able to help him that day—"

"He went into your room without your permission?"

Ms. Laurent made it sound like Donovan had done something unconscionable. "He knew I wouldn't mind. He wasn't trying to snoop. It was my fault—"

"Don't finish that sentence." Another stern look had Angel playing back what she'd said. "It wasn't your fault. That's the whole point. Because if it was..."

"I go to prison."

They talked through the story. No, not the story. The facts. Everything she told Ms. Laurent—and would eventually tell Routhier and O'Donnell—was the truth.

She didn't have to lie. She'd done nothing wrong.

When she was finished filling Ms. Laurent in, the woman stepped out.

Unfortunately, unless God directed the hearts and minds of the cops and the judge, it wouldn't matter that she'd told the truth or that she'd done her best to uphold her end of the bargain. She was going to end up in prison after all.

Lord, please...

She didn't want to go to prison, but if it was between her and Donovan, it had to be her. *Not him, Father.*

Finally, the door opened, and Ms. Laurent walked back in. She closed the door and took the seat across from Angel. "Your boyfriend told the same story you told me. You didn't tell him what was going on. He snooped and figured it out on his own."

"He didn't really know, though. He only suspected."

"What matters—"

"Donovan matters to me. Keeping Donovan out of jail—"

"Is our second priority." Ms. Laurent's lips rubbed together in that disappointed look Angel had come to know. She'd been Angel's attorney since the first arrest. She knew her history. Knew and didn't judge, at least not aloud, but the looks she gave Angel often communicated what she wouldn't say. "I'm glad you found someone you care about. He seems to care about you, too. And he seems like a really nice guy. He agrees, and his attorney agrees, that you're the first priority."

"I didn't agree."

"Don't let everything you've done be in vain, Angel. If he knew about the robbery and didn't report it, then he's going to have to deal with that. You can't help him. Going to prison won't help him."

That was true.

"You didn't violate your contract," Ms. Laurent said, "not on purpose, but the police will argue that you didn't protect the operation as you should have." She pulled some papers from her briefcase and set them on the table. She scanned them, then turned one to face Angel and tapped it. "Right here... This little clause may save you."

Angel studied the paper. It was the contract she'd signed. When she'd first seen it, she'd been focused on what her responsibilities were, and she hadn't paid much attention to the detectives' responsibilities. Hope sparked in her heart as she read. "That might help."

Ms. Laurent stood and knocked on the door. It opened, she stepped out, and a few minutes later, she stepped back in, followed by Routhier and O'Donnell.

Ms. Laurent gathered her things and sat beside Angel. When she was settled, she squeezed Angel's hand while they waited for the detectives to sit.

Routhier's smug smile stretched across his face. "Guess who's going to prison."

"Anton Turner, I hope," Angel said.

"Him, too," Routhier said. "But right now—"

"Turner's going away for good," O'Donnell said. "When we heard you'd been abducted, we arrested the man driving the SUV and recovered the statue. His name is Carpenter... Bradley Carpenter. Ever heard of him?"

Angel shook her head. "Never."

O'Donnell nodded once. "We picked up the kid, Mason, and he swore he'd known nothing about Carpenter."

"I hope you guys'll go easy on Mason." Angel felt bad for the kid. He'd had no idea what he was getting into when he signed up to work with Anton. If only she could have warned him.

O'Donnell didn't smile. "He's a criminal. He'll probably spend time behind bars. This was his first arrest, though. Maybe he'll get a break. And maybe he'll clean up his act. Like you did."

Routhier scoffed, and O'Donnell shot him a look before he continued. "Turner had a wheelchair in the backseat of his car along with a handful of plastic zip ties."

How odd. Angel glanced at Routhier, who looked bored, and then at Ms. Laurent, who seemed to be working to keep her neutral expression in place, though her skin had paled. Angel focused again on O'Donnell. "I don't understand."

He gave her a gentle smile. "There were a few hand weights, too. We think he was going to use the wheelchair to roll your body down the dock. He could fasten you to the wheelchair with the zip ties, attach the hand weights to it, and then roll you into the water."

"Oh." Acid filled her stomach, churned. She pushed away from the table, held her arms across her middle, and bent over.

The image of what could have happened... Maybe her body would never have been found.

Anton would have gotten away with it. Maybe he'd have been arrested for the cop's murder, for the museum jobs, but Angel's murder would have gone unreported.

Her parents would never have known what happened to her.

Donovan would never have known.

Thank You, Lord, that he was there. Thank You for protecting me and my family from that tragedy.

O'Donnell said, "I didn't mean to upset you. I thought you'd want to know what happened. And to understand that we got him. He's going to prison for good."

She took a deep breath and looked up. "Thank you for telling me."

O'Donnell gave her a quick nod. "We hope Carpenter will tell us where Turner's stash is. When he does, then we'll be able to get Turner for the cop's murder in Boston."

It had worked out. Routhier and O'Donnell didn't care about what Anton had done to Brittney, but Angel did. Her friend's attacker would go to prison.

The sober living houses Anton owned? She didn't know what would become of them, but the men and women who'd put their faith in Anton Turner would be protected from him in the future. God would have to work all of that out. With His help, Angel had done her part. She had no doubt God would manage the rest.

Routhier drummed his fingers on the table. "All that's lovely, but it doesn't change anything. You violated your contract."

Angel tore her gaze away from O'Donnell and focused on Routhier. She told him how Donovan learned she was casing the museum, but the man only shrugged those over-large shoulders. "Doesn't matter. The point is, he knew. You were supposed to keep the information hidden. You blew it, like I knew you would."

Beside him, O'Donnell shifted away from his partner. Angel glanced at the younger detective, caught the derisive look he gave Routhier.

Ms. Laurent sat back, focused on O'Donnell. "Where were you, Detective, when Ms. Rossi was shoved into the trunk of Anton Turner's car?"

Routhier said, "We're asking the questions here."

She kept her focus on O'Donnell. "You can answer now, or you can answer when you testify. Either way, you will answer."

"I'm happy to," O'Donnell said. "I was following the SUV."

"Mind if I ask why?" the lawyer said.

"That's none of your business," Routhier said.

Ignoring Routhier, O'Donnell said, "My job was to follow the statue."

Ms. Laurent turned her gaze to Routhier. "And what was your job?"

"If Angel'd told us the whole plan—"

"It's a simple question, Detective Routhier. Where were you when my client was dragged down an alley, beaten, and shoved in the trunk of the suspect's car? Where were you?"

"The job was to follow the statue, find where Turner kept his stolen goods."

"And you were where, exactly?"

"I don't have to answer your questions."

"He followed Mason," O'Donnell said.

"We didn't think Angel or Turner had the statue"—Routhier shot Angel a smug look—"despite your obvious attempts to trick us with all the extra bags. If you'd told us everything, none of that would have happened."

Routhier was trying to rile her, but the longer they talked, the calmer Angel felt.

Ms. Laurent turned to Angel. "Did you neglect to tell the detectives anything?"

"I told them everything I knew. Obviously, Anton didn't tell me the whole plan."

"You expect us to believe that?" Routhier asked.

"Hmm. He did try to kill me. I think that might lend credence to my story."

Routhier shifted his bulk in the wooden chair and focused on Ms. Laurent again. "All that matters is that she told her boyfriend what was going on. She's in violation of her agreement."

"You're with the Manchester PD, right?" He only offered a smirk in response. She continued. "Were the Portsmouth police aware of your plans tonight?"

"Of course. They knew all about it."

"Were they involved?"

"That has nothing to do with anything," Routhier said. "Our procedures aren't your business."

"Considering my client was kidnapped and almost murdered tonight, I disagree. Why were there no Portsmouth police involved?"

"There were," Routhier said. "The guard at the Nightingale was a local cop."

He was? Angel hadn't had any idea the museum was aware of what was going on. She started to say something, but Routhier cut her off.

"You didn't need to know."

And here she'd been proud of her ability to pull off the job.

How foolish.

How funny. Because it didn't matter. God created her for far better things.

"No other Portsmouth officers were involved?" Ms. Laurent asked.

Routhier huffed. "We didn't need anybody else."

Angel glanced at her lawyer. Ms. Laurent's eyebrows were raised. She set the contract on the table. "What happens if you're in violation of the agreement?"

"What?" His gaze flicked to the papers.

"If she's in violation, she could go to prison. I wonder... If you're in violation, what happens? A mark on your record, if it's a small thing, but if it's a big thing?" She tapped a pen against the contract. "If it's, say, a life-and-death thing?"

"We did our jobs," Routhier said.

"I don't think you did." She turned the papers around and scanned them. "According to this, it was your job to 'make every effort to secure the safety and protection of the confidential informant.'" She turned to Angel. "Do you think they made every effort?"

"Not even close."

"Nice try," Routhier said, "but—"

"You could have had more police there, couldn't you? More local cops could have been stationed around the area."

"We didn't want to tip anybody off."

"Come on, Detective," Ms. Laurent said. "With all those alleys and side streets, surely you could have managed to get one more cop there. Was there not enough manpower?"

He crossed his arms.

"Or did you want all the glory? You didn't want to share your collar with the local cops, right? Bringing down the guy who murdered a cop—that's a big deal."

"It is a big deal," Routhier said. "I wasn't in it for the glory, I was—"

"Oh, I think you were. You see, after you offered my client this deal, I did some research on you. Looks like you've been trying to get hired by the FBI for years. You're too old now, but bringing down a cop-killer they couldn't nail? Wouldn't that show them what they'd missed out on?"

Routhier's look was cold. "You have no idea what you're talking about."

She shrugged. "Maybe, but it'll play well to a jury."

He laughed. "Come on, Ms. Laurent. You know how they're going to see her." He waved toward Angel as if she were no more significant than a fly. "She's a criminal. A crook, and thanks to you, they'll believe she's a druggie."

"My client doesn't matter," Ms. Laurent said. "That's why you followed the statue."

"I'd assured the museum owner and the local cops that it wouldn't get away. If she'd told us everything—"

"You're saying," Ms. Laurent clarified, "that you felt it was more important to follow the statue than to protect my client?"

Routhier stood. His words were measured, but the red face and the bulging veins on his temple revealed his fury. "I'm saying if she'd told us everything, none of it would have happened. This was"—he jabbed his finger toward Angel—"all her fault."

Angel's heart pounded, not in fear, though. She couldn't identify that feeling that had her itching to stand, to speak. A few weeks ago, Routhier's words would have made sense to her. The statue was priceless.

The cop's life, the one they were trying to prove Anton had taken, was priceless. Angel was just... Angel. A crook, a con, a liar.

But everything had changed in the last few weeks. Or maybe nothing had changed, but Angel was seeing everything differently.

You think everyone's worth fighting for except yourself.

Routhier's fat finger pointed from O'Donnell to himself.

"We were trying to bring down a murderer. We'd allowed a priceless statue to be stolen. We couldn't let it get lost."

Angel shoved her chair back and stood. She glared across the table. "The statue was priceless? Is that what you said?"

"Yeah. The statue. And we had to get Turner for the cop's murder, and the only way—"

"What about me?" Angel asked. "What am I worth?"

The loud *pfft* that escaped gave her all the answer she needed.

But his opinion of her was irrelevant.

Beside him, O'Donnell looked up at his partner, mouth agape.

Ms. Laurent stood and placed her hand on Angel's upper arm. "Let's sit down."

"No." Angel shook off her attorney and glared at Routhier. "That statue is worth a few hundred grand. It's not priceless. The cop who died? His life was infinitely valuable, but it was already lost. The only thing at risk this morning that was priceless was me."

"You wish." Routhier rolled his eyes. "Nobody sees you that way, Angel. You're trash."

The room seemed to blur at the edges until the only thing in focus was Routhier, Routhier and the hate wafting off him like the scent of a dumpster on a sweltering day. She wouldn't back down to that hate. She had Truth on her side. "I am a child of the Most High God." The Spirit filled her, spoke within her. Her voice rose, carried beyond the walls and the ceiling to the One who held her in His hands. "He died for me. And you will not speak to me that way."

Routhier took a step back, bumped into his chair.

O'Donnell smiled at Angel. Then, he stood and focused on Ms. Laurent. "You're absolutely right. Angel might have inadvertently broken the terms of her agreement. We did it intentionally." He barely glanced at his partner. "He assured me he would stay with her. I was furious when I found out he hadn't. I'll be taking this to my chief and the chief in Portsmouth."

Routhier huffed. "You're all nuts."

"We're looking forward to going before the judge," Ms. Laurent said. "We'll tell him how you left your informant to fend for herself against a murderer. The judge'll be on our side. And then, we'll file a suit against the Manchester PD and the Portsmouth PD. We won't stop until we have your badge."

"I'm on Angel's side." O'Donnell turned to Routhier. "If it goes before the judge, I'll tell him you said you were going to protect her and didn't."

Routhier's face darkened from red to purple. Then, he spun, yanked open the door, and stormed out.

O'Donnell turned to Angel and smiled. "Glad you stood up for yourself. He's had that coming for a while."

She was too overcome to speak, so she nodded, swallowed the emotion clogging her throat.

O'Donnell looked at Ms. Laurent. "Our chief is reasonable. The chief of this department is already furious about what happened this morning. When I tell them everything that went down, he'll agree with us."

"You're sure?" Ms. Laurent asked.

"I'll talk to him now. Sit tight."

"Wait!" Angel called.

O'Donnell turned back to her, one eyebrow raised.

"Donovan had nothing to do with this. He was only trying to protect me."

He studied her a moment, then nodded. "I'll see what I can do."

"Thank you."

After he left the room, Angel and Ms. Laurent sat again. The anger that had launched Angel to her feet had escaped with her words. Her declaration that she was priceless—it had sounded crazy, but it wasn't.

It was truth.

~

Angel paced in the interrogation room for what seemed like hours. Ms. Laurent had left to speak with the local chief in hopes of getting her released. Before she left, she'd warned Angel she might have to spend the night in jail.

Unfortunately, judges didn't work on weekends.

So, she waited, trying to be thankful she was in an interrogation room alone and not in a jail cell with the Saturday night crowd of drunk-and-disorderlies, addicts, and prostitutes.

At least she was safe. At least here, she had the freedom to close her eyes and pray.

Finally, the door opened, and Ms. Laurent stepped in. "We did it."

Angel stood. "What?"

"You just have to sign this agreement promising not to file a suit against either department." Ms. Laurent set a sheet of paper on the table and sat. "Sorry for the long wait. It took some time to draw it up."

Angel pushed the paper away. "What about Donovan?"

"The Portsmouth PD has decided not to pursue charges against Mr. Gilcreast." She nodded to the agreement, and Angel read it.

According to the deal, no charges would be brought against Donovan Gilcreast, and the Manchester PD would honor their agreement with Angel. When she looked up, Ms. Laurent offered a rare smile. "Your record will be expunged. You're free."

Could it be true?

She was free?

"Can I tell Donovan everything?"

"You can tell anybody anything you want. No more secrets."

She closed her eyes. *Thank You, Father.*

She signed the agreement, stunned at how it had worked out, and followed Ms. Laurent out of the interrogation room.

O'Donnell was leaning against the wall with a plastic bag gripped in his hand. Her impression of the man had shifted. She'd thought of him as Routhier's lapdog when she'd first met him—irrelevant. Now, though he resembled Opie a little with the red hair and freckles, she saw maturity and strength in his eyes she hadn't recognized before. He was... handsome, actually. How had she missed that?

He pushed off the wall and faced her. "I'm sorry I didn't protect you."

Ms. Laurent said, "I'm going to deliver these," and disappeared around a corner.

Angel focused on O'Donnell again. "You trusted your partner."

"He won't be my partner from now on. I never liked him. After this, I don't trust him either." He looked past her, shook his head. "I don't think this job is for me."

She hadn't expected that. "You're a good cop."

"I wanted to help people, but ever since I became a detective... By the time I get involved, the crime's been done. Justice is important, but I'd rather be involved in a way that prevents the crimes from the start." He lifted one shoulder. "I need to pray about it. Anyway, I wanted to apologize."

"I'm free, thanks to you," Angel said.

"No. You're free thanks to you." He offered his hand, and she shook it. "You did well."

"Thank you." She stifled a yawn, then a laugh.

"Long night." He held out a little plastic sack. "Your keys and cell phone."

She looked inside. Sure enough, her things were there.

"We found them in Turner's car. He probably planned to drop them into the water with you."

A cold chill crept up her spine, weakened her knees. The beating, the lack of sleep, the need for food—it was all catching up with her.

He gripped her elbow, steadying her. "You're safe now."

She was safe. Safe and free. She could hardly believe it.

O'Donnell walked her to the front door. "Call me if Routhier gives you a hard time. He was convinced from the start he'd send you and Turner to prison. This is going to be a tough loss for him."

"I'll take you up on that," she said, "but I don't plan to give him any excuse to arrest me again."

"I have no doubt," O'Donnell said.

He left to deal with paperwork, and she walked outside alone.

It was a beautiful October day. Angel stepped off the small concrete entrance of the police station into the sun. Past the half-full parking lot, water sparkled in the harbor. A church steeple rose in the distance and, beyond that, she could just make out the outline of Memorial Bridge.

All around, trees wobbled in the cool breeze, and the changing leaves danced, showing off their splendor.

She was free. Free of her felony convictions. Free of all her arrests. Free to love the Lord and go wherever He led.

Where would He lead, though? What would her future hold? She could keep working at the restaurant, maybe go back into hairdressing. Maybe go to culinary school. She liked cutting hair, but she loved cooking.

What about Donovan? Now that Anton was behind bars,

she had no reason to stay at the house. She could get an apartment. Would Donovan be glad to be rid of her? He thought her a thief. Had that changed his feelings for her? Knowing about the deal she'd had, knowing she'd been deceiving him all along... Would he want to keep his distance from her now?

She'd done it all to secure her freedom. Had it cost her the man she loved?

The thought of it, the fear of it, stole her peace.

Where was he?

He'd been released. She knew that. He'd probably left. Gone home. Forgotten all about her.

Behind her, someone cleared a throat. She turned, and there he was, standing in front of a small bench in the shadows.

"You're here."

His eyebrows rose. "Did you think I would leave without you?"

She had, and now she realized how foolish the thought had been.

He moved toward her, arms open, and she stepped into them.

He held her tight, held her as if he feared she'd get away. "You're okay?"

"I am now."

He backed up, brushed her hair away from her face. She'd long since pulled out the ponytail, which had only contributed to her headache. She had no idea what she looked like. Terrible, she figured. Bedraggled hair, no makeup, dark circles.

He touched her left cheek gently, and she felt the tiniest pain. That was where Anton had hit her in the alley. It seemed that had happened long ago. Was there a bruise forming?

"I didn't hit him hard enough to pay him back for all he did to you." Donovan's voice was low, angry.

"It's not your job to repay, right?"

He smirked.

"Isn't that God's job?"

"Yeah." Donovan's smirk slipped to a frown. "I guess I have to leave it to Him. Although you did a fine job when you whacked him."

The memory of that moment caused a shudder. She was glad she'd stopped Anton hurting Donovan, but hitting him like that... What kind of person could get pleasure from inflicting pain? Anton had deserved it, and she still felt sick.

"Are you injured? Does anything hurt?"

With Donovan's arms around her...? "Nothing hurts."

He lowered his forehead to hers. "I was afraid I was going to have to say this through a phone with plexiglass between us."

"Which one of us did you imagine would be behind bars?"

He shrugged. "Either. Both. I didn't know."

"We're free," she said.

"I love you."

She gasped, leaned back, studied his intense gaze. Her heart filled to bursting. "Even after everything? After I almost got you sent to—"

He pressed his lips to hers, cutting off her words, her ability to think. She opened her lips, explored his mouth. Slid her hands up his strong shoulders and into the hair at his nape.

He pulled her closer, deepened the kiss.

Behind him, the precinct door opened. "Oh."

Angel recognized the voice from the single word and would have happily ignored it.

But Donovan backed up, keeping her hand in his, and turned toward Ms. Laurent. "Sorry. We were just—"

"Celebrating. I get it. Though you might find a more romantic spot." The attorney's smile was wide. "Don't let me stop you."

He reached his hand toward her. "Thank you for all you did. And for sending Mr. Franklin."

She shook it. "You're very welcome." She squeezed Angel's shoulder. "Stay out of trouble."

"I promise."

The attorney walked away, and Angel looked at Donovan, who was studying not the lawyer but her. He gripped her shoulders, turned her to face him. "Did you hear what I said? I want to make sure there's no confusion here."

"You love me?"

"I love you."

Tears stung her eyes. Emotion rose, brought a tremor to her lower lip.

Donovan's eyes narrowed. "Maybe I should have—"

"I love you, too," she said. "I can't believe..."

But her words were cut off when he pulled her close. Then he chuckled, the sound coming from deep in his chest. "Your lawyer's right. This isn't the most romantic place."

"We're together." Her words were muffled by the fabric of his jacket. "That's all the romance I need."

"That'll sure make my life easier." He stepped away, took her hand. "We'll see if you feel that way in twenty years."

Twenty years?

He was thinking twenty years down the road?

The thought of it could have brought anxiety or fear, but only a sense of peace and rightness followed her across the parking lot. This was exactly right.

She froze when they reached the first row of cars. "Wait. Your truck is—"

"Right there." He nodded past a minivan. "My lawyer had someone pick it up for me this morning while we were waiting."

"That was nice of him."

Donovan shrugged. "I'm sure his kindness will be reflected in my bill."

She chuckled. "I'm sorry about that. I'll pay you back."

He froze, and his face took on the scowl she'd seen many times when she'd first met him. "You owe me nothing."

"You saved my life, and it almost cost you your freedom."

"I don't think you understand how this love thing works." The scowl disappeared, and he squeezed her hand. "You'll learn. We'll figure it out together."

He walked her to the passenger side, helped her in, then kissed her forehead. "Food or sleep?"

"Yes?"

He chuckled. "We can do that."

CHAPTER TWENTY-NINE

The following Sunday morning, Donovan put the finishing touches on Katie's painting and stood back to stare at it. He'd captured the scene—the lake, the colorful trees beyond it. In the foreground, he'd added a dock and, farther out, a floating platform.

And there was Katie, not as a child but as a young woman. She wore a peaceful blue bathing suit over a healthy body. In the picture—and in his mind's eye—she'd run across the platform and jumped. He'd caught her mid-air, dark hair flying behind her, arms and legs flailing, expression joyous. She was the woman God had created her to be.

Donovan imagined it was who Katie was now, in heaven, free from her sins and addictions.

It was how Donovan would always remember the sister he'd loved.

And maybe it didn't make any sense. People didn't swim in October in New Hampshire. It was far too cold for that, but if anybody would have done it, Katie would have. And maybe Angel, come to think of it. And Donovan would have watched from the sidelines. He'd done far too much watching life, capturing life.

He'd done far too little living it.

Behind him, the old plaid sofa creaked. He turned to see Angel pushing to her feet. She stood beside him, took his hand, and gazed at the canvas.

When she said nothing after a minute, Donovan glanced at her face.

Tears coursed down her cheeks. She wiped them and sniffed. "It's her. It's absolutely perfectly her."

The feelings clogging his throat kept him from responding. When he'd swallowed the emotions, he said, "Ian's coming this week to see what I've done. I hope that's okay."

"He's going to love them all. And your show is going to be an amazing success."

He dared to hope maybe she was right. Donovan kissed the top of her head. "It's all thanks to you. You knew what was missing."

"You'd have figured it out."

He wasn't sure about that, but there was no point in pressing the point. Angel had helped him get his heart back, helped him see beyond the colors and shapes to the depth of life. She'd never know all she'd done for him, but, if she would agree, he'd spend the rest of his life showering her with gratitude.

"Are you hungry?" she asked.

"I can cook something."

She took his hand and pulled him toward the kitchen, where they prepared breakfast together. When they'd eaten and cleaned up, he asked, "You mind if I shower?"

She gave him that irritated smirk he'd seen too often this week. "I say it's ridiculous you moved out. If either of us should have left—"

"It's your brother's house. He wanted you to stay."

"But you could have, too. It was fine with both of us living here."

He took the washrag from her hand, tossed it in the sink, and rested his hands on her hips. "It wasn't fine. And when your brother found out about us, there wasn't a choice."

"Mr. Protective needs to back off. We don't have to do what he says."

Donovan chuckled at her frustration. He and Angel had gone to see Jack a few days before. Angel had told her brother and Harper everything that happened in Portsmouth. Harper had seemed impressed. Jack had been furious. Not with Angel for agreeing to the plan but with the police for not protecting her.

It had taken them a good ten minutes to calm him down after he'd heard the whole story. And then, Donovan had told him the truth about his feelings for Angel.

Jack had found him an apartment the same day, even given him a discount on the rent. Anything to protect his sister's virtue. Donovan appreciated how Jack felt.

"We're being wise," he said. "Knowing you were sleeping under the same roof did not lead to restful nights."

"Oh." She bit her bottom lip. "I didn't see it that way. I liked having you here."

He kissed her forehead. "It's not as if we don't spend almost every waking minute together."

"True."

"So... the shower?"

"Help yourself. I need to get cleaned up, too."

"What time should we leave?"

She backed away. "Uh, I'm not sure—"

"We're going. I'm not letting you back out."

After a swallow, Angel nodded. "Nine o'clock should get us there in plenty of time."

Donovan showered, praying the Lord would help this day go well. Angel was worried, but Donovan didn't understand why. Her parents would welcome her with open arms and, if her mother was anything like Angel, probably tears.

Donovan had gone to see his folks the day before and told his mother about his relationship with Angel. It hadn't been an easy conversation. Mom had been blaming Angel too long for Katie's addiction to let it go easily. It would take time for her to get over that, but she would. She promised to do her best to love the woman Donovan hoped would someday be her daughter-in-law.

A few months before, the news that he was seeing Angel Rossi would have sent Mom into a tailspin. God had done a work in Mom's life like He'd worked in Dad's, and Donovan's. And Angel's, too.

God was working on all of them, maturing them, guiding them through the hardships to make them stronger, more faithful believers every day.

This was only the beginning. And, if he could get a private conversation with Angel's father, it would be a spectacular beginning to a beautiful future.

CHAPTER THIRTY

───────────

Angel stared up at the church that had been hers throughout her childhood. White siding, tall steeple, green trim. The annex on the back had been added in the nineties, but the original structure had been in Nashua for over a hundred years. It had been her family's church home as long as Angel could remember.

Donovan opened her door, and she stepped out of the truck and held his hand. He was here with her. She could do this, as long as Donovan stayed by her side.

No. That wasn't right. She loved Donovan, and she longed for his presence, but the truth was she could do anything as long as God stayed by her side. God's was the presence she truly needed. Donovan was a beautiful blessing.

"You ready for this?" he asked.

"Nope."

He kissed her forehead. "We'll do it together."

From deeper in the parking lot, she heard a shouted, "Donovan!"

They turned and caught Jack's wave. He and Harper approached, and he shook Donovan's hand and kissed Angel's cheek. "Figured you were here, sis, but I couldn't see you over the truck."

"Short jokes," she said. "Real mature."

"Glad to see you."

"Did you know we were coming?" Angel asked.

"He might've mentioned it." He nodded to Donovan. "Thought you could use the moral support."

Jack and Harper worshipped at a church in Nutfield, a solid forty-five minutes from here. "Thanks for making the trip," Angel said.

"We're happy to." Harper rubbed her belly, where the baby bump was more noticeable. Angel couldn't wait to get her hands on that little one this winter.

"Let's go." Donovan squeezed her hand and led her toward the open door.

Clouds had moved in, and with them, moisture. It was chilly and would probably be raining by the time they left, but Angel could hardly focus on the weather as she walked toward the church.

This was going to be good. She knew it was. And when shame and embarrassment niggled at her heart, she pushed them away. She was forgiven. A lot of folks here knew her story, and maybe some would whisper when she walked in. The ones who mattered, her family, would love her. They'd never stopped loving her.

They climbed the steps and moved into the foyer. The scent —old books, dusty furniture, beautiful people—reminded her of so many Sundays as a child. She should have listened to the lessons instead of dreaming of adventure and scoffing at the church ladies. Turns out, the church ladies knew what they were talking about.

Angel wanted to be a church lady. She'd be one who could teach from experience. That was worth something.

They entered the sanctuary, and there were Mom and Dad, near the front, chatting with the couple in the pew ahead of them. They'd saved enough room for three to sit comfortably. Jack and Harper must've called, said they were coming. That accounted for two.

The third... that was for Angel. The seat Mom had promised years before to save for her every week until she came back.

And now she was back. And she was going to need another seat. Jack and Harper preceded them down the aisle, and Mom and Dad stood, greeted them, and let them pass. Jack whispered to the people in the middle of the row, who scooted down.

Simple as that, there was space in the pew for Donovan. As if he was meant to be there.

Now, the hard part.

Dad was focused on Jack, chatting. People were visiting with each other like they did every Sunday before the service began. Nobody pointed. Nobody whispered. The few people whose eyes Angel caught smiled at her. Welcomed her.

After a deep breath and a prayer for courage, Angel tapped her father on the shoulder. He turned, saw her, and his jaw dropped. It wasn't as if it had been that long since she'd seen him. A couple of months, maybe. But in church, in this church she'd sworn she'd never set foot in again...

He wrapped her in his arms. "Baby girl."

"Hi, Daddy."

He let her go, then scooted out of the aisle. He and Donovan spoke, but Angel couldn't focus on that.

Her mother turned to her. Her mouth opened, and her hand covered it. Tears filled her eyes. And then she pulled Angel into a hug. "I knew you'd come. I knew if I saved you a seat..."

"Sorry it took me so long."

Mom said nothing, just hugged tighter, sniffling in her ear.

The music started, and everyone around them stood. Mom let her go. Angel scooted past her, and then Donovan scooted past both of them.

Angel couldn't focus on the service, not with Mom on one side, Donovan on the other. Dad's arm was around Mom's shoulders, and every once in a while, he looked over her head at Angel as if to assure himself she was really there. Jack and Harper sent encouraging smiles.

Her family surrounding her, the man she loved at her side... This was the life she wanted. This was the adventure she'd craved. This was the legacy she wanted to leave. Not a legacy of crime and shame, but a legacy of faith and love.

Thanks to the grace of her Savior, hers was a legacy restored.

EPILOGUE

Six Months Later

Angel studied her reflection in the oversize gilded mirror propped against the wall in an upstairs bedroom. She'd insisted she didn't need an expensive gown, but her parents wouldn't listen. And when she'd tried on this Victorian style, she'd known it was the one. Long, lacy sleeves, sweetheart neckline, full skirt—it was perfect.

Mom sighed. "You look like a princess."

Angel's eyes filled, and Harper handed her a tissue. "Don't you dare ruin your makeup."

The stern tone made Angel laugh.

Angel's older sister, Gloria, made a final adjustment to the veil, then met Angel's eyes. "I'm so proud of you."

More tears, which Angel dabbed away. Her family, proud. It was a new idea she was learning to get used to.

A knock sounded at the door, and one of Angel's new Nutfield friends, Ginny Powers, popped her head in. "Everybody's..." Her words trailed. "Wow." She stepped all the way into the room and took Angel in from head to toe. "You're gorgeous. Donovan's going to be speechless."

She hoped not. She really needed to hear two little words. *I do.*

"Is it time?" Mom asked.

"Everybody's in place," Ginny said. "We're ready whenever you are."

"I'm ready," Angel said. "Send Dad in."

Ginny left, and a moment later, another knock sounded.

Angel opened the door, and there was Dad, beaming at her. "My angel."

Oh, but she was going to have to get a handle on the crying. She hugged her father, who held on a long moment. "I never doubted you'd come back to the family."

He hadn't? Because she had. There'd been times when she'd wondered if the family would want her back. How could she have doubted them? These were her people. Of course they loved her. Of course they'd welcomed her home.

She pulled back from the hug and turned to Mom. "We'll be right behind you."

Downstairs, the music started.

Mom stepped into the hallway, and Harper followed. Just a few months after giving birth, Angel's sister-in-law was thin and more radiant than ever. No surprise, that, though. Their new baby girl, Angel's niece, was a precious addition to their family.

Gloria squeezed Angel's hand and followed Harper.

Angel's dad gestured to the door, and she stepped out. Donovan hadn't quite completed the house's renovation, but the hallway's refinished floors gleamed in the reflection of the new overhead light fixtures he'd installed a few days prior.

The downstairs was completely restored and absolutely gorgeous.

Today, the common rooms were decked out for the wedding, thanks to the help of Angel's parents and her soon-to-be in-laws. Satin and lace and tulle adorned tables and chairs and banisters. Flowers on every surface filled the house with their glorious scents.

Angel couldn't believe this house was theirs. After Donovan's successful gallery showing in December, he'd floated the idea that they buy it and run it as a bed-and-breakfast. She'd be the pretty face, he'd joked, and he'd be the grumpy maintenance man who painted in the attic.

She'd laughed at the vision, but it hadn't taken long for her to catch it. She could run this place. She loved to cook. She loved the house and the property. She loved people. And this would be the perfect place to raise a family.

She'd continued to live there, and Donovan had continued to come over every morning at dawn to paint. Angel had quit her job at the restaurant and dedicated her time to restoring the old furniture and helping Donovan make this dusty old house into their home.

She and Donovan had sealed it when they'd hung Katie's painting over the fireplace in the parlor. He'd decided before the gallery showing to display it but not to sell it. He couldn't part with it. It was the first of Donovan's art that would fill this house. The first, but certainly not the last.

Today, the downstairs rooms were filled with café tables. The caterer had set up in the kitchen. The reception would begin as soon as she and Donovan were pronounced husband and wife.

Mom squeezed Angel's hand, then slipped her hand into her escort's elbow and disappeared down the stairs.

Harper and Jack followed. Then, Gloria joined her escort, Ian Hawkins, who charmed her with his Australian accent as he gestured to the staircase.

"You ready for this?" Dad asked.

"Just don't let me trip on my gown."

"You're safe in my hands." Daddy winked. "But I was talking about the marriage, not the wedding."

She faced her father. "Donovan's a good man."

"He is." Daddy kissed her forehead. "He's also a lucky man."

She didn't know about that. She was the lucky one. Blessed beyond belief.

She held onto Daddy's elbow, and he escorted her down the stairs. She didn't trip. In fact, she practically floated.

The pastor stood in front of the door, and the guests lined either side of the wide corridor, all gazing up at her.

Donovan's mother dabbed at her eyes, beaming at Angel. It had taken some time for the woman to accept her, but in the months since Donovan's proposal, Angel had worked hard to forge a friendship with her. That friendship was young and tender, but it would grow.

She glanced past the guests and the wedding party until she found the one she sought. Donovan. He was stunningly hand-some in his tuxedo. She could hardly believe he was real.

Their eyes met. Hers filled as she neared him. She brushed the tears away so nothing would blur the vision of the man she loved.

Daddy led her to Donovan, and she took his hand and stepped to his side, unable to take her eyes off him.

The pastor spoke, Donovan spoke, she spoke. She'd never forget a moment of it. But not until the pastor's final pronounce-ment, "husband and wife," hung in the air, not until Donovan placed his hands on the sides of her face and leaned close, did she allow herself to truly believe. He was hers. This strong, talented, loving man was hers forever.

It was time to begin the greatest adventure of her life.

~

IF YOU ENJOYED Angel and Donovan's story, you'll love reading about Dylan O'Donnell (also known as "Opie") and Chelsea Hamilton. Turn the page for more about LEGACY RECLAIMED.

ONE MORE THING... Did you grab your free book? Visit my website at http:// robinpatchen.com/subscribe to get a copy of *Escaping with You,* the edge-of-your-seat prequel to Robin Patchen's best-selling Wright Heroes of Maine series. You're going to love it!

LEGACY RECLAIMED

She'll risk anything to save the company her parents built. He'll risk anything to save her. The murderer will stop at nothing to make sure they both fail.

Chelsea Hamilton spent her life preparing to run the international clothing business her parents started, but she's not ready when she learns of her mother's untimely death. Chelsea returns to New Hampshire, buries her mother, and prepares to take the helm at the floundering business. When a stranger attempts to kill her, she realizes somebody doesn't want her to inherit her legacy.

Since quitting the police force and opening his own private investigation business, Dylan O'Donnell has spent most of his time searching for lost teens. He doesn't know what to think of the beautiful woman who shows up at the food bank, and he's even more surprised when she tells him her story. Hers isn't the kind of case he's accustomed to handling, and she isn't the kind of client he quit his steady job to help, but something about the woman—with her high-end purse and designer clothes—pulls at him. She's in danger, and he can't turn her away.

Together, they dig into her family secrets. The closer they get to the truth, the closer they grow to one another. Can Chelsea save the legacy her parents fought to leave her? Can Dylan save Chelsea from the enemies determined to see her dead?

The Wright Heroes of Maine

Running to You

Rescuing You

Finding You

Sheltering You

Protecting You

Capturing You

Defending You

Fighting for You

Anchoring You

The Coventry Saga

Vanished in the Darkness

Redemption for Ransom

Betrayal of Genius

Traces of Virtue

Touch of Innocence

Inheritance of Secrets

Lineage of Corruption

Wreathed in Disgrace

Courage in the Shadows

Vengeance in the Mist

A Mountain Too Steep

The Nutfield Saga

Convenient Lies

Twisted Lies

Generous Lies

Innocent Lies

Beautiful Lies

Legacy Rejected

Legacy Restored

Legacy Reclaimed

Legacy Redeemed

Sleigh Bells & Stalkers

One Christmas Night

Amanda Series

Chasing Amanda

Finding Amanda

ABOUT THE AUTHOR

Robin Patchen is a *USA Today* bestselling and award-winning author of Christian romantic suspense. She grew up in a small town in New Hampshire, the setting of her Nutfield Saga books, and then headed to Boston to earn a journalism degree. After college, working in marketing and public relations, she discovered how much she loathed the nine-to-five ball and chain. After relocating to the Southwest, she started writing her first novel while she homeschooled her three children. The novel was dreadful, but her passion for storytelling didn't wane. Thankfully, as her children grew, so did her writing ability. Now that her kids are adults, she has more time to play with the lives of fictional heroes and heroines, wreaking havoc and working magic to give her characters happy endings. When she's not writing, she's editing or reading, proving that most of her life revolves around the twenty-six letters of the alphabet. Visit robinpatchen.com/subscribe to receive a free book and stay informed about Robin's latest projects.

9 781950 029082